M000208799

TRADE: BANGKOK

BY TIM BROST

This book is a work of fiction. Unless otherwise noted by the author, all references to people and historical events are spun from pure imagination. Any resemblance to actual people, living or dead, is coincidental.

For information about distribution channels and marketing opportunities for this novel and other works by this author, visit timbrost.com.

ISBN-13:978-0-9978614-5-7

Printed in the United States of America

@Copyright - 2016 - All rights reserved.

To Dave
Best Wishes
[signature]

Acknowledgements

Chief technical advisor:
Rod McKay

Additional technical advisors:
Brian Burns, Gene Payson, Alex Baldon,
Mark Steiger, Chip Dorsey

Chief editor:
Bruce M. Brown
Additional Editors:
Jim Morrison, Gabriella West, Geraldine Buchanan
First readers:
Daniel Halladay, Val Pendergrast

Contributors to the success of *Trade: Bangkok*
Patrons: Joncleir, Peter and Sheila
Additional contributors in alpha order: Ryan Baldon,
Geraldine Buchanan, Joel Buder, Leann Chapman,
Dan Halladay, Lawrence Hanson, Patti Hanson, Dan Iverson,
Elizabeth K. Johnson, TKs, Jeffrey T Kropelnicki,
Jeffrey K. Lundgren, Nick McCune, Jeff Nugent, Valerie Reilly,
Avi Taylor, Robert Wagner, Trish Walton,
Carol Zapfel

Cover design: Tim Brost

Cover photo: Florian Blümm
(Sathorn Unique Tower)

More from Tim Brost

Trade Series
Trade: Bangkok (a novel)
Trade: Azerbaijan (a short read)

High-Rise Crew Trilogy
High-Rise Crew: Dirty Money (a novel)

Dedication

S, R, J, and C. I love you all.

Testimonial

In over 22 years of service I planned, coordinated and participated in many operations with the most elite fighting forces in the
world. We always are at the end of a very sophisticated lifeline
and, relatively speaking, did not want for anything, but on occasion we had to adapt to the curves thrown at us. Trade Bangkok
expertly, and in realistic detail, portrays the exciting and very
dangerous business side of armed conflict where men and wom-
en with unique skills have to think on their feet every day. Just
as with the Special Forces who serve with distinction around the
Globe, this story weaves a tale of intrigue, ingenuity and suspense
centered around a select group of professionals who are dedicated to mission success and to each other. I could easily see myself
being part of this group. Instead of focusing on equipment and grit
as many authors do, Brost touches on the one thing that separates
a true operator from a "wanna-be"—resourcefulness. Trade Bangkok honors the men and women who served and continue to serve
long after the uniforms come off.

> *Brian J. Burns, Lieutenant Colonel, United States Army*
> *(Retired) served as an Infantry Officer and Logistics and*
> *Acquisition Specialist in every engagement from Operation*
> *Urgent Fury to Operations Enduring and Iraqi Freedom.*
> *In his last 10 years Brian was assigned to various Army*
> *and Joint Special Operations Commands.*

Introduction

Trade: Bangkok is the first release in the Trade series. Trade novels feature Tuck (Web) Webber and the operatives, shadow agents, technicians and lawyers that make up his teams. Primary characters in this novel are inspired by the lives of real people.

Through writing I've had the privilege to meet exceptional subject matter experts in criminal and patent law, commodities trading, special operations, finance, cyber security, avionics and law enforcement. Each meeting has been informative and memorable, but few encounters compare with an exclusive introduction to the world of an international arms dealer, a world I intend to explore in this series.

I hope you find *Trade: Bangkok*, and the other novels in this series, to be informative, entertaining adventures.

Above the entrance to many buildings in Thailand there are sentiments that read: Country, Religions, Monarch and People. Long live the King of Thailand, a force for peace in difficult times.

- Tim Brost

PROLOGUE

Two battle-hardened men of Middle-Eastern descent deplane at Changi Airport in Singapore. They walk to a departure gate for the Island of Penang, on the northwest coast of Malaysia near the southern tip of Thailand.

When they arrive a man in a Yankees cap drives them through dark streets to a dockyard known locally as the Weld Quay Clan Jetties. They park out of view behind a weathered warehouse. The driver hands the men a sealed envelope and points them toward one of the nearby docks. When the driver leaves they read Perso-Arabic script beneath a streetlamp. Waves lap against moorings in the near distance. Next to the warehouse the air is densely humid and laden with the smell of salt brine, fish and diesel fuel.

They roll and light cigarettes then walk to the end of the wooden dock, where they throw the note into the water and wait for passage north, across the border into Thailand.

A fishing boat arrives minutes later. The boat's gunwale slaps hard against the dock's edge as the captain frantically signals for the men to board. When they are on the boat they pass through the wheelhouse and climb downward into the musty berth, out of sight of prying eyes.

This stage of their journey ends hours later at the mouth of the To Reang River in Southern Thailand. The captain, like the driver before him, hands them an envelope. They read it, discard it into the water, and wait.

A long-tail riverboat arrives to carry them upriver. The breeze they enjoyed on open water yields to thick inland air.

They travel into the heart of farmland and are given final instructions beneath a gondola at the edge of the river. Another driver takes them north into Bangkok and they wait for final instructions near the Victory Monument in the Ratchathewi district. The driver nervously rolls beads through his fingers. Joggers pass within feet of the van, oblivious to what is about to happen.

A green and yellow taxi arrives, accompanied by two motorcycles. The man in the taxi drops keys and a phone on the seat before he walks away. The assassins take his place in the taxi.

The phone between them rings at 0706 military time. As planned, they receive their final instructions from the caller and enter the stream of traffic on Phahonyothin Road. They drive slowly by crowded shops and sidewalks on their left and the massive concrete pillars of the Bangkok Transit System to their right. Bangkok is a busy, crowded, industrious and inviting city, especially in the morning.

Driving slowly past the Thai Border Police Headquarters, the driver makes the shape of a pistol with his right hand and points his angry fingers across his chest at the guard shack. He pretends to fire a round. His partner laughs. As instructed, they drive slowly and watch the sidewalk for a man in a green shirt and Yankees cap. They find him standing in front of an open-air coffee shop. The spotter sees them too, and acknowledges their arrival by removing his cap and turning deliberately toward the open mouth of the café where a swarm of morning customers sip coffee, drink tea and eat pastries.

A colonel from the Thai Border Police is in line there with his aides. The assassins pull to the curb and park a few meters from the café crowd. The driver turns off the engine and throws his keys under the seat. The motorcycles pull up next to them and idle their engines as the assassins climb on. They speed away.

Six seconds later the taxi explodes, cratering the street and sending shrapnel into the crowd at velocities approaching 20,000 feet per second. Twenty-three people die instantly. Seventy-nine others suffer injuries. Windows rattle half a kilometer away.

The man who meticulously planned and financed the attack watches from the window of a luxury hotel nearby. Dust, smoke and ash rise into the sky and drift north. Within minutes, every television station in the city reports on the most devastating Bangkok terrorist event of the year—thus far.

CHAPTER 1

Tuck (Web) Webber leaves the Dirksen Senate Office Building in Washington, DC and walks through the Senate Subway Tunnel to Capitol Hill. Sweat accumulates on his forehead and across his chest and stomach, mostly from heat and humidity, but also from stress and exertion. The pressure of having to testify, yet again, in front of the Senate Armed Services Committee is palpable.

He stops momentarily to wipe his brow with a handkerchief. The subway rolls by and he looks with envy at the comfortable passengers. His feet feel like they are on fire. Six feet two inches tall, weighing nearly two hundred forty pounds, his doctor says he's overweight, needs to get his BMI down and needs to accumulate at least ten thousand steps per day if he wants to remain healthy. Reaching for that goal here feels like a mistake.

His walk ends in the relative comfort of the Capitol Building, where lawyers Harold Stein and Barbara Hemming wait. They greet Web at the top of an escalator and escort him to a hearing room. Haglund, Teller & Stein has been his main DC law firm for eighteen years. They've made enough money off of his company alone to put the partners' kids through private schools. It's common for Tuck Webber LLC to spend more on the lawyers required to vet a sale than on parts for the product being sold.

Footfalls and quiet conversations echo across the floor and ceiling as they walk. Web says, "Thought Hines would be with you." The retired general he refers to has a long history at the intersection of the law and military incursions, especially where special operations bumps dickheads with Washington politics.

Like a bothersome know-it-all, Harold touches Web's shoulder. He says, "Everything is going to be just fine. The general is already in session, something about Eastern Afghanistan. He spent a hell of a lot of time over there, you know."

Web shrugs. "I'm the guy who filled you in on all that, Harold. We've both known the bastard for years."

An embarrassed smile creases Harold's face, and he laughs nervously. "So you did. Just remember the three Cs and stay cool, calm and collected. End of the day, they are all just people like you and me."

Web's heard it all before. Harold's pandering is the worst. It grates on his nerves, how Harold pushes him to say and be what

Congress wants to hear. It's as if anyone appearing before the committee should not have an opinion.

What amazes Web most is how some of these senators struggle to understand even rudimentary technical issues, and yet make pronouncements and draft laws that affect the lives of men and women overseas. But without lawyers, he'd not be in business, so Web tolerates the scrutiny, pandering and expense. Seems unfair. His firm, Tuck Webber LLC, is a minor player in the military-industrial complex. Small arms and light aircraft are the bulk of his trade, making the expense of dealing with regulations a decisive factor in whether he turns a profit.

They wait outside the hearing-room door in the company of portraits of legislators and men of history, wall trophies peering down on them. History is interesting to Web, but not at the moment. He's tired, anxious to leave DC and immune now to the trappings of power.

Today, Barbara is on point for his legal team. She's spent years on the Hill developing relations and mapping political shoals. Her connections with members of this and other congressional committees, including Commerce, are invaluable to him and others beneath her wings. No one chooses lightly to overlook Barbara's talons and attack her clients. Moreover, she's a brilliant legal strategist, one of the most expensive lawyers inside the Beltway.

Web turns to her. "Is Hines sober?"

She smiles and shakes her head. "He consumed his share of cocktails last night, but yes. He's a trooper. It's you I'm worried about."

"Me?"

"Don't ad-lib, Web. You're no good at it."

Web rocks on his heels, an unconscious nervous tic. He checks his watch again. Like Harold earlier, Barbara touches his shoulder. "How's Samantha doing these days?" she asks, referring to Web's wife and changing the subject. Around Barbara, Web always feels led.

Before Web can answer, the hearing-room doors burst open. A stream of suited men and women pour into the hallway. Web recognizes executives of multinational corporations and wants to talk with them, maybe exchange cards, but a young man in a blue suit points toward Barbara.

"We're up," Barbara says. "Remember to smile and breathe."

Web affects a necessary smile designed to exude confidence. "Oh my God," Barbara says, and looks away. "Try to be natural, confident. You smile like that and they're all going to think you're being arrogant or worse, nervous. The sharks smell blood, we're sunk."

A guard glances at Web's visitor badge as they enter the stuffy room. Close quarters, tense people and poor ventilation make him wish he'd turned down the invitation to testify, but he knows better. Turn down the committee and you get subpoenaed. Being subpoenaed is inevitably far more expensive. Showing up also says he has nothing to hide.

Four massive, rectangular wooden tables form a single surface in the center of the room. As the room empties, a senate staffer replaces placards on the tables. Microphones rest in front of every chair so that everything said can be heard, recorded and played back at inopportune moments in the future.

General Hines rises from his seat to greet the team. He looks haggard. They all shake hands. "Ready for this?" Hines asks as Barbara and Harold sit and prepare notes.

"Never ready for this," Web says.

Hines sits to Web's left, Barbara then Harold to his right. The aide in the blue suit says he'll bring water and asks if they need anything else. Barbara says no and places a blank legal pad in front of Web. He knows the drill. He will answer precisely and volunteer nothing. He's coached again, Barbara whispering into his ear not to embellish or extrapolate. She says, "I'm serious about this today. They will try everything. Don't add commentary. And for God's sake, no jokes. You're horrible at telling jokes. Just stick to the facts."

"Why are you on my case all of a sudden?" Web says, but before Barbara can react, Hines leans into him from the other side. "Good day to keep your pie hole shut, let me do the talking. Don't elaborate."

Web laughs and shakes his head. He's getting it from both sides now. A few years earlier he tried to educate Senator Acker on why aid to countries without an adequate police presence was ineffectual. He may have used the word stupid and compared the practice to planting potatoes in September. Whatever. Barbara kicked him hard that day, caught him on the anklebone, hurt like hell.

Except for the presence of the chairwoman seated directly opposite of them, all of the senators' chairs are empty. Web leans toward Barbara. "Conn going to be here?" he asks, referring to the only senator he believes will have field experience enough to be on his side.

Barbara places her hand over his microphone and whispers that he's probably got his penis in a urinal with the rest of them. Web chuckles and asks if he can use that during the session. Barbara gives him the look.

They wait in silence, Web doodling some on his legal pad,

meaningless squares and triangles. The doodling helps reduce the flow of adrenaline. He turns to the general for assurance, but Hines ignores him. He's focused instead on something in a thick printout of the National Defense Authorization Act. Sticky-notes protrude from every side.

Web looks behind him. Two young, suited men sit there with laptops, ready to track down any bit of information Hines asks for. Two other aides sit behind him to his right. He speaks behind Barbara's back, to Harold. "They yours?"

Harold whispers, "Just in case."

"In case of what?" Web asks, but no one answers. The legal entourage for this hearing alone will cost him many thousands of dollars. Much of the cost can be charged off of taxes, and sometimes forwarded on to customers who also know the routine, but his time is never compensated. Worse yet, there's always a risk of being manipulated into perjury.

The senators enter through a door opposite them. Senator Conn is not among them. A gavel sounds. Everyone stands. The chairwoman, Senator Tibbit, calls the session to order. As senators adjust their chairs and tap their microphones, the chairwoman reads from the agenda. Web's mind drifts during the opening remarks, overwhelmed by the gravity of the moment, but he remembers to smile. Tibbit says how she hopes to keep it short. Web is all for that.

Names of those present are read into the record and Tibbit begins. "Mr. Webber. Thank you for taking time out of your busy schedule. Your testimony is vital to national interests and to the security and welfare of our troops overseas. General Hines, welcome back. I also want to thank Ms. Hemming for appearing today. How are you, Barbara?"

"Doing well, Madam Chairwoman."

Tibbit lifts reading glasses from lanyard to nose and reads a prepared statement. "Mr. Webber, you have appeared before this committee on numerous occasions to testify on conflict zones, including those in Africa, Latin America, Eastern Europe, and Central and Southeastern Asia. Your statements about the delivery of various supplies are the subject of this hearing, specifically shipments of weapons intended for Kurdish fighters in Iraq." She stares at Web as if expecting a response.

Web doesn't speak.

"We're simply having a conversation," Tibbit says.

Barbara intercedes. "Mr. Webber has been a valuable asset to DoD and various agencies, in Iraq and elsewhere."

Tibbit replies, "But Barbara. A valuable asset would not supply IS." Two of the congressmen chuckle. Web wants to fight back, but holds his tongue.

"I'm sure Mr. Webber has an explanation for why supplies fell into the wrong hands," the chairwoman continues. "We've invited you here, sir, to lend your perspective. You'll tell us what happened and we'll follow up with questions. Take as much time as you need. Mr. Webber, you have the floor."

Web folds his arms, rests his elbows on the table, and leans toward his microphone. Before he reads from the script edited by his lawyers, he says, "First of all, I feel compelled to point out that only a fraction of the supplies fell to the Islamic State."

Web clears his throat and reads from his script. "I was one of a few contractors to supply authorized light arms and ammunition to Kurdish forces. Our planes followed a complicated flight pattern to the coordinates given. We conducted an airdrop. Some of the parachutes fell into the wrong hands."

Tibbit glances at her notes, looks to her right and hesitates. She has a quiet conversation with a senator for two minutes. Web leans forward again, but Hines clears his throat. Web waits.

The chairwoman continues. "Mr. Webber. You are a pilot, is that correct?"

"That is correct."

"Pilots are trained to understand coordinates, the effect of wind and so on?"

Web hesitates again. General Hines speaks before he can reply. "Web was not the pilot for this mission. Highly experienced pilots delivered the package as instructed, precisely to the coordinates given. The result was unfortunate, but no fault of Mr. Webber or his team. Lines between ISIS and the Kurds were changing at that time, often more than once in a single day."

Tibbit continues. "So it is your testimony, Mr. Webber, that the mission was conducted flawlessly, at least in so far as you executed the plan."

"That is correct," Hines says, again speaking for Web.

"I'd like to hear from Mr. Webber, please."

Web says, "We conducted the mission using the timing and co-ordinates supplied."

"I see. In your estimation, then, the flaw lies in the planning that went into this mission. You used the words *timing and coordinates supplied*." Before Web can answer to the statement the chairwoman passes the conversation to her left. "Senator Johnson, you have three minutes."

The senator sips water before speaking. "You're probably a competent guy. Yet, your name has come up in the past." The senator hesitates as he reads something in front of him. "You testified that your pilots used a set of coordinates. Were those coordinates flawed?"

Web says, "I did not use that word. Action on the ground can change in any conflict. It was a fluid situation."

Barbara pushes a note at him. It reads "Just the facts!"

The senator continues. "If things on the ground were fluid, as you say, you must have sensed the danger. Wouldn't it have been better to wait for updated coordinates?"

"I was not responsible for the coordinates," Web says. "Only the delivery. We delivered to the coordinates given, on the timeline provided."

"Thank you, Mr. Webber. I yield the floor."

"The chair recognizes Senator Acker."

As Senator Acker formulates his questions, Senator Conn enters the room and takes his seat. Acker says, "You dropped supplies at the coordinates given. In your expert opinion, if different coordinates were used, the weapons you supplied would not today be in enemy hands. They would be in the hands of the Kurds, for example. Is that correct?"

"I can't engage in speculation," Web says.

"Who supplied the coordinates?"

General Hines interrupts. "The coordinates were supplied by the Kurds, with the assistance of US special operations personnel on the ground."

Senator Acker scoffs. "Oh, hell. Let's blame the Kurds. We have a private international arms dealer from the Midwest dropping arms into enemy territory based upon coordinates supplied by mystery men. That about right? I've said from the beginning that we need the Pentagon to step up. Madam Chairwoman, I have no further questions."

Senator Tibbit thanks Senator Acker and yields the floor to Senator Conn. "Thanks for coming in, Web. I know you're traveling to Thailand today. I'll keep my comments short." Conn adjusts his papers, sits back and takes off his glasses. He speaks in the amicable tone of a true southern gentleman. "We're talking about a regrettable incident but these things happen in war. If my fellow congressmen, and woman, had war experience, they'd know. By the way, the same people the good senator accuses of being incompetent with their coordinates took ground and recaptured the damn shipment from the jihadis, so no, Senator. The arms are not at present in the hands of IS. We determined that earlier today in this very room. Let's get our facts straight and keep things in perspective.

"Mr. Webber, I don't get it. There's no good reason for you to appear here today. The country has solicited your services in the past and will again in the future. You delivered to the coordinates provided. By the way, Madam Chairwoman, the facts are in the record. I see no fault in Web's actions. I have no more questions and suggest that we move to more pressing matters."

"Thank you, Senator Conn," Tibbit says. "I tend to agree. The floor is open to further discussion." The committee members remain silent. "Thank you for your time, Mr. Webber. We'll be watching. We are adjourned."

The gavel sounds and Web turns to Barbara. "That's it? They'll be watching?"

They stand as the senators exit the room. "They got what they needed," Barbara says as they gather up papers and head toward the door. "They established that you dropped at the coordinates given. The real fire is under the feet of planners."

Harold and Barbara accompany Web to the parking lot and limo that will bring him to Dulles Airport. Before he leaves he removes his tie and opens his shirt collar. "I thought for sure I was going to get raked over the coals," he says.

"We got lucky," Barbara says. "Enjoy your trip."

CHAPTER 2

Web's first impulse at Dulles is to tell the operative hired to travel with him to go home. His elbows rest on his knees. He plays with something like a kid would, thumbs on the keys of some game or other. They sit in the airport waiting for their flight to Narita, Japan, a layover on the flight path to Bangkok.

"Your name is Tallis, right? You should look up once in a while."

Without looking up, Tallis tells Web he's on a break.

"From what? You're on personal protection duty."

Web hates the perpetual travel that an international arms dealer enjoys. Frequent trips to distant locations are particularly arduous, and the bigger the deal is, the less sleep Web gets. Less sleep means his medical issues flare up. Anytime there's a mound of cash at stake, whether from equipment sales or brokering of precious metals, sleep and calm run distant.

In the weeks leading up to this deal, Web popped pills, manned up, and logged thousands of miles meeting with suppliers and working on logistics. That's what it takes to move metric tons of munitions and equipment around the globe. The accumulated stress of his profession over almost two decades has taken a toll.

"I hate flying commercial," Web mumbles. He's not sure Tallis is listening, but it doesn't matter. There are more pressing things to worry about. He attributes his hot feet, tingling legs and a twisted spine to being in his fifties. Doctors say it isn't age. Something else is wrong. Two EMGs and a gallon of blood drawn in the past year proved nothing except that healthcare is expensive. So the neurologists have concluded that perhaps his autonomic nervous system is out of whack. He's not supposed to stress about the stress of not having an actual diagnosis, but he does. Web's blood pressure has more dips and spikes than a fitful stock chart.

He glances at Tallis again and realizes he can't take any more. "Lesson one. The pros have their heads on a swivel to see if a hatchet man is lurking. You'll do that if you want to stay in the biz."

"Good idea," Tallis says, but he doesn't look up.

"Just saying."

Patch Riggs, one of Web's associate partners, hired Tallis a few weeks earlier. Raves about him. As far as Web is concerned, the new guy is a wash. Everyone under thirty is a kid to Web, but Tallis showed up in a *South Park* T-shirt and that alone makes Web suspect that Patch may be pranking him. The kid's frame is right for the job—6'3" and cut, but he has long, scraggly hair. Might even lean left. Web likes his guys to look and act sharp.

Tallis rocks with the action his thumbs create on whatever the hell it is—Gameboy or Nintendo—Web suspects one of those gaming devices. Tallis says, "I've never worked for an arms dealer before." He says it loud enough for people around them to hear. A few turn their curious meddling necks toward Web.

"Import export."

"That either," Tallis says.

In Web's estimation, they've turned a corner. The kid is cut from burlap rather than rip-stop nylon. He's as bad as Web's nephew— jacked-up gamer, high-adrenaline, no accomplishments to point to outside of a computer display. The kid lacks substance. "Real world move too slowly for you?" Web asks, more of an accusation than a question. As soon as he says it, he realizes that the frustration of the day is about to erupt in molten syllables.

"Sometimes," Tallis says coolly.

A young boy sits in the facing row of seats between his hefty mother and querulous older sister. Mother and daughter speak incessantly over the boy's head while he slumps calmly, chin in the palms of his hands, elbows on knees, engrossed with Tallis. Web shakes his head. When he gets to Bangkok, he will confront Patch.

Then Web remembers how he is supposed to take deep breaths or something, but screw that. Thailand is his largest customer in Southeast Asia. He's headed for the biggest equipment demo he's ever conducted there, and everything has to go perfectly.

Web hears an alert notification on his phone. He pulls it from his pocket, presses his thumb into the screen, opens the encrypted app and finds an update on a substantial ammunition order.

Tallis's shoulders wrench. He writhes with the controller as if possessed. "Shit!" he barks.

Waiting travelers scowl in their direction, and the boy across from them laughs. His mother gasps. Tallis seems unaware of his surroundings, which causes Web to take a breath and close his eyes for a second. *The hell with it!*

"Excuse me," Web says. He stands and walks a few yards away.

It's four in the morning in Thailand, but he punches Patch's name in their communications app and lifts his phone to his ear.

The call rings three times. When Patch Riggs answers, he says, "Who the hell did you hire? Sitting in the airport over here and the guy is playing with toys. First thing he said, right here in the airport, is how he never worked for an arms dealer before. I don't need this crap, Patch."

Patch's deep voice cracks into laughter.

"You played me, right?" Web insists.

Patch says, "He was potty-trained in combat, for Christ's sake. Don't like what he's doing? Tell him. You don't need to wake me up in the middle of the night to hold your hand on this one."

"He has the maturity of a fifteen-year-old."

"You wouldn't say that if you'd read the damn resume I sent. You really need to eyeball that stuff. Anyway, he might be a quirky prankster, but he has a hell of a lot of tactical experience. Hand-to-hand is outstanding. You wanted stealth, right? I'm not even there and I can tell you no one would think he's an operative. No one. I'd love to BS with you, always fun, but I'm going back to sleep. We good?"

Web glances back at Tallis and adjusts his glasses. "You're right about one thing. No one would think he has any idea what he's supposed to be doing, especially me. You hired this guy to prank me, right?"

Patch laughs again.

"I wouldn't put it past you," Web says. "Anyway. If you say he's all right, I'll give him a chance. Everything on track?"

"All good," Patch says. "See you when I see you."

Web returns to his seat and tries to make out the thing Tallis plays with. Tallis cusses under his breath.

Web says, "No more questions about what I do, where we are going, any of that. And no more cussing."

"Got it."

"Gives people the wrong idea."

Tallis doesn't respond or look up, so Web continues. "We can talk later on the plane when passengers are sleeping or something. Better yet," Web says, angry now. "Wait until we're in Bangkok."

"Sure."

Three minutes later Web is still obsessed. He asks Tallis what he's playing with.

Tallis ignores him at first, engrossed by something on his little screen. In time he says, "Maybe on the plane. Better yet, Bangkok."

"Wiseass," Web says. *OK, maybe the kid is all right.*

"Jerkwad," Tallis says, not batting an eye but smiling, thumbs and index fingers flying.

The child across the aisle laughs. Web smiles at him and twirls his finger around his right ear. He points to Tallis and they snicker together.

A few hours into the flight Web sets aside his novel and removes his loafers to rub his gold-toed socks and painful feet. To hell with the comedian across from them who earlier had something to say about him taking off his shoes.

Tallis takes a break from his device. He turns toward Web and places his controller on the seat between them. "What are we doing in Bangkok, boss?"

Web removes his glasses, rubs his eyes and glances at some of the other passengers. There's only one other reading light on in the cabin. Everyone seems to be at or near sleep. He says, "We probably shouldn't talk about it in depth right at the moment, but Patch is joining us for a meeting with a Thai general."

"Just trying to make conversation."

"I appreciate that. Just saying."

Tallis hands his controller to Web. "It's in beta."

Web takes the hand-held unit. It's much heavier than he thought it would be. He turns it over. A worn label on the back reads, "Mission Aircrew Training Systems." Web realizes Tallis is training to pilot highly specialized military drones.

He laughs and asks Tallis a question he's been dying to ask since they met. "What's your body mass index?"

CHAPTER 3

Jawad is not his real name. He doesn't yet know anyone in the Haqqani network, Lashkar al Zil, Boko Haram or the Uighurs of Western China. He's never met a Chechen fighter and certainly did not secretly orchestrate, nor have anything to do with, attacks in Egypt, Belgium or France as he once implied while holding an AK-47 for the first time.

Counter-terrorist professionals in Europe and regions of Southeast Asia, outside of those engaged with insurgents in the Southern Border Districts of Thailand, are not yet familiar with his slight frame, dark hair and scraggly beard. They don't know that he often wears a green cap or that he took the name Jawad from Mohammed Jawad An-Neifus, a celebrated figure among the most radicalized Sunni detainees at Camp Bucca, where he was held by US Navy military police in the mid-2000s.

He didn't enter the camp as Jawad. His birth name was Sarab Najjar. He was the well-educated, light-spirited son of wealthy Kuwaiti citizens. Of course, Camp Bucca terrified Sarab, as it would anyone. But Sarab was intelligent, well-spoken and persuasive. His easy style and intellect earned him the title of teacher and his captors eventually treated him more as a friendly. They allowed him access to multiple compounds for the purpose of encouraging a particular form of literacy among the detainees.

There were other teachers who did not confine their teaching to literacy. Sarab learned from men like Abu Bakr al-Baghdadi and kept his mouth shut when in the presence of the most outspoken prisoners. When he was asked for an opinion, he debated the true meaning of Jihad with passion, arguing at first that true Jihad was an interior holy war, a battle with the lower self.

In his first month in the camp he argued playfully with anyone, even the few guards that would argue back, but he soon realized that was dangerous. Another man was caught doing something similar. During the night his tongue was cut out by the faithful. Others lost their eyes for spying on things that were none of their business. Within months, Sarab espoused a theology of reckoning, the more violent the better. Adopting jihadist rhetoric was a way to survive in the camps, and he was determined to survive.

Thousands of detainees prayed together before dawn and again at noon, afternoon, sunset and evening in the shadow of razor wire, guard towers and raised walkways. Dust got into everything. Sarab often looked toward his home in Kuwait, just across the border to the south, and dreamed of what he would do if ever freed.

Sarab Najjar entered Camp Bucca a terrified man, cowering to and appeasing his captors, but the constant threat of violence changed him. He fashioned himself after Jawad An-Neifus, took the name Jawad and grew in confidence, cunning and defiance.

Thirteen months after he was imprisoned, the Americans surprised everyone. They closed the camp. They just left. After Washington yanked the US military from the country with only a few of the most hardened prisoners in their clutches, he was released and returned to Kuwait. Filled with a new sense of mission, he begged his father to support the overthrow of the bloody dictator Bashar al-Assad of Syria. It was part of a plan discussed in confidence, in the shade of block walls behind the razor wire. His father and others agreed. Funds flowed north toward the Levant, with good intentions, but ended up in the hands of those who formed the Islamic State in Syria.

With considerable political intervention from his parents, and a minor modification to his name and passport, Sarab entered the United States on a student visa. He enrolled in DePaul University's department of economics in Chicago. He never told anyone about his time behind the wire.

Wealth made him popular. A small group of economics and political science students joined his lavish dinners and weekend parties. He enjoyed their company and big ideas. "Inequity pervades every corner of the globe," Sarab often argued. "Rise up! When the Islamic State is fully realized, it will need men like us to govern."

Friends joked that zealots like Sarab were exactly the kind of leaders the world did not need. They followed his reasoning, but pointed to innumerable anecdotes from the war-torn Middle East. Indonesian students argued that Southeast Asia was the epicenter of true Islam, because true Islam leads to peace, not violence. They argued that in their home countries, places like Indonesia and Malaysia, faith grows with equanimity, without the need for revenge. Sarab disagreed. Even then he felt the hand of destiny guide him toward a leadership position on the global stage.

Near the end of his second year, well short of a degree, Sarab wrote his family that he'd finished his studies. He drafted business plans that described Southeast Asian capital markets as golden opportunities. He flew to Kuwait and charmed millions of dollars from parents and uncles so that he could go into business.

With funds secured, Jawad moved to Singapore where he read everything he could find on regional politics. His studies included Indonesia, the Southern Philippines, Myanmar, Malaysia and Thailand. Thailand enticed him most. In the decade prior to his arrival, nearly seven thousand people died in escalating violence between the Thai government and Islamic secessionists, actions most often referred to as an Islamist insurgency. Another fourteen thousand were injured in the struggle, rendering the area largely ungovernable and ripe, in his opinion, for a more coordinated and successful uprising.

At Camp Bucca he had learned that the Islamic State would rise from vacuous instability. Everything fit and soon Thailand was all he could think about.

Jawad chose to use his millions to support the most effective groups of the insurgency, but his motives were not pure. Through his generosity he learned how they worked. He took notes. He doled out cash more generously than the moderates, quietly supporting families of the dead and injured throughout Southern Thailand, instantly winning the trust of many families. But he was also more decisive and bold in his statements of violence than were his brothers in the BRN, National Revolutionary Front and Gerakan Mujahidin Patani.

To the faithful, his efforts are known only as Ja. Ja funded this and Ja funded that. Ja attacked yesterday. Ja will attack tomorrow. Ja is the future.

Jawad reduced his expenditures to other groups in favor of his own. Ja is simple, he explains to his followers. Ja will never attack a Muslim, even if that brother struggles in his faith. Ja is not a threat, now or in the future. Ja is for the common family.

Only the closest followers know his name, and then only after a long vetting process. None of them, not even his inner circle, ever hear his birth name, Sarab. To them he is Jawad the generous, their gateway to the coming Islamic State. Founder of Ja, the ghost of Southern Thailand and the embodiment of true faith.

Today, Jawad meets with his closest followers on the slopes of the rugged Tenasserim Range. They stand in a dense tropical forest, at the shoreline of the Gulf of Thailand, within miles of the South China Sea. Some of his followers have had little rest for days. Jawad knows the thoughts of his men will have strayed after the emotional impact of their most recent attack. He has called the meeting to review what took place and discuss a new course of action.

Jawad congratulates his followers. "This is our battlefield. I have funded your mosques and families," he says "We have struggled together, brothers, and I will happily die to set you free.

"We have done something very important. This month you fulfilled your duties with dedication and precision. Remain strong. Go about daily routines as if nothing has happened. People will talk about the bomb, but don't engage with them. Don't listen. Walk away. Any word, the slightest gesture, could give you away and place us all in danger."

Jawad hands envelopes to each of the men, but pays special attention to Akara, barely twenty years old, a thin, dedicated man in need of dental care. He was recruited after his sister was severely injured traveling in a car with their father, the target of a rifle attack. Akara was devastated, reached out to Ja and soon became one of Jawad's most trusted aides. "You now all have enough money to live quietly for a month or more. But Akara, because you completed training abroad, and because of your bravery in confronting the border police, I am putting you on salary. The envelope you have includes money for your sister. Pay her bills. God cares for the faithful."

Akara gratefully takes the money. A tear forms on his cheek. Jawad touches the young man's shoulder then addresses all of his men. "We haven't been together as a group since Akara came back. I want him to tell you about his wife. When you were in Syria, Akara, they gave you a wife?" Jawad asks.

"Yes. I was given a wife," Akara says. He smiles broadly and receives the envy and congratulations of the young men around him.

"Did you kill?" Jawad asks. The young men look at Akara expectantly.

"I killed," young Akara says. "I killed four times."

Jawad addresses the rest of his men. "I need more like Akara. Look at his confidence, his strength and determination. He can love. He can kill. His skills are strong. This is a holy warrior. Embrace him."

In turn, each of the young men embrace Akara, a ritual Jawad learned from his time in the camp. Jawad continues. "Our fight is here, secession from Thailand. Elsewhere others carry bread, water and swords, but here, we are the leaders. I have given you the right understanding. No one else in Thailand is as well connected to the global stage as we are, and no one else has the training I offer you. Soon everyone will praise the All Merciful. Allahu Akbar. Be strong!"

The men repeat his words. "Can a man enter the gates of heaven with words?" he asks. "No, brothers. Every man must prove himself with actions. Men like Akara are blessed with a salary, training, authority, a place in the Islamic State in Thailand and a home in heaven.

"Boys, look at him. Akara is worthy. He is proven. He is a man. In the coming weeks I need the rest of you to prove yourselves worthy. When you do, I'll pay for the airplane, the training in weapons and for your wife.

"Is your wife faithful?" Jawad asks Akara.

Akara smiles. "Faithful and beautiful."

The other young men voice their approval. "Good," Jawad says. "You deserve her. And you deserve the salary. When our work is complete we will send for her. Does anyone have a question about the training? We will not be together all at once like this until next month."

One of the older recruits, a man named Sakda, asks, "Was it necessary?"

Jawad squares up to him. "Necessary?"

"So many died to kill so few."

Jawad inches closer. An angry expression softens as he speaks. "It was already written in the womb. Every soul shall have his taste of death. The faithful are blessed. The unfaithful, no matter where in time, are damned. Don't worry, brother. The hand of God guides us. Take no delight in death, but be strong."

Sakda says he understands. Pressed, the other men say they understand, too.

"Everyone should go now, but I need to speak with Akara. *Assalamu alaikum*," Jawad says.

When his followers have gone, Jawad tells Akara he has a job for him. "A dog that cannot be trusted must go," Jawad says. "You saw it yourself. Sakda is weak. He cannot be trusted. We can tell everyone he has gone to fight with the faithful in Aleppo. Do you understand?"

"I understand," Akara says.

Jawad embraces Akara and tells him how proud he is of his accomplishments, and how important he will be in the coming attacks. "God willing," Jawad says, "the network will bless us and the faithful will learn from our deeds."

CHAPTER 4

Patch Riggs waits for Web and Tallis to arrive at Suvarnabhu-mi Airport. Thousands of travelers pass through the massive steel-and-glass structure of BKK on a daily basis, making Bangkok one of the most important tourist and business destinations in Southeast Asia.

Patch is just over six feet tall, but he weighs two hundred and forty-five pounds. He sports a barrel-chest and carries himself like the seasoned special ops command lieutenant colonel he was for many years. Even though retired now, Patch is approached frequently by military, agency and private entities for his considerable connections and experience. Today he's clean shaven, but if the mission calls for it he'll grow a beard. Hard men are forged from hard duty. Patch has been shot on multiple occasions and yet considers himself to be among the lucky.

After nearly twenty-four hours of travel, Web and Tallis deplane. They walk toward customs and the baggage area. Web is relieved to see Tallis gradually assume personal-protection best-practice protocols, leading him to believe his initial impressions may have been mistaken. Even so, Patch is going to hear about it. Can't let his best friend play him if that's what actually happened.

They connect at baggage claim area twenty. "Everything on track?" Web asks as the men shake hands and head toward the exit.

"You'll have to tell me. I met with everyone you wanted me to see. Wrote a few orders. It's been a good trip so far. When do we meet the general?"

"Tomorrow afternoon, late. I'm going to need every minute of rest for this one."

"Hell of a long way to travel for a single meeting. What's it about?"

"Neither General Phang nor Choochai would say, just that they have a big project they want to discuss in person."

As the men near the exit door, Web stops walking and turns to his men. "You two pranked me, right?" Web asks, a wry smile on his face.

Tallis smiles and Patch laughs. "Let's just say you were never in any danger," Patch says.

CHAPTER 5

Intercontinental Hotel, Bangkok, 0630 hours the following morning.

Web's phone alarm buzzes and vibrates on the nightstand. Despite heavy medication for his legs, he found it impossible to sleep. They burned and twitched deep into the night. He feels physically out of balance, but is determined to stay mentally positive and on track.

A Thai monk once taught him to stand when he first opens his eyes in the morning, and to briskly rub his shoulders, legs and arms into action. Web reaches for his glasses before he turns off the alarm. He kicks off his covers, adjusts his jones, and comes to his feet. Mental images of the upcoming day mingle with deep breathing and a couple squats as he vigorously rubs his chest and arms with a wadded-up sock. Then he picks up his phone. This day starts with an encrypted call to Patch.

"I need you both ready to roll by noon. We good?" Web asks.

"All set. We're meeting here, right? Breakfast first?"

"I haven't heard otherwise. I'll be talking to Choochai in a minute."

"What are the roles?"

"I need you to stick with Choochai. He always knows more than he lets on. Maybe he'll open up to you. Tallis doesn't have a role except to keep his eyes open. No funny stuff, Patch. Not today."

Web ends the call, splashes cool water on his face, then cranks the faucet to hot. When the water forms steam, he shaves. After showering he pulls granola bars from his luggage, checks the time, and reviews notes and spreadsheets.

At 0900 he calls Choochai Mookjai, a lieutenant colonel in the Thai Army. They've known each other for many years. Choochai is General Phang's closest personal aide, an indispensable liaison between Web and the Thai military command.

"*Sawadee krup*, Choochai," Web says. He muses over how the colonel prefers to be called by his first name, and yet, Choochai often calls him Mr. Webber instead of Web, preserving a layer of formality common in Thai dealings.

Greeting each other with the term *sawadee* is everyday life in Thailand, that and the slight bow with palms together called *wai*. *Krup* adds a tone of respect, which in Choochai's case is well earned. Choochai is slight in build, always calm, yet spirited under pressure. He can be incredibly amusing when it suits him, but typically prefers to stand humbly in the shadow of others. More than a military aide, Choochai is sensitive to, and informed by, the cultural and political landscape of Bangkok.

"Sawadee krup, Mister Webber. Welcome back. We will pick you up at 1300 hours. Are you traveling alone?"

"Patch is with me, and one other. I thought we were meeting at the Intercontinental? Are you picking us up or sending a driver?" Web asks. The Thai military often provides an escort for Web when he travels on official business. Arms dealers, Tuck Webber LLC included, have enemies. His customers' enemies are among the most dangerous in the world. The list includes nation states, drug lords, radical jihadists, secessionists and common criminals. They are scattered across continents. Attempts to intercept shipments are common in the arms trade.

"The venue has change," Choochai says. "There was an incident yesterday. All the schedule have change. You will attend a gathering that is already secure."

"I heard about a bombing last night. Fill me in."

"Very bad. Part of the meeting."

The fact that Choochai conflates the bombing with the meeting elevates the anxiety Web already feels. As they talk he turns on the television and lowers the sound. Video of a horrible bombing is on both of the main news channels. He sits on the bed facing images of bloody victims covered by shirts and jackets or being helped away from the scene. It is reminiscent of the Erawan Shrine bombing, but the death and injury toll are likely much worse.

"I'm looking at it now. I can easily see the need for heightened security," Web says.

"Very bad. Your driver will have a red patch on his left sleeve."

"Got it, Choochai. I look forward to seeing you again."

Web fires up a morning cigar and thumbs a text to his wife, Samantha, who travels internationally as a flight attendant: *Things are going well, Sam. Wish you were here.*

Sam is the love of his life—gracious, always at ease, physically and spiritually beautiful. He misses her whenever he travels alone, but bringing her on this trip just didn't work out.

A curious fear enters his mind. Web has never doubted his vocation or role in a mission, but in a weak moment he recently told Sam time has run out. He doesn't even know why he said it. She'd replied that maybe it was time to retire. It's a theme he gets from her more often these days, her stating the fact that they have more than enough money to retire comfortably. Every time she brings it up, he says he'll think about it, but rarely does.

Now, sitting on the edge of yet another hotel bed, cigar smoldering in the tray, he tries to imagine a life where he is not chasing sales on a global stage. With great risk comes the possibility of substantial reward, but it's no longer about the money. It's about the excitement and challenge. Web's teams find success where other teams fail; to that adds another dimension to the decision—pride. Where's the pride in sitting on a couch?

"It's about how a man spends his life," Web says aloud, as if Sam were standing right there in front of him, waiting for his answer. Web's career has given him a view of international affairs few men are blessed, or cursed, with seeing, but maybe Sam's right. Maybe he should wind things down and step away.

"Can't do this now," he says aloud, and stands. He draws from his cigar and mumbles to himself. "Not today anyway."

CHAPTER 6

Military-dispatched BMW motorcycles arrive at Web's hotel. Web, Patch and Tallis ride side streets in the comfort and security of a Range Rover Sentinel from the Intercontinental to Hotel Muse, where the meeting with General Phang will take place.

When they arrive, even Web is surprised by the level of security. Humvees and two armored Unimog troop carriers block parking in front of the hotel for a block in either direction. Soldiers in full gear direct them onto Ban Lang Suan Alley and check the undercarriage of their SUV before allowing them to open the doors and exit. When they do step onto the pavement, guards bow deeply, surround them and escort the team around the corner to the entrance.

"Is this usual for Thailand?" Tallis asks Web quietly. His attention moves quickly from object to object as they walk.

"No. Stay sharp," Web says.

They enter the small, dark front lobby through floor-to-ceiling wooden doors. Choochai greets them wearing light white cotton clothing, typical casualwear for men in his position, especially in hot humid climates. Tallis gazes upward at ornate wrought iron and wood appointments as they walk across an intricately detailed parquet floor. Web has been to this hotel many times, but Patch and Tallis have not. Hotels like the Muse are more like boutiques, small in size, a showcase for craftsmanship and amazing service.

Patch gives Tallis lobby duty and tells him to be on his best behavior: no pranks, no fuckups, respectful of anyone on the general's security team. He hands an earpiece to Web and they leave Tallis near the elevator. Choochai takes them to the 24th floor. On the way up Choochai answers questions about the heightened security. "Very bad, yesterday. Today many new threats, but you are safe here. The building is clear.

"Tonight you meet friends and family members of General Phang at the Speakeasy Bar lawn terrace." He smiles when he says this, emphasizing the word *speakeasy* for some reason. "General has reserve the Blind Pig cigar bar for private meeting."

"I watched news all morning," Web says.

"So many dead and injured. We have to do more," Choochai says.

The Speakeasy lawn, as Choochai calls it, is an exposed rooftop terrace with sturdy all-weather furniture and a reasonable view of the city. The general's guests bow to or salute Web and Patch as they arrive. They are never seen together in the media, but there have been times where he appears in the background at gatherings. Today he is very sensitive to individuals taking photographs.

Choochai walks Web from guest to guest, making introductions. The mood of the gathering is appropriately subdued, as nearly every conversation recalls the terror of the most recent insurgent attack. As they circulate, Choochai explains which of the guests are merely friends and which are relatives. Web is given the respect of celebrity, knowing full well that many do not know who he is, only that he is important to the general. He makes a point of talking about his business in general terms, mentioning water projects often.

Su Tha Ros chefs, from the restaurant of the same name on the nineteenth floor, serve Thai and European delicacies.

Web and Patch sample seafood and roast duck curries, coconut rice and noodle dishes. The Thai food is more than enough for everyone, but there are also sterling silver plates of French hors d'oeuvres. It's a pleasant distraction as his mind races forward to the discussion he is to have with the general.

The head tobacconist from the Blind Pig cigar bar offers the general and his guests an assortment of aged cigars. Web selects a Montecristo No. 2. Immediately one of General Phang's day-wives approaches and lights his cigar. Gorgeous young escorts are a measure of affluence among powerful Thai men. The general is no exception.

Moments after Web and Patch light up, the general steps onto the terrace. A third day-wife escorts him, hand positioned lightly under his arm. She totes his briefcase and steps away as guests stand and bow in unison, Web with them.

The eyes of every guest follow General Phang as he walks directly to Web. They greet each other and the general asks for a few minutes to visit with his friends before they adjourn to a private conference area. As the general catches up with visitors, Choochai and Patch refill their plates. Web braces mentally for the meeting. He's learned that when the general asks for a special session the commitment can be anywhere from a few minutes to many hours, even days. He gratefully accepts any face time he can get.

Patch brings a plate of food to the lobby for Tallis as Web studies the general's interactions. Everyone knows his or her place in this dance—bowing, smiling, laughing, sometimes whispering in confidence.

Thirty minutes go by before the general returns to conduct business. Day wives gather around them, and Choochai and Patch follow Web and General Phang to a private room.

When they arrive, the women sit apart from the men. Choochai and Patch step onto an adjoining private balcony leaving the general and Web in facing dark-leather chairs.

Pleasantries precede business in Thailand. The general expresses his interest in how Web's business is progressing in Thailand and elsewhere. He seems sincere in his concern that Web succeed, and interested in capacity.

As if scripted, four or five minutes into their conversation, the general's focus shifts. He describes how his position in Thailand's political pantheon has changed. His standing with peers and the royal family has risen. "I am very happy, but I have much responsibility. Finding the people responsible for the bombing is now on my shoulders, as is protecting the people. Being able to prevent attacks in the future is very important."

"I speak for my family, and everyone who works for me, when I say that our thoughts and prayers go out to all the victims. If there is anything we can do to help, please just let us know."

"We will get to that," the general says, and his face floods. This is new for Web, seeing this man in an emotional state.

The general looks away momentarily and seems to contemplate something. When he returns to the conversation he speaks with renewed resolve. "The bomb was left in a taxi cab on Phahonyothin Road near the Border Patrol station. The news reports a random attack. That is probably not true. Four of the victims were Border Patrol officers who participated in recent peace talks. All those deaths, to send a message."

"Choochai says you went to the site."

The general's eyes immediately moisten. "Bodies torn into many pieces, shredded corpses pasted against walls and each other. I can't get it out of my mind, Web. The smell of the disemboweled and explosives together is the worst."

"I'm sorry you experienced this. Some of those images will be with you for the rest of your life. I didn't know that officers were killed. That explains heightened security. I hope you are successful in tracking down the killers."

"We will find them, but finding attackers should not be the priority. Even before Erawan we have been increasing our capabilities to prevent such attacks. Web, Thais are peaceful, inviting and industrious. We love it when you come here to enjoy yourselves. It is good for our economy and Bangkok is the most popular tourist destination in the world. We cannot allow a few misguided insurgents to destroy the peace."

"Terrorism is a cancer that nearly every country faces. My heart is with you."

The general reaches for his briefcase. He pulls it close to his side, but doesn't open it. "I cannot cure violence with a hammer, Web. A scalpel is needed. I only have hammers. Excuse me for a moment."

The general stands and dismisses his day wives. He slips a few thousand bhat to one of the women and returns to his discussion with Web in a more relaxed state.

"Now we talk openly." As he speaks he pours a glass of Scotch for himself and offers one to Web. Web declines. "We have known each other many years," General Phang says. He sets his cigar aside. "The country needs your help. I've been talking to suppliers and advisors for long time about a new surveillance network. Progress is too slow, Web. Too much research. Too many excuses. No action! You understand?"

"I do," Web says.

"People injured and dead. Investigators from all over the country have tracked the cowards from the bombing site into a market, but that is the end of the trail so far. In the future I need better tools. That is where you come in."

The statement surprises Web. "I'm not sure I follow."

The general puts his hand on his briefcase handle. "Last week I made an important decision, to place all new intelligence contracts under one management team. You will set up the operation. If I don't have new capabilities soon, violence will escalate. It's a big problem what a few determined terrorists can do."

Web takes a long, smooth draw from his cigar. He knows what a project of this magnitude could mean for his organization and weighs that against his team's skill sets. "I'm honored, but what I do is procure weapons, helicopters and UAVs—some marine equipment. A good portion of our work here in Thailand isn't even military. The water projects in the north, for example. I'm not sure we are the right organization for a big ISR project."

"Before we talk about intelligence, surveillance and reconnaissance, we have unfinished business. Two payments."

Web is surprised. "Only one payment, and it is not even due yet."

General Phang waves off the suggestion and calls loudly to Choochai. Choochai comes in from the terrace and receives signed payout documents from the general. They speak in Thai for a moment, then the general adds in English, "Let us know when the transfer is complete." Choochai smiles at Web and leaves the room.

"I appreciate your business very much, General. Thank you. Very generous to make both payments." Web mentally adds three million dollars to his corporate account and tries to show neither surprise nor excitement. In the corner of his eye, there in the near distance, he sees Patch raise his glass to the occasion.

"You trust me to pay. I trust you to deliver," the general says. He opens his briefcase and pulls out a thick folder, knocks an inch of ash from his cigar, and invites Web to join him on the balcony.

Patch steps inside so they can remain alone. The setting is intimate, just a few square meters of space with a table and two chairs available to them. Web follows the general to the railing and notices a man on the rooftop of the neighboring building. "General!" he says, alarmed, pointing, placing himself between the general and the figure.

The general smiles and reassures Web that the man he sees is his. Web relaxes and apologizes.

"It's a good omen that you looked up," the general says." We need better technology, including advanced sensors and a more advanced class of aerial drones to carry them. How do you say it? We need eyes in the sky."

He turns to Web and leans his weight against the railing. He flicks his finger toward the slowly sinking sun. "To our west, Myanmar has signed with one of the world's biggest suppliers of both armed and unarmed aircraft." He points south. "A secessionist insurgency has raged in the southernmost provinces and districts for far too long. Thousands are dead and many thousands are injured. And here, all around us, protesters organize, disband and organize again."

"UAVs can only do so much," Web says.

The general hands Web a folder and motions to sit. "Our digital assets are scattered across too many data centers. We need strategies and tools that link land, air and marine intelligence. Wherever targets travel, we should be able to follow. Some experts say that proposal is too difficult. I say, too much talk! I just want it done."

Web reads as the general paces. If the general can achieve half of what is asked for in his executive summary, Thailand will have one of the most sophisticated surveillance networks in the world. But Bangkok is a sprawling and fast-moving city. Thailand is a big country. He sees dozens of unmentioned obstacles within the first two minutes of reading the report, but fights the urge to agree with those who have come before him. Wanting to make better use of his time with the general, he quickly flips through dozens of detailed pages until he is at the end of the text.

"Who are these people?" Web asks. A section near the back of the folder is reserved for photographs, head shots mostly. He holds up one of the sheets.

The general walks to him and sits. "Insurgents and drug lords. Some just common criminals. There are descriptions on the back of each print. As soon as possible, I want new tools to hunt for the one called Jawad."

"I assume he has something to do with the bombing?"

"We think so." The general reaches for the folder, pulls out one of the photos, and hands it to Web. "Jawad is an outsider," he says. "No one claimed responsibility, but we believe Ja did this. Even if not Ja, he is a person of interest for us."

"I hope you get him. What about these other photographs, Rosyid and Achwan?"

"Right now, Jawad is our main target. What is your assessment of the plan?"

"I know you are anxious, but honestly, this will take weeks of evaluation before I can give you a detailed reply and cost estimate," Web says. "I understand the basics, though. You want a team to collect data from all public transportation systems, then sync that data with aerial fleets and other feeds through an operations center. Where there are gaps in the grid, you need cameras or other sensors installed. All that data needs to be turned into actionable information and streamed to your teams on a need-to-know basis. Is that about the gist of it?"

"That and new tactical capabilities. Will your government take issue with the equipment lists? They have been reluctant with us since we shut down the protests."

"I have people in Washington that deal with Commerce Department regulations on a daily basis. Are you familiar with our Arms Export Control Act?"

"ITAR. Is that the same thing?"

"International Traffic in Arms Regulations. Their annual update comes out next week. It's shifting sand, General. I won't lie. We may not know definitively until your specs are nailed down. If you want me involved I'll get on it right away, but it will still take the better part of a month before I can get back to you with precise costs."

"Of course, but please speed things along. I trust you'll figure out. what to do"

"One final question. Why me?"

The general raises his glass to toast the moment. "The answer is simple. You get things done."

"I'll do my best," Web says.

The men stand. "You came so far for such a short meeting, but I think you will agree it was worth the trip. Here's to a long and productive future," the general says.

Web accepts the responsibility with a handshake.

Web spends one extra day in Thailand before returning to the States. Under other circumstances he would stretch that to a week. For him, two long flights in such a short period of time are especially grueling, but he can't lose any time on a project of this magnitude.

CHAPTER 7

To the rare visitor, the lobby of Tuck Webber LLC looks like a war museum. Photographs of military and civilian dignitaries line the walls. Each photo tells a story—Web with the president, Web with various generals, Web with prime ministers and unnamed operatives and security personnel from the US, Thailand, Israel and many places in Europe and Africa. There are photos of Web and Patch with special-forces personnel on every continent, many faces deliberately blurred out or otherwise redacted.

Gold bars sit on Web's desk, tokens of his years as a commodities broker. Insiders in the arms trade know the name Tuck Webber very well, but the person on the street, stateside and abroad, knows little or nothing about his line of business. That's how Web likes it.

Wanting to help out, his wife Samantha drives to the airport to pick up Patch and a new contractor, Imrich Kolec, a Czech émigré. Web is excited to meet him for the first time. According to Patch, they won't find a better super-tech to run the data center. When they arrive, the new hire gets a short tour of the weapons room and fabrication shop. Rich, as Imrich prefers to be called, marvels at the varied collection of rifles, pistols, machine guns and small artillery, but they quickly get down to business in the planning room.

Web summarizes the day's agenda while Patch pulls papers from his laptop case and arranges them on the table. He says, "This is the largest technology project we've ever attempted, guys. But, I can't think of a better place in the world to spend a couple years. I expect light duty, but even Bangkok doesn't come without risk. I had Patch tap government back-channels so we know better what to put into operational security. Patch, what'd you find?"

Patch shoves paperwork toward both Rich and Web. He says, "Thailand is stable and well regulated, but the insurgency is still very active, especially in the southernmost provinces. They've attacked officials and advisors even in the north, so we have to be on our toes.

"The FBI has recently linked bomb fragments with IED attacks in Malaysia, Myanmar, Southern Philippines and now Thailand. Signatures have a definite Middle-Eastern flavor."

"The Internet is a sandbox," Rich says.

Web picks up papers from the desk. "I briefly went over your resume, Rich. Says you lived in Thailand for a while."

Rich speaks with a faint, lingering Czech accent. "I was born in the Czech Republic, lived in Germany for five years, then I worked in Thailand. Now, I live in Evanston, Illinois, but work in Chicago.

I've been strictly a consultant for the last three years."

"Anything tie you to the States?"

"No wife and no children. I know Bangkok pretty well, but I spent most of my time in Pattaya."

"Ever wrestle the orangutans?" Web asks, straight-faced.

Rich appears to be flummoxed. Web laughs.

"He's just messing with you, Rich," Patch says.

Rich takes it in stride, doesn't even ask what the joke is about. "I read about that explosion. They catch the guys yet?" Rich asks.

"Not as of yesterday. If they don't have it wrapped up by the time we arrive, you can bet it will be among our priorities," Web says.

"Let me cut this short. If you are asking if I understand the risk, I do," Rich says.

"Okay, then. Enough of that. There's a section of the contract you need to sign, standard stuff. Just wanted to address risk one more time before we get started," Web says. He turns toward a whiteboard and scribbles the letters T-ISROC.

"Quick overview," Web says. "Our main contact, General Phang, is asking for enhanced tactical intelligence. They've painted themselves into a corner with technology. Like many places, their legacy systems don't all work together, certainly not quickly. Among other things, we have to fix that."

"Thailand is wired better than most countries are, but centralizing data anywhere is like turning an ant farm into a phone book," Rich says.

"What he said," Patch says, and laughs.

Web draws a box around the acronym and draws another box

near it. "The general uses the name Thai Intelligence, Surveillance and Reconnaissance Operations Center. We'll just go shorthand. We're building an op center. We will build it, perfect and codify systems, and then gradually turn over control. Probably be in the country twenty-four to thirty months. If we can get out in twenty months, I'll be ecstatic."

"What's our cover story?" Patch asks.

Web points to the second box and scribbles the word COMMS. "Telecommunications. Part of the operation will run out of an innocuous warehouse. For the avionics and data collection, we need a data center attached to a hangar. It would be nice to have those facilities close to each other, but that may not be possible. Bird barn has to be adjacent to the operations center. Warehouse can be anywhere.

"Back to our cover. We're just another company hired to wire cell towers and whatever. That's the warehouse and linemen. But for UAVs, I'm thinking repair shop. Fixed-wing commercial repair, maybe draft a logo of an airframe flying over a rice field or something. We could get shirts made up with that agrarian focus."

"I assume the two of you will handle the actual airframes and ground control. My expertise is on the data side," Rich says.

Web shakes his head. "You need to know UAVs inside and out, Rich. Their capabilities, anyway. Of course we'll hire pilots and a ground crew for operations, but you will have to orchestrate all that."

"Back up a second," Patch says. He looks confused. "Did the general actually lock up a hangar or are we still looking?"

"Choochai thinks we will be near the Royal Thai Air Force Academy training center. What's the airport called? D something."

"Don Mueang," Rich says. "Can I see the equipment list for the op center? Maybe I can fill in some blanks."

Web points to a stack of documents at the end of the table. "Two-thirds of our fleet budget will be spent on avionics and sensor components. The balance will go into airframes and launchers. I set up a phone conference for you this afternoon to bring you up to speed on the avionics side.

"Thai Border Police already have birds in the sky, as do navy ships in the Gulf. Our operational objective is that we be capable of following bad guys wherever they go, coordinating with police and navy where possible. It's a big order."

Rich taps keys on his laptop, and sighs. "There are thousands of cameras in Bangkok. Most of the systems date back to the early nineties. We know what we're getting into?"

"You're not being paid to know, Rich," Web says. "You're being paid to figure it out. And it's not just land cameras and UAVs. Throw in all kinds of signals intelligence including phones, human asset management, media feeds and 911 calls. Ready for sleepless nights, Mr. Kolec? It's a massive undertaking."

Rich closes the lid of his laptop and pushes it a few inches forward. He rests his face in the palm of his hands, elbows on the table.

"You all right, champ?" Patch asks. "Need a hug? Maybe I have more faith in you than you have in yourself."

"I need IT requirements by end of day, Rich," Web says. "Job descriptions first, equipment lists later. Patch will find the pilots, ground crew and installers. You just have to focus on technicians."

Rich looks shell-shocked. "I don't have any sense of volume. Make the list now?"

"You really are a newbie," Patch says. He snaps his fingers a few times. "Big. Think big. Pick it up a notch, all right? We're counting on you to get up to speed quickly."

Web chuckles. "You'll get used to him," he says. "Anyway, Patch and I are going to work on some things in my office. You can use this room until lunch. Get on with it."

Web hands Rich a business card for Mikhailo Chownyk then checks his watch. "Give this guy a call in thirty minutes. He'll give you a hell of an education on avionics. Take your time. Be thorough. The information will help you understand things later."

CHAPTER 8

R ich catches up on notes for a half hour, and creates a list of questions. He opens an audio recording app, a browser and word processor to capture the phone call he's about to make. "Mr. Chownyk, my name is Imrich Kolec," Rich says. "Tuck Webber suggested I call. Do you have time now?"

"*Rád vás poznávám*. Pleased to meet you," Mikhailo says, apparently recognizing the name and slight accent Rich has as being Czech. "Call me Halo. If Web told you I know everything about aircraft, he's lying. Total BS."

Rich laughs. "You know more than I do. Web says you worked for some of the biggest names in the business."

"I'm just a consultant now, like everyone else from my generation."

"But a consultant with contacts and contracts. There's a difference. Let's start with applications. I'm familiar with hand-held UAVs. I collect micro versions, actually. But today I stepped into the world of medium-range rail-launched fixed-wing drones. Web suggested I tap your knowledge."

"You said drones. I thought we were only doing surveillance? Weapon platforms are a whole different discussion," Halo says.

"No weapons. I'm confused."

"That word *drone* implies weapons. On TV any unmanned vehicle is a drone, but technically that's not true. We can use the word drone if you like, as long as you remember the difference."

"Good to know."

"Let's get on the same page. UAVs don't fly themselves. Well, actually some do, but experienced pilots and a qualified ground crew are needed. If we are talking about rotary-wing craft instead of fixed-wing aircraft, you wouldn't need the retrieval systems. For your needs, the advantages of fixed-wings far outweigh any disadvantages.

"Point is, you want launching mechanisms and you need to retrieve your aircraft in one piece. Sometimes you crash aircraft on purpose, but you know what I mean."

"Why would you crash on purpose?"

"When you face enemies with fleets they can follow you home, right? Anyway, the retrieval system dictates modifications to the airframe. When you add reinforcement to one or another wing, you reach structural limitations and that affects performance. Every component, launch, flight and retrieval have to work in sync."

"How is performance affected?"

"If these little guys were indestructible, retrieval would be a no-brainer. You know. Just smash into the ground. Some of the sensors, even the cameras, can withstand a one thousand-G impact, but not the airframes. That's another situation where a crash makes sense. I know of cases where special forces just needed the sensors. They destroyed the aircraft, buried the pieces and carried home the avionics.

"Engineers have perfected flying a reinforced wing into a nylon tether suspended in the air on a hydraulic mobile crane. There are other systems that use springs, but I recommend the wing-capture method."

"I've seen them in operation," Rich says. "The pilots are amazing. The span of a single wing is only like a couple feet wide, but they hit the landing every time."

"That's actually software and avionics. Pilots fly close, then angle of attack, pitch and yaw are all managed electronically through precise GPS. A miss is very rare. An amateur could miss, I suppose. A wave under a small ship could rock the landing gear at the wrong second, but a miss under any conditions is rare. All right. You lose electronics, or fry a servomotor you're done, but failures won't happen if your ground crew is properly trained."

"What about hacks and GPS spoofing? Scares the crap out of me."

"Pilot flies out of range or overrides protocols, you'll have problems, but you won't do that. The pilots Web will hire won't lose flight controls. When the bird breaks digital connection, a homing device in the sensor package will direct the bird homeward. Just remember, unless you are using satellite feeds, the farther you fly, the weaker your signal. That increases the chance of your avionics being lost to jamming or rain fade.

"Now, let's talk sensors. You'll never regret paying for the highest resolution optics. You have to be able to see things clearly on the ground. That means the deluxe burger with radar, laser, pickles and cheese. Lots of cheese.

"Cameras should spec in at 30 megapixels or better. But, resolution is a balancing act. High-resolution cameras put pressure on your data link. Imagine streaming seven-by-five thousand pixel images in real time. I'm old enough to remember how sending two or three images of that size over a standard modem would take half an hour. It's all microwave now, but there are transmission challenges in that part of the world. It can rain buckets. Figure out early on whether you are using K-u or K-a band comms before you lock in specifications on the sensors. Whatever you do, factor in the possibility of rain fade.

"My other piece of advice is that you know your theater of operation inside and out."

"How experienced do the pilots have to be?" Rich asks.

"Web will hire the best. Pilots are not your typical joystick jockeys. The flight team also manages sensors. They learn angles of approach and how to take advantage of lighting conditions. When the situation calls for it they turn up the juice and send high-res, high-bandwidth images or video.

"The Net output relies on equipment, software, experience and technical support. It's the burger, fries, shake and coleslaw."

"What do you mean by specialized equipment?"

"Narrow your thinking to two kinds of missions. Set up high-altitude long-endurance autonomous units for the coastline. Program them and away they go. HALE capability with pattern recognition gives you a continual feed of video and stills. Any number of things you're flying over can be monitored, all the way down to flashes of light, then played back.

"That's one mission category. But most of your tactical work will be done with remotely controlled units. You need everything from hand-held units to jets—no gaps in your tactical options unless you can't afford to do anything about it. If you can't afford something, you can be sure that will be the one thing you need. Murphy's law, right?"

Over the next hour, Halo covers solar-powered HALE units, sensor quality, protection against hacking, geolocation technology, 3-D imaging, license plate readers, and radar tagging for boats, cars and people.

Deep into the conversation, Web and Patch return. As the door opens the smell of curry enters the room. They sit.

"Web and Patch just walked in," Rich says.

"Now I'm in trouble," Halo says. "Web, I'm talking your guy into expensive toys."

"How are you, Halo? At this stage price isn't even on the table. We're just gathering requirements. And thanks for doing this, by the way."

"No problem," Halo says. "Like I said, Rich. We can use email for questions. We're getting to the data side anyway. Anything else?"

"Any parting advice will be appreciated. Don't hold back," Rich says.

"You're an IT guy so you're used to drafting scenarios. Do that. Write dozens of them and then overlay requirements and specifications until you see the sweet spots."

"That's pretty much what we're doing today," Web says.

"Good," Halo says. "Here's my other advice. Spend money, okay? You need reliable equipment, the best stuff out there."

Web laughs at the implication that he might not do that. "The word value comes to mind. Before you go, speak to integrating new data sources with Thailand's legacy systems. Maybe Rich already mentioned it, but that's going to be our biggest challenge."

"Data integration is like three-dimensional chess. One hundred and seventy countries are building UAVs and drones now. Screw it. Everyone is building something, and with differing technologies.

"A little story. At one point the CIA transformed itself from an intelligence-gathering agency into a paramilitary unit. They've run hundreds of missile strikes in Afghanistan, Pakistan, Yemen, all over the place. Now they're trying to switch most of that capability back to the Department of Defense."

"Rich worked in Stuttgart for a while," Web says.

"I heard that. So you probably know some of the challenges JSOC faced. There have been serious mishaps during joint missions.

"What did you do in Stuttgart, Rich?"

"I did a few things for Joint Special Operations Command, but I was formally attached to US Africa Command as a private contractor. There were a few of us over there."

"Huh. I always wondered if the German KSK engaged in any of our kill-capture missions. Ever hear anything?"

"If I did I wouldn't say."

"I shouldn't have asked and it doesn't matter. Ever get back to Czech Republic?"

"Not in many years."

"I'm thinking of a trip to Brno. Maybe we can meet in person sometime and have a few too many Pilsners, smoke cigars and compare notes."

"I'm all for it. If I had my way, we'd sit down tomorrow."

"Thanks, Halo," Web says, interrupting the conversation. "We appreciate the help. Say hello to your boy for me."

"It's been a pleasure."

Rich ends the call then sits back and smiles. Web smiles with him then says, "Halo has a photographic memory. Pick that up? You talked avionics and data with him, but he's just as knowledgeable about propulsion, hydraulics and a dozen other topics, all in depth. He's a force of nature. Ready for lunch?"

The men move to the conference room. As they walk, the aroma of Thai food and the sound of Web's wife Samantha singing to herself, lighten their mood.

A dozen delicacies rest on a large walnut table. When they enter, Sam says, "This is about as close as I could get to the real thing."

As the team eats, Sam searches Bangkok locations on her iPad. She wonders aloud about shipping items to condos in Bangkok. Wants to be near the Bangkok Transit System.

"What's going on?" Patch asks. He's looking at Web, but it is Sam who replies. "Well, I'm not living in a hotel for a year," she says.

"I haven't told Patch yet," Web says to her.

"You're going? This isn't going to be a vacation, Sam," Patch insists. "We'll be working six- and seven-day weeks."

Sam doesn't look up. "Not me," she says. "You guys can work

all you want. I'm going to play."

"She told you, tough guy," Web says, and chuckles.

Web's phone rings. He steps away. A contact in Israel wants a face-to-face meeting and asks how soon Web can be there.

CHAPTER 9

Web and Samantha fly commercial from Minneapolis to
Washington, DC for a meeting, dinner and a night on the
town. The day doesn't begin well. Their departure is de-
layed by over an hour because of a mechanical issue on the plane.
By the time they land in DC, Web is anxious. He urges their limo
driver to hurry all the way to the Army and Navy Officers Club,
Seventeenth Street. They arrive at ten past the hour, which means
the lawyers waiting for him in the Daiquiri Lounge, one of Web's
favorite bars and the headwaters of many crazy nights and stirring
conversations, are already on the clock.

When they enter the lounge, Web observes a common social
phenomenon. Men can't take their eyes off of Sam. As she and Web
approach their friends, General Hines and Harold rise from their
seats to greet them. Barbara, smiling, remains seated next to Harold and across from the General. Web is happy to see Barbara, but
hopes she is not logging time. His business today is with Harold,
and possibly with Hines.

"Sam! What a great surprise!" Hines says. He gives Sam a hug.

"So good to see you, Samantha!" Harold says.

"I'm here too," Web says. He throws his arms into the air in
mock disbelief and feigns awaiting a hug from the general. He often plays off of how Sam attracts all the attention, but secretly loves
it.

"Web!" the general says. "You have no personality. We didn't
even notice you." He turns to the others. "Did anyone see Web

come in?"

Sam replies for her husband. She creates a visual innuendo by adjusting her bra. "You need a bigger set of personalities, honey. How are you, Barbara?"

Barbara gives Sam a thumbs-up, and Sam leans down for a quick hug from her. "Drinks are on me," Hines says. "What can I get for you?"

Web orders a Scotch but Sam passes, saying she only stopped in to say hello.

"I hear you're taking a leave of absence, Sam," Harold says. "Did I hear right? You're running a duathlon or something over there in Bangkok?"

"I am," Sam says. "I'll be in the fitness center in a few minutes to get a workout."

Web brags a bit to Harold and Barbara about Sam's fitness and determination, comparing her to his Olympian brother, Sonny.

Hines returns from the bar, places drinks on the table and asks if he missed anything.

"We were just talking about Sam's fitness training," Harold says.

"Speaking of that," Sam says, scooting her chair backward. "Time to go." She kisses Web on the cheek, says goodbye to all and leaves. As she does, a man approaches the table and whispers to General Hines. Hines excuses himself, promising to be right back.

Web, Harold and Barbara sit and Web opens his briefcase. He places a folder on the table in front of Harold. "That's what we have so far," he says. "If you have questions, let me know. Should have the rest next week."

"We've gone through General Phang's order with a fine-toothed comb. Big project," Harold says.

"It is," Web replies.

Harold puts Web's folder in his briefcase. He uses his napkin to dry off the condensation rings collecting on the table, then pulls folders and documents from his briefcase. He pages through an executive summary, apparently reviewing key findings.

"No big surprises, Web. You're up against ITAR in a few instances, but we already knew that could happen."

"Don't mince words, Harold. There are always surprises. I see yellow tabs," Web says.

Harold smiles. "Everything is correctly coded. If we were shipping to Syria or somewhere we'd have major issues, but this is Thailand." He puts on half-frame reading glasses and grasps a yellow tab marking a section of his document. For whatever reason, habit probably, Harold carries a full printout of the Department of Commerce Control List.

"If they enlarge the font, you won't be able to lift the thing," Web says, a bit of a dig that Barbara gets but Harold does not. The document is available in digital form.

Harold laughs. Missing the point, he says, "Exactly. I don't know what's wrong with them. Anyway, here we are. Do the drones you specify have quartz rate sensors integrated into either the primary or standby instrument systems? Whatever that means."

Barbara checks her watch, pushes her chair back and stands. "Gentlemen, it's never good to keep a senator waiting. Time for my next appointment."

Web and Harold stand. They thank her for stopping by and she leaves.

"Where were we?" Harold asks mindlessly. He places his hand

on the documents.

"Technically, they are not drones. They're UAVs. You were talking about quartz sensors. Are you sure they are not referring to inertia sensors?" Web asks.

"You'd have to tell me," Harold says. He opens the control list and shoves the heavy document toward Web.

Web reads from the Aircraft and Associate Equipment section, Category 8, Section E. The entry is marked NS.

"I don't see how a quartz sensor evokes national security. Huh. I'll check into it. If it's an issue for us, it's probably been an issue for someone else. The manufacturer will have a workaround. What's next?"

Harold lifts another yellow tab in his document. He sips Scotch and adjusts his glasses. "Do any of your drones, sorry, UAVs, require a flight distance of more than 300 miles? If longer, we have an issue."

"Come on, Harry," Web says. "You can't be serious. The big guys sell UAVs all over the planet. Something's wrong with that assessment. Don't bring me simple reads without digging. Please. Some of these aircraft fly thousands of miles."

"I'm just reporting what we found."

"Well, you found a roadblock that doesn't exist," Web says. "Dig. There has to be a precedent we can leverage. No way they won't allow us to sell an American manufactured airframe with a range over 300 miles."

"If there's a way, we'll find it, Web. You know that."

Instantly Web knows he made a mistake flying to DC. Should have been a video conference, as Sonny suggested. "Anything else? I see more yellow tabs."

"No showstoppers. You'll have all this with you on the trip."

Web looks away. A couple of the military brass at a far table nod in his direction. "Drinks are on the general's tab. You heard him, right?"

"Yeah. Why?"

Web goes to the bar and orders a round for all the officers in the room. "Put it on our tab. Tell them it's all courtesy of General Hines."

Hines returns to the table. "I need to borrow this guy for a minute, Harry. We'll be right back."

"By all means. I have reading to do, anyway," Harold says.

Web reluctantly excuses himself, knowing his bill will continue to climb for as long as he is away.

The general leads Web into the hall, where he briefs him. "Don't give me one of your goddamn hissy fits. I need to introduce you to some buyers from Kenya—a couple businessmen and government guys. They're pissing themselves over there, scared to death they're going to lose everything to Somali clans. Showed them around town last night. Hot for equipment and maybe training contracts. Right up your alley."

"A little heads-up would have been nice. I'm on the clock in there."

"See? Hissy fit. Screw the goddamn bill. We're talking real money, Web. I've got 'em in a private room sucking liquor. They're ready to sign." And then the finger comes out and taps Web on the chest. "Do your thing. You're a closer. Good money for both of us!"

"Stop it with the finger."

"Goddamn! It's a simple sit-down." The general turns back toward the lounge to leave. Web grabs his arm. He wants to know more, to understand the gist of the Kenyans' needs, but the general wants to get back to his drink. "At least tell me where the hell I'm going," Web says.

"Oh." Hines leads him to a closed door at the end of the hall. "I'd join you but really I can't know the details. Understand? Company stuff. I don't talk trade anywhere in Africa right now—conflict of interest, blah-blah. Big order, though. Counting on you. I'll be in the lounge."

"If you can't talk business, why can I? We play by the same rules."

"Degrees of separation. Besides, I'm no good at sales. You can do that side in your sleep. Get in there and do it."

The general brushes his palms together and flicks his wrists as if to throw away any responsibility. "When you're done I'll take them to a strip club or something. Musa likes that kind of stuff."

The general leaves. Web shakes his head. He takes a breath and opens the door of a private meeting room. Four men sit at a table with drinks. Web presumes them all to be Africans, even though a stoic Caucasian sits in their midst. They stand simultaneously to greet him. One of the visitors, the man closest to him, speaks for all.

"Pleased to meet you, Mr. Webber," he says. "Join us."

"Thank you," Web answers. "General Hines says we have something to discuss?"

CHAPTER 10

Web takes a seat with friends and staff of General Thabiti Mburu, the top man in the Chief of Defence Forces, Kenya. The military men are Musa and Umoja, both colonels. Musa looks familiar, but shows no sign of recognizing Web. The thin man has bright eyes and dark facial scars.

Umoja is stern and disinterested, reminiscent of combat veterans who have witnessed too much violence. The long scars on his scalp and arms are nothing compared with the injuries to his psyche.

The other guests are Rashid and Jacob. Jacob is a Kenyan businessman. Web guesses Jacob funded the trip on the chances of purchasing weapons and other materials for civilian defense. It's a pattern he sees more often every year, and in every corner of the globe. The battlefront in Kenya is now the entrance to malls, the gates of cul-de-sacs, the busy lobbies of train and bus stations.

Following introductions, Web says, "I just now was told of your needs. Forgive my lack of preparation. How can I help?"

The initial spokesperson is Musa. "We came to DC at General Hines's invitation to meet with suppliers. You were not on our list, but we are happy to meet. The general says you have a history in our country."

The general's motivation makes perfect sense to Web now. He has introduced the Kenyans to other resources and will take a cut from anyone who can close a sale. Typically, Web pays a higher commission. "Yes," Web says. "We've done business before, and I've been to Kenya on multiple occasions."

Musa speaks for the group. "We learned that you are improving surveillance systems in Thailand. Our situation is different, but this capability interests us."

"I am. You conducted a Naval ship-to-shore bombardment against Somalia in 2012, as I recall," Web says. "Something to do with Al-Shabab commerce? Is that why you are looking for weapons now?"

"Kismayo. Al-Shabab uses that port for selling charcoal and receiving arms shipments. The military denies access to the coast and does its best to keep clansmen from crossing the borders. We have no plans for additional incursions. Our motivation is defense."

Web is pleased to hear it. "Border security is expensive. In that arena I don't have anything new to offer except perhaps for aerial reconnaissance. I recently looked at some very interesting solar-powered systems that could be of value. As for the shoreline, your Navy already has sophisticated equipment."

"The military is preoccupied," Musa says.

Rashid leans forward. He is visibly impassioned about their needs. "They attack business centers. Clansmen threaten our families. Once rats are in the house, it is too late to shut the door."

"I understand," Web says. "What specifically are you looking for?"

Musa has a look that says he gets it. "General Mburu wants Kenyan businesses, militia and the military to work together. In your country, you have the Homeland Security department. We need equipment for business and local leaders to conduct surveillance. This is how you can help."

Web inches his chair forward. "Just so you know, DHS doesn't provide substantive support to businesses. You mentioned Bangkok. The general shouldn't have mentioned any of that to you without my approval, but we can talk in general terms. The project is very expensive.

"Here's my advice. Businesses can contribute their exterior surveillance equipment to the government's network. Military and private entities all rely upon the use of surveillance, so a combination of systems is probably your best option. If we work together we can discuss other methods for countering terror, dissuading poachers, and reducing pirating and theft. It won't happen overnight, but better intelligence is one of the best paths to reducing violence."

"Like your NSA, but with respect," Umoja says, a wry smile on his face.

"Many of my countrymen share your concerns. I don't happen to be one of them," Web says.

"Tell us more about Thailand," Musa says. He leans back in his chair and folds his arms across his chest.

Web never discusses his customers' work in detail. "I can say this much. We have the expertise to do what you want. If you don't find help elsewhere, our company will be happy to talk with you in depth, in Kenya."

Musa is the first to push his chair back and stand. He holds out his business card. Web exchanges cards and handshakes with the men. Musa says, "You have other engagements. We understand."

Before leaving, Web says, "I'll let General Hines know you're waiting for him."

CHAPTER 11

Two days later, back in the Twin Cities office, Web and Patch spend the morning developing equipment specifications for a buyer in Indonesia. Short on time, Web asks Patch to take a group of prospective customers to the shooting range and then join him in the evening at The Perfect Ash for a cigar.

Web sits at the counter laughing with Ryan, one of the employees, when Patch arrives. Patch grabs a Padron from the humidor.

"You're in a good mood," Patch says, clipping his cigar.

Web raises an eyebrow and reaches into his pocket. He grins as he hands a bankcard to Patch. "Don't spend that all in one place," he says. Web and Patch often use stored-value cards not tied to any one person. Some international cards allow huge balances, handy for large purchases.

Patch kisses the card and puts it in his wallet. He opens his laptop case and pulls out his MacBook. "I got another briefing from the State Department this morning." Patch reads aloud. "Our ability to assist U.S. citizens in an emergency, and provide routine consular services, remains limited for any one of the following three southern districts. It goes on to list military excursions, police actions and so on."

"Thailand? Probably overreacting, don't you think?"

"They're usually on the mark. You reduced the number of operatives for our project last time we talked. Maybe we should bump things up again."

"I'll have to think about that one. Long engagement. Who do you have for the two positions we agreed on?"

"Sean is at the top of my list. How about Tallis?"

Web is confused. "Wait a minute. Our strategy has always been to blend into populations, hire indigenous people where we can and look-alikes where we can't. We've never strayed from grayman techniques, so how do a couple of lanky Caucasians like Sean and Tallis fit the model?"

"Bifurcation," Patch says through a mischievous expression.

Web laughs so loudly others in the cigar bar want to know what's up. Web waves them off. "Don't use your verbal Kung Fu on me, Patch. We're not splitting the crew. To what end?"

"We are still using grayman. Hear me out. Everything outside of the operations center itself is as blended as it can be. Our line workers and installers are all Hmong, for God's sake. There's no better cover than that for Bangkok. And the general expects US and European technicians to be in the operations center, no matter what. We can't get around bringing in our own people on this one. Same thing for the hangar crew."

"I was thinking we would get our bodyguards out of Black Talon in Hong Kong. Maybe use Pinkerton in Thailand."

"We can. My point is that we're going to be in Bangkok, not Central Africa. There will be white guys all over the place where we spend our time. Throw a hard hat and reflective vest on just about anyone, they become invisible. One more thing, we won't have to worry about loyalty. These guys will stand between you and a round any day of the week."

"It's counterintuitive, but I think you're right. We can use our own guys for the op center and hangar, escorting between that and the apartments, but not the warehouse. It's probably a good plan, but I'm a maybe on Sean."

"Why? Good shooter. His tradecraft is top of the line."

"The tattoo thing bothers me. Too many of them. He's even got them on his neck now. I tell you what, we use our own people for office, dwelling and commutes, but contract with a local firm for travel outside of our comfort zone. It will give us local intel. Tallis has been through evasive driving, right?"

"Driving, bomb detection, all of that. Back to Sean. You have something against art now? People wear freaking tattoos. Get over it."

Web laughs, but says no again, to Sean.

"What about Brick, then? You want brute force, he's a monster. I have a list here somewhere—Chad, Ryan, Wags. What about Texas Tommy?"

"Texas is fun, but you're right about Brick. Can we afford to feed him?"

"Six-four, two hundred and sixty pounds of pure muscle? You might be right," Patch says as he laughs. "I'll deduct carbohydrates from his paycheck. His uncle lives in Bangkok. Could be useful."

"Tail Gun, right? Gunner has experience on riverboats."

Patch updates his list. "A biker now, as I recall. Okay. Unless you're going to change my mind again, I'll call Tallis and Brick, let them know they're in."

"You'll also negotiate a contract with a local firm for the rest of it. Sign us up for weekly reports and semi-dedicated service. Here's the deal on Sam," Web says. "She's coming. Nothing more to discuss."

"OK then, here's the other deal on Sam. She can't wander off like she does. Every time I turn around she's off somewhere. You know I'm right."

"She's coming. She'll wander. Get used to it."

"Might as well not hire security at all, then, but whatever," Patch says.

"I like how you did that, Patch. You caught up to me in under four seconds."

"Jerk," Patch says.

"Try to understand my point of view. You're the best security guy I've ever met, but Sam likes to move around. I'm stuck in the middle and don't like it. If she wants to take in the neighborhoods and sample local cuisine, we just have to let her go. She's been a flight attendant all of her adult life. It's not Syria, for God's sake."

"Brick and Tallis have been all over the world, too. So have you. I still worry. It's my job to worry."

Web takes a draw from his cigar. "I'm asking you to let it go. Anything else?"

Patch doesn't answer. Web has known him long enough to realize it's his way of processing, looking ahead in time, solving problems before they arise.

Finally, Web decides it's time to change the subject. "Remember that tech group we met at the Shot Show last year. Bright kids. I'd like to contract with them, either that or just hire them away from whomever signs their paychecks."

"Anish something and that funny one, the Vietnamese guy. Good idea. I'll have Rich look into it. By the ways, we really lucked out with Rich. Works around the clock. Outstanding! He forwarded a resume to me a few days ago for an operations and repair specialist certified in Apache helicopter support. She knows small airframes inside and out."

"She?"

"Inge Rush. Goes by Ginger." Patch hunts through electronic files then spins his laptop in Web's direction. "She was on multiple tours in Afghanistan and Iraq. Here's a photo. Amazing stuff. Purple Heart and Silver Star."

"Give me the highlights."

"You can't read now? Whatever," Patch says and spins the laptop back around. "Picture Iraq. Lead Humvee is flipped on its lid by an IED. The explosion kills two instantly and seriously wounds another. They come under fire for nearly a half hour. The fifty cal machinegun is hard bent and their shooters have about a foot of ditch to hide in. It's a regular ranger grave out there, but they stay low and fight.

"Long story short, she drags the injured under a Humvee with her and tucks everyone behind the wheels. She's drilled in both legs, ruptured eardrum and concussion. Still has the sense to send rounds at the jihadis until a gunship shows up. She and one other guy survive."

"Wow." Web pulls Patch's laptop closer and looks at her photograph. She stands in the open door of a hangar. A C-130 and two or three drones are parked behind her. "Good mechanic, I assume."

"The best. Like I said, her work history and fortitude are worth every penny. Aced everything at Fort Eustis and Fort Riley. Occupational specialist. Only a couple of women in history have her awards. Hell of a story."

"She definitely doesn't blend, but I trust you. When do we ship out?"

"The techs meet Rich and me in Atlanta next Monday for orientation. Rich wants to put them through a couple days of training before we go wheels up. I'll let you know when we land in Bangkok."

CHAPTER 12

While preparing for their move to Bangkok, Web spends a morning at the private hangar where he stores airplanes and his collection of cars. One of his mechanics is there with him, receiving instructions and working out a budget for projects to be conducted while Web is away. The weather is a balmy seventy-five degrees with very few clouds. Even collectibles need to be driven on occasion and Web feels like driving fast. He elects to drive his Cobra, removes his shoes, crams his large frame into the small space, buckles in and spends an hour on city streets and the highway.

When he returns to the hangar he wheels an office chair to the massive open door at the tarmac side of the building, lights a cigar and sips from a bottle of mineral water. He checks the time and places an encrypted call to Dyna Stavros, Romanov Agency, Sofia, Bulgaria.

Dyna answers on the third ring. "Mr. Webber. So good of you to call. Are your ears burning? We've been talking about you."

"Interesting. I called to let you know I'll be in Thailand for a year or more," Web says.

"Planes fly in and out of Thailand all the time. Your point?"

The relationship between Dyna and Web is complicated, to say the least. Web has been read in on three agency projects in the past four years, two of them involving both Israeli and US assets. He's just a supplier, not much more than a pawn in her world, but she acts as if she owns him. "I'm trying to be courteous here," Web says.

"I appreciate that," Dyna says. "Business or pleasure?"

"ISR, avionics, we'll be setting up an operations center."

"Good experience to have. Best of luck to you. Don't forget to check in every once in a while."

"That's what I'm doing right now," Web says. "Why did my name come up?"

"Have a good trip, Web," Dyna says, and ends the call.

CHAPTER 13

After grueling weeks of penetrating interviews and detailed background checks, Patch sets about integrating new-hires into his team. Among other responsibilities, it's his job to manage people. Web relies on him every day to find and fix personnel problems before they get out of hand.

Systems engineers, technicians, launch crews, pilots and repair staff spend most of a week processing orders, gathering essentials, receiving last-minute training and getting to know each other. Patch continually asks tough questions and applies pressure. As he does, he closely studies moods and interactions to ensure he's made the right hiring decisions. He makes sure everyone takes their anti-malaria drugs, and in follow-up one-on-one meetings asks again if the employees understand the risk.

When the team arrives in Bangkok, Rich assures everyone that the interviewing and vetting is over. Patch, however, knows that true vetting has just begun.

Crews are moved into assigned apartments in a complex close to Don Mueang International Airport. Ginger is the first female employee to arrive, so she gets her own room, but everyone else shares an apartment.

James (Picasso) Palmore and fighting Joe Bloomquist billet together. James got his nickname from a compulsive habit he developed after an auto accident. For years, he's created three or four pieces of art every day from anything at his disposal, just like Picasso did. He makes art of paper clips, paint, clay and charcoal. He went through a glue and dirt phase. Jimmy, as Ginger calls him, openly admits to clinically diagnosed obsessive-compulsive behavior. Like many in his position he claims he can stop any time he wants. He just doesn't want to stop making art. Hopes to be helplessly addicted to creating objects for the rest of his life. What he does best for the team, as he aids pilots and reviews data, is pattern recognition.

In offhand comments, Patch branded Joe and James the odd couple. Picasso is a proud African-American artist. Joe is an ex-fighter from a large East Coast Italian family. He calls himself Champ too often. Everyone knows he took too many shots to the head and his glory days are behind him, but he's a never stay quiet kind of man. What got him hired was that Anish, James and Lee said they would not go to Bangkok without him. He's a handyman with the title operations specialist.

Michael (Brick) Patrick Doyle's contract came with an exercise equipment stipulation and the possibility of an advance. In Web's outfit, operators get special treatment so Patch budgeted for thick rubber floor mats, free weights, a squat rack, and a few extras. Patch knows Brick will always want more weight. He has added muscle ever since they met in Columbia years earlier. Technically, Brick got the free-weights as a signing bonus. Tallis and Joe got electronic gear and a heavy bag that takes a severe beating nearly every day of the week. The exercise equipment sits in one corner of the hangar.

Miles away from the operations center, and even the warehouse, Patch, Brick and Tallis move into rented apartments on floors below the Webbers' condo.

Patch uses team-building techniques he developed in the military to bring the team into a viable rhythm. The first few days in Bangkok are a vacation, everyone setting up their apartments, touring the hangar, enjoying fine cuisine. Then the twelve- and sixteen-hour days begin. For two weeks everyone works with few breaks and little sleep. Heavy stress and an unrelenting workload expose issues that otherwise could remain hidden until the wrong moment. In the way expansion and contraction stresses steel, Patch tests the mettle of his crew.

The team works around the clock alongside construction workers hired to do the heavy lifting, and technicians lent them by the Thai military. It's noisy, chaotic work, but in the second week of operation, the data center is already receiving data. Carpenters have finished work on storage areas, a minor revamp of the lobby and a feature for the control room dubbed the sky deck is in place, and pilots and the ground crews are able to test avionics on a daily basis, at least for the hand-held units.

It's day fifteen. Patch sits with Rich and his operatives in the op center, reviewing progress and discussing next steps while everyone else finally gets a day away from work.

"Sure you don't want to come, Patch?" Brick asks. He and Tallis have had their eyes on the exit door for the past hour. All the techs, pilots and most of the ground crew left earlier in the day, ready to party.

"Stay safe, guys. Rich and I will be here if something comes up. Have a good time."

"Which is it," Tallis asks as he walks toward the door. "Stay safe or have a good time?"

The team's R&R begins with a party in the apartment shared by Joe and Jimmy. Picasso has decorated every square inch of wall space with paintings, drawings and paper sculpture made from objects collected during the build. Hours into the event, Lee stands with one leg on a coffee table littered with empty beer cans and pizza crusts. He extends his arm into air above him in a statuesque pose and toasts repeatedly to anyone who will listen. His favorite toast, "Here's to fucking Bangkok!"

Systems administrators are usually the quiet men at a party because their thinking tends toward analytics and reservation. This afternoon they are all out of their minds, especially Lee. He is a Vietnamese American from Alabama who frequently corresponds with distant relatives in Vung Tau. His grandparents fled the country in 1975 and never went back. Until arriving in Bangkok, though, Lee had never been out of the United States.

Joe tells everyone the crotch of the city is slippery Sukhumvit Road. He strays into Freudian territory when he repeats how he's never seen a lady boy, the term for young men dressed and sometimes medically altered to look like ladies. Some of them trade favors for cash. He goes on to say he would never let one do him. Repeats himself too often for Lee's taste.

Brick and Tallis arrive late in the day with Chang Beer. According to Tallis, any beer with elephants on the label kicks ass—630 milliliters at 6.4% alcohol, double the volume, and four times the alcohol, of a typical American beer.

As one of his final sober acts, Anish tells Brick that Lee needs adult supervision. "I've got him," Brick says. He takes Lee's bottle away, grabs him by the back of the neck and marches him into the kitchen. He finds a half-empty jar of instant coffee then fills it with tap water. He stirs the mixture with his finger and drops two pieces of bread into a toaster that has been dialed to its highest setting.

Three minutes later he forces Lee to drink instant coffee the thickness of syrup, and eat two slices of charred white bread. "You're cut off until you can count from zero to ten and back in Thai," Brick tells him. Lee can't find his phone to translate the numbers, let alone count backwards.

More crew members arrive. The apartment shakes with drinking and loud music, but Ginger is still missing. Lee earns another small glass of beer, not for counting in Thai, which Brick can't do properly either, but for reciting his mailing address backwards, one alphanumeric character at a time, while standing on one leg, arms outstretched, looking at the ceiling. Tallis calls it remarkable.

Joe leaves the relative comfort of their air-conditioned living room to have a cigarette on the sweltering balcony. Moments after he lights up, he jumps back into the room. "Guys," he says in a loud forced whisper, palms pressed to the side of his head in disbelief. "You have to see this!"

Young men race to the balcony with him and simultaneously look to their right, gawking at the curvaceous presence of Ginger hanging laundry on her balcony in the next apartment. It's Bangkok hot outside, high nineties with unwavering humidity. She wears only a bra and low-cut sweat pants.

Ginger glances in their direction and shakes her head, but continues to pin items to her makeshift clothesline.

"We have beer," Tallis yells. "Get over here."

"Doing laundry."

"We can see that," Lee shouts. "Whoo!"

"It's pronounced Whooha, dildo," Ginger yells back.

"Seriously," Tallis shouts again. "We're going out on the town. It will be epic."

"Goddamn, she looks good," Joe says under his breath. "I'd go a round with her just for the pleasure of getting punched in my face."

"Knock it off," Picasso says, always the philosopher. "It's hot and humid. She's doing laundry. What's the big deal?"

"What's the big deal?" Joe says to his roommate. "Look, you moron!"

"I'm coming to you," Tallis yells and heads for the door.

Everyone except for Joe follows Tallis to the exit, but as he grabs the handle he spins about and shows his teeth. The techs stop in their tracks.

"Whatever," Lee says. He pops the top of another Chang Beer and takes a long gulp before Brick snatches it away.

"Forget it. He's not coming back," Anish says. His Indian accent has been tempered by five years in Dallas, Texas, and years of playing first person shooter games with online teams. Anish is the most accomplished of the systems admins, a virtual sponge. He earned a master's degree in distributed processing at the age of twenty-two. Rich says that if he ever matures, a fate that so far has eluded him, he'll be able to work anywhere in the world.

Within seconds of Tallis's departure, everyone but Joe has forgotten about Ginger and nearly everything else. Lee tries to crush an empty beer can on his forehead. He gives it all he has, but only creates a deep circular indentation. "You're an idiot," Anish says to him. "You press the top of the can, not the bottom. Go look in the mirror."

Ginger hangs the last of her laundry. She flips Joe off again for staying on the porch staring at her so long. "You don't have a prayer, Joe. Everyone knows that. Even you."

"Doesn't matter," Joe yells. "I've got the memory of you locked up here forever." He points to his head.

Ginger laughs. Over the weeks she's actually come to accept Joe as something of a sidekick. "We're in a Buddhist country, Joey. The cause of suffering is desire." She reaches behind her back and unclips her bra. Upon removal, it hangs from a single finger.

"Suffer, little man," she says, like a chiding sister delivering an object lesson.

Joe acts faint. "Oh my God," he shouts and glances toward the room of guys.

Ginger leans over, picks up her laundry basket and returns to her apartment.

Joe runs inside to tell the others, but no one believes him.

Twenty minutes later Tallis returns. Ginger is with him. Everyone cheers that she's finally in party mode. By 2100 hours, opening time for the club they want to visit, everyone in the apartment knows they are into a night they will never forget.

CHAPTER 14

Mostly because Tallis is already half in the bag, he gets out of being the second designated driver. Brick tries to get his uncle Tail Gun to help, but Gunner says no. He is willing to tag along as a sober chaperone, but wants to ride his motorcycle. He explicitly wants no part of hauling inebriated inexperienced delinquents around Bangkok, his words.

One of the older techs reluctantly volunteers. He and Brick fetch the vans and drive to the front of the apartment complex.

Drunk and drinking passengers get into one or another van and head south toward the Insanity Nightclub off Sukhumvit Road. No one can stop Lee from yelling, "Whoo!" A couple of times Joe yells with him, adding the "ha," a symphony of silliness brewing in the back seats. Ginger says, "Enough already." They yell louder.

Just past the Sirat Expressway Brick yells at Lee to shut the hell up a minute. The team goes silent. "Our warehouse is over in them buildings," he says. He looks to the side of the road and over the edge of the elevated freeway as they motor by.

The overpass takes them across a once-bustling rail yard. To the techs and ground crew it looks more like an abandoned lot in an otherwise energetic city. Lights reflect off rooftops. They see rows of unexceptional and possibly empty buildings.

"Lovely," Ginger says in a tone of voice that makes Brick laugh. Ginger mostly gets anything she asks for, especially from Brick. Tonight she rides shotgun. She says she relates better to Brick and Tallis than her coworkers. Brick says trash talk in her German accent turns him on, which gives her the impetus to do more of it.

"This Chang Beer is all right," Ginger says. Her staid and distant professional leader persona fades as she rides deeper into the city.

They continue onto Sukhumvit Road, parallel to the overhead BTS. Brick shouts, "Almost here. I just seen a sign." Having gotten the attention of his riders, he adds, "Anyone wants to join my uncle and me for a steak? You get in free if you eat."

Ginger asks what the dance club costs. If it's a hint for Brick to pay her admission, it doesn't work. "Price of a drink or something," Brick says. "Come have a steak first."

Ginger passes on the offer, saying she can't wait to get on a dance floor. She wants Brick to join her as soon as he's done eating. Says she'll work up a sweat for him, teach him to mambo.

Brick barks at the crew as he pulls the van to a stop. "Working-women in there will tell you how handsome you are and smart. You ain't neither. No matter what, don't leave the club with anyone but us."

"One last time!" Lee yells. This time two of the other riders join him. "Whooha!"

Brick points to the New York Garden. "The club is just back behind them tables. Everyone get out here and stay in the club till I get there."

A dozen half-soused, laughing pilots and technicians walk past open-air tables, a pizza place, and the DHL service center. They enter the deafening nightclub. Insanity is the perfect name.

The second driver unloads his passengers and follows Brick into the nearby Times Square Building parking ramp. They backtrack together on foot, Brick heading for the diner, the driver for the club's entrance.

Brick joins Gunner at a table in the diner. They catch up on family gossip and talk about the future. Their history together starts with family, but they talk mostly about the military and their motorcycles. Like his uncle, Brick is falling for Bangkok. He incessantly talks about the people he's met and neighborhoods he's explored. He has a dozen questions. Gunner listens for a while then says if Brick likes Bangkok so much maybe he should do something about it. And he tells Brick to eat slower. Says he eats like a starved wolf, but that doesn't happen.

After dinner they leave the sweet aroma of curries for the intense smell of stale beer and dance sweat. Inside the club, the other designated driver, tired of dancing or wanting to hang with an operative and a biker, joins them at a table. They sip soft drinks and flirt with one woman after another.

Tallis joins them in an alcohol-fueled gregarious mood. They speak loudly over the pandemonium as the DJ rocks the club without mercy. Strobe lights and disco balls further stimulate the dancers. Joe is entranced by a go-go dancer on a raised chrome-railed platform. He stands below her station motionless.

Tallis yells something to Brick.

"What?"

"Monkeys," he yells.

"What about them?"

"Orangutans," he yells. "What do you think?"

Brick frowns and gives him thumbs down. "Not this group," he shouts.

"What about monkeys?" the other driver wants to know.

Gunner laughs and shakes his head. "I think it's illegal now, but I know a place. Different rules, same concept."

Brick yells to the other driver. "You wrestle them. Stay in the ring for a couple minutes and you get paid."

"Yeah!" Tallis says. "Let's go."

"I have to see this," the tech says and leaves the table.

"Bad idea," Brick yells, but no one seems to hear or care.

Fifteen minutes later, five guys stand in front of Brick arguing in favor of seeing men wrestle with primates. Two more crew members join them. These two either want to see the apes or hit the strip clubs at Soi Cowboy up the street.

Brick says hell no to the strip club. They have a lady along. Eventually he says okay to the orangutans. "Somebody rescue Ginger and we're out of here," he says. She dances with two Thai men at once, possibly twins.

Joe runs to Ginger as Tallis rounds up the crew. A couple of hookers cling to the arms of Anish and one of the pilots like giggling barnacles on a ship.

They walk together to the parking ramp, where everyone piles into the vans again. Gunner leads the way on his scooter.

"Whoo!" Lee hollers. Everyone in the van tells him to shut the hell up or else.

"What are we in for?" Ginger wants to know. She's returned to the front passenger seat. Strands of her hair are stuck to the side of her cheeks, embedded in the thick sheen of sweat she's worked up dancing.

"Ever seen a sleazy fight club on television? Gunner says this one is in an old busted-down factory. You'll see Muay Thai, MMA and orangutans in there. Smell will stay with us for days," Brick says.

"They totally have apes fighting?" Ginger asks.

"The apes don't fight each other. More of an act to entertain the crowd between real fights."

Ginger wants to know if Brick is going to get in the ring and kick some monkey ass.

"Hell no. Professionals show up sometimes. You can get your teeth kicked in by a guy half your size. I'm too pretty. Don't you think?"

Ginger smiles. "Never been to a fight club."

"If it's too much let me know."

"No one could push you around," Ginger says. "Fight the orangutan. I dare you."

"Definitely not going to roll with them orangutans."

They have to walk two blocks from the closest parking spot. Gunner, Brick and Ginger enter together. "I told you," Brick says as their nostrils fill with the smell of cigarettes, and the humid, pungent sweat of fighters and audience. The unmistakable essence of urine is present in the air as well.

"You sure that's monkey piss?" Ginger says.

The main floor is packed. Although a few women are scattered among the guests, the crowd is composed of tough men, standing shoulder-to-shoulder. They cheer for their favorite fighters. A violent, bloody martial arts battle rages in the center of a circle reminiscent of a Sumo wrestling platform. No ropes, cage, or fence separates fighters from the audience. A few shirts in the crowd wear blood spatter.

"Oh my God," Ginger says to Brick. "This is crazy." They follow Gunner through the dense crowd to the balcony stairs. The balcony offers little more than standing room against a back wall, and along the steel railing that overhangs the action.

Gunner and Brick push through spectators along the narrow walkway, which is just a few feet below the rafters. The dirt floor below, and the raving fans and cigarette smoke wafts at eye level, accentuating the coarseness of the event.

"They wear them ribbons on their arms over here. Muay Thai style," Brick says to Ginger. "National sport."

"I prefer to grapple," she says, and startles him by grabbing his arm. He laughs and taps out on her shoulder. Ginger softens her grip, but doesn't release his arm. She also touches his back as they look over the railing.

Below, Tallis takes bets on when Lee will puke. Bettors fork over B100 per time slot. Tallis jots bets on his forearm with a Sharpie and stuffs cash in his shirt pocket.

Anish and his hooker have also made it to the balcony, where they continue to make out madly. No one seems to notice or care. A ground crew tech looks up at Ginger every once in a while until he sees her arm interlocked with Brick's. Picasso draws figures on a stack of napkins lifted earlier from the dance club. His pen pierces the napkins repeatedly. He tells Tallis that holes show the futility of man's reliance on technology.

"Whatever," Tallis says. "You going to bet or not?"

Picasso carries his Thai bhat in a money belt around his waist, something like an old man at a casino. He bets B100 on 0330 hours.

One of the fighters throws a vicious roundhouse kick that knocks the other fighter unconscious. Gunner yells, "Yahtzee!" and laughs. The fight ends. The winner's arm is raised. His nose bleeds like a faucet and he touches a lump the size of Arkansas on the side of his forehead, but he is ecstatic.

With barely a moment's delay, a trainer and his beast of a male orangutan emerge through the crowd.

This orangutan is huge, which becomes more apparent as he walks upright for a few seconds. According to his trainer he weighs 100 kilograms, about 220 pounds. He takes the center of the ring smoking a cigar and drinking from a bottle of beer. He squats on haunches and blows a raspberry.

Ginger becomes excited. She says loudly that she's never seen anything like this. The ape's flaccid face, a massive plate of dark flesh with small, intense eyes and a huge mouth, seems undisturbed even as the humans around him convulse with excitement. He calmly watches what to him must be madness. Drunken loud locals and a few wide-eyed Caucasians surround him. They suffer fanatical anticipation. The laughter is infectious.

Probably on a gesture from the trainer, or because orangutans are the most intelligent of all primates, the red-haired ape flips off the crowd. Cheers erupt. Lee pukes into his pocket at 0215 hours. His hooker slaps his sloppy face, forces him to remove his shirt, wipes his mouth, then sucks a third massive hickey onto his neck.

The trainer taunts the frenzied audience. It's all part of the show. He wants challengers. Staying in the ring will be easy, he says, for a real man. The line of prospects extends into the crowd for six or seven meters. Men struggle through the chaos to retain their place in line. More men, friends or employees of the trainer, run in stained white shirts through the audience. Cigarettes hang from their lips as they wave cash and betting slips. The trainer's wife, sagging breasts and a fat hand-rolled cigarillo in her mouth, barks instructions to the challengers.

For reasons unknown to anyone but her, she pushes some of the men aside and chooses a huge Brit as the first contender, a tourist apparently, light skin, Manchester United T-shirt. He raises his arms and cheers for himself. His friends are cheering too, urging onlookers to bet. They wave cash. Everyone either laughs or boos their antics.

Bets pour in. On the command of the trainer, the orangutan faces his challenger. His face changes and he lets out an ear-splitting roar. If he were on the street, or free in the jungle, the sound would carry a mile. The crowd mimics the roar in puny human voices, riling each other to a fevered pitch.

Brick yells to Ginger over the noise. "They repeat the same routine every time."

Ginger gets into the action. She roars and raises her arms, jumping up and down. Brick glances at her breasts a few times. He is not alone in his ogling.

"I'm for the ape!" she yells, and tries to place a bet.

"You can't bet on the ape," Brick yells to her. "You just bet if challenger will last two minutes."

"Yes! I'm for the ape."

She pulls a wad of cash from her bra and waves it in the air, yelling at the Brits. "Pulverize Manchester United," she yells. The Brits glance in her direction but turn away.

"What the hell is she yelling about?" Gunner asks.

Brick just laughs. "Soccer fan."

When all bets are in, the trainer steps into the ring and takes the cigar and beer from his hairy friend. He whispers into the ear of the ape. The ape nods awkwardly and flips off the challenger.

Then the trainer steps out of the ring and picks a plate-sized gong off of the dirt floor. He dusts it off and holds up a wooden mallet for everyone to see. The yelling subsides slightly as the challenger prepares. His friends laugh so hard they can barely speak. The challenger circles toward the ape's back, tiptoeing.

"These hapless yahoos all think they have it figured out, but nothing works. Watch this," Gunner says. He points at the challengers.

The trainer points to his wristwatch, checks the time and bashes the center of his gong with the mallet. The ape just sits as the human becomes animated. For a few seconds the ape seems to look in the direction of Ginger. Brick says he thinks she has an admirer.

The human crouches and spreads his arms for balance, ready to dash this way or that. His friends yell that he can do it. He'll be fine. He just needs to stay light on his feet. They are so sure he'll win that they start counting backward, with obvious difficulty, from one-hundred and twenty.

The trainer says something in orangutaneze and the ape reels. He stretches his long arms to either side like giant wings. His red body hair, Spanish Moss hanging from a Southern Carolina shade tree, waves from his open arms as he advances.

The ape corners the Manchester man in a flash. Valiant and composed as the Englishman once pretended to be, he soon flies awkwardly out of the ring, landing on his knees.

Gunner laughs so hard he falls into a coughing spell. "The bigger they come," he says, gasping.

"Twenty-eight second!" the trainer barks in English. He steps to the center of the ring. He waves his watch, proof that the Englishman failed. He raises the ape's arm in victory. He hands the still-lit cigar to his friend and begins taunting the next contender. The Brit, however, a real a-hole according to Ginger, returns to the ring and pushes the trainer aside. Jeers erupt. He demands a rematch.

"Oh hell," Gunner says. "This shit doesn't fly around here. Seriously. Collect your crew. I'm out of here." He abruptly leaves for the stairs, the door, and the safety of the street.

Friends of the challenger enter the ring, talking sense to their man. The trainer misunderstands, or so it seems, and gives some signal or other to the orangutan. Either that or it could have been the ape's idea. He throws Englishmen. As they fall this way and that, angry locals jump forward and stomp them. The challenger grabs the ape's beer bottle from the trainer and turns toward the ape when another orangutan howls and races into the ring. The toothless smoking assistant howls too, and runs with him. She waves a golf club in her right hand and brandishes the cigarillo in her left.

Chaos ensues from every corner. What started as orangutans against anyone in a soccer uniform becomes every man for himself.

"Tallis! Out. Everyone out," Brick yells toward the main floor. He places one hand on his holster and turns toward the exit.

"I've got your six," Ginger says and grabs a fistful of the shirt on Brick's back. He violently clears a path through anything that doesn't move the hell out of their way.

At the edge of the arena below, Joe fights with four or five men at once. Anish and his hooker play suck face through most of it, oblivious to the mayhem. Brick will have none of it. He slaps Anish on the back of the head and pushes him forward toward the crowded stairs. Men ahead of them race upward as others fight to go down. Someone falls over the balcony railing onto the crowd below. On the ground floor, Brick and Tallis push everyone in their company toward the exit as Ginger helps Joe to his feet. Brick on point, they press forward as a group against the wall of struggling flesh.

The trainer gets smacked in the forehead with a bottle and bleeds profusely. The orangutans panic right along with most of the audience. It is bats in a bottle as people stream into the street. The apes run with them.

Fools left in the fight club cower in a ball, are unconscious, or simply frozen in their tracks.

Just outside, Brick and Joe get into a scuffle with four locals waiting for targets of opportunity. They make quick work of their opponents as Ginger pushes team members toward the vans. Brick sends Joe to join them.

Down the street, the Brits get their faces handed to them. Tallis pulls out his sidearm, ready to run to their aid, but Brick yells for him to stop. "Them Brits is on their own," he yells. "Make sure we didn't leave nobody in the club and let's get the hell out of here."

Tallis runs back inside as Brick heads toward the vans.

The toothless woman and trainer emerge from the building yelling for their apes and waving fruit, but the apes run off on knuckles in different directions. Tallis follows the trainers out of the building. Anish and his hooker are close behind, arm in arm.

Tallis shouts to Brick. "Got everybody?"

"Fuck if I know. Doing a head count now."

They have everyone but Lee.

Chaos in the street subsides as people run for their cars and leave. Brick and the other driver load everyone into the vans and drive to the fight club entrance. Brick curses, then sends Tallis back into the building, saying how Lee is probably passed out somewhere.

Sirens approach.

Ginger pushes people out of her van and tells them to get into the other. Everyone but Joe and Picasso pile into the other van and it leaves. Gunner drives his Harley to Brick's van window and says good luck. He also leaves.

Brick lays on the horn. He yells toward the entrance for Tallis to hurry as Ginger and Joe repeat how they need to get going.

Moments later the police arrive and block all hope of escape. Tallis emerges with a semi-conscious, slobbering drunk named Lee over his shoulder. Police whistles sound. Lee yells, "Whooha!" and asks if he got it right.

Within a few minutes, Brick, Ginger, Joe and Lee are bound with nylon cuffs.

"Anybody get a call off to Patch?" Lee asks. Brick kicks the side of Lee's leg in disgust. That they are hanging with apes, fighting with angry locals, and now dancing with the police is just part of being over the top in Bangkok. But no one wants to experience the wrath of Patch Riggs.

CHAPTER 15

Jawad spends days hunting for followers in the streets of Kuala Lumpur. He's come to the financial and spiritual center of Malaysia looking for bright, malleable young men willing to join his cause in Thailand. He spends most of his time near the National Mosque, Masjid Al-bukhary, Masjid Alam Shah, and farther east in the Desa Pandan neighborhoods.

He becomes frustrated. A small margin of success is found in a less affluent area of the city, near the tin factories, but in truth he has failed. As he shares the evening with a potential adherent, he realizes the prospect does not have the required mental toughness.

Jawad abandons his quest and decides to spend a day enjoying himself before returning to Thailand. He checks into the Piccolo Hotel. In the evening he has dinner at L'Opera and sits under awnings in the small mezzanine street-side watching the steady stream of passersby. It's a habit for him now, to consider how he would attack this or that building, wherever he is. And it's also a habit to be wary of anyone that looks like a government official.

At sunrise the call to Morning Prayer echoes through the city, and he smiles. He showers then dresses in jeans and a Harimau Malaya Football T-shirt. He opens his smartphone and scans the *Bangkok Post*. The explosion he masterminded has already gone from the top of front page. A mention of his work appears far down the page, saying only that the hunt is still on for the perpetrators.

He scans articles about corruption, the energy grid and disgraced leaders. He places a call, as Sarab, to Al Rajhi Bank to verify his appointment and ensure they are ready for him. Finally, he sends an encrypted text to Akara in Thailand and pockets his phone. Personal items from two nearly empty duffel bags go into a grocery sack. He takes the sack and empty bags with him to the bank entrance, just minutes away, and hails a taxi. When the taxi arrives he pays him to wait, places his sack of personal items in the car, then enters the bank.

An important customer, Sarab reviews the status of his investments. He's liquidated a small number of his Islamic financial certificates. The Sukuk yield RM 650,000 MYR, Malaysian ringgit, or just over $200,000 dollars US.

A bank officer approaches with an armed guard and asks that Sarab accompany them to a side room. There, an assistant counts out the cash. The assistant is sent away and Jawad stuffs money into his duffle bags. The guard accompanies him out of the building to the waiting taxi.

Jawad pays the curious driver nearly double the fare for a ride to the bus station. During the 357-kilometer bus trip north to Penang, and across the bridge to George Town, with many stops along the way, Jawad speaks to no one. He never releases his grip on the duffel bags. In the dead of night, when he steps onto Akara's friend's fishing boat at the island's north side, they dispense with formal greetings.

"I need water and food," he says weakly.

Akara hands Jawad a sack of food and a canteen, then he starts the engine.

"Slowly," warns Jawad. "Speed attracts attention."

As Akara steers the boat north toward Thailand, Jawad drinks, eats, drinks again and falls asleep.

Jawad awakens when engine power is cut. It's still dark as Akara guides the boat to the side of a dock. It rocks against the pylons. Three of Jawad's trusted followers secure the hull from shore. On land, they split up. A driver, Akara, Jawad and the cash go in one car. The others take a second vehicle on separate routes to a home where four others wait.

After formerly greeting all guests, Jawad talks excitedly through the half hour that remains before sunrise and Morning Prayer. He tells his followers that the network has blessed them with a mission that will change the world. He says the men he has placed in positions of authority will soon possess keys to victory, God willing.

"You are disciplined and well trained," he says. "Some of you have gone to the Middle East, some have lived in Philippine jungles. In a few weeks, your training will end and glory will begin. Remain vigilant. Be patient. Pray for strength."

After Morning Prayer, Jawad issues final instructions for the day. His crew travels in two trucks. Jawad holds the duffel bags. Late morning, in a village near the southern border, they arrive at an abandoned building chosen for its innocent appearance and remote location. They park near a small warehouse that once served as a garage, get out of the vehicles and take up positions suggested by Jawad. Their best shooter carries an AK-47 to a thicket of tall grass on a mound overlooking the entrance to the warehouse. Jawad unlocks the building and opens the overhead doors. His men gather inside to wait.

Two hours later, a step van arrives. It backs into the building and stops. The driver pulls on a ski mask to cover his face and removes the keys from the ignition.

An armored SUV arrives seconds later and waits for the truck driver, its engine idling. It's clear to Jawad and the others that armed men are in the SUV.

The driver of the delivery truck approaches Jawad and his men, then holds out his set of keys. In a thick Russian accent, he calls out, "Is for you. From Indonesia."

Jawad pulls a sack from one of the duffle bags. Akara carries payment to the Russian and the masked man checks its contents. He looks at Jawad then at the waiting SUV. He shrugs.

"The other half," Jawad says, holding up a second sack. "You get it after we confirm the contents."

The Russian brings the first payment to the SUV and discusses the situation quietly. He then waves for Jawad to do the inspection. Jawad sends Akara to move empty boxes out of the way and hunt for what they are looking for. When complete, Akara hands over the balance of the payment. The Russian does a quick count and gets into the back seat of the waiting SUV.

When they are alone, Jawad and his men remove three crates of AK-47s and 74s, along with blocks of ammunition. They carry these weapons to one of their waiting trucks. Jawad and Akara stay at the warehouse while everyone else leaves.

When the men are gone, Jawad and Akara carry marked boxes to their truck and secure the warehouse. "Is that everything we need?" Akara asks as they drive away. "If not, I've found someone that can help."

Jawad smiles. He appears to be relieved that the transaction came off so well. "Drive, brother," he says. "We have been blessed with everything we need."

CHAPTER 16

Jawad sits in the front passenger seat of a Toyota Yaris. He is riding with three of his closest followers, philosophizing as they drive through the streets of Bangkok.

"Of the many secessionist movements worldwide, we will be the first to succeed," Jawad says. "Beginning in Southern Thailand, your generation, or the next or the one after, will force democracies and communists back into their borders. China and the West will eventually implode and Islam will reign supreme throughout Southeastern Asia, the Middle East and across much of the global south. Know this, brothers. History will remember our accomplishments. All of you, give me your phones."

The men nervously hand over their cell phones. They don't understand, and Jawad doesn't explain, why he flips through their call histories. He says they can no longer connect with each other unless they use encrypted applications. As they ride, he downloads apps onto their phones and explains their use. "The US hears everything, but with these apps we think they cannot yet break encryption.

"Cell towers show where you are, and where you have been. I'm found in Bangkok today, somewhere else tomorrow. The phone they probably believe is mine travels every day, even when I do not."

Jawad holds up a burner phone to demonstrate a communications technique. He asks Akara to pull to the side of the street for an important conference call.

When they've rolled to a stop, Jawad dials a number and steps out of the car. He talks with his back to the Yaris, speaking in Arabic and occasionally in English, a language one of his followers understands perfectly and quietly translates. They all understand the words, *"Assalamu alaikum."*

"Wa alaikum assalaam.

"Yes. Peace upon you, too.

"I've been well. Thank you.

"I can hear you, brother. The connection is weak, but I can hear."

Jawad appears to listen to a lengthy proposal.

"Yes.

"Okay.

"I accept your guidance on the matter." Jawad turns toward the his men, each of them attentive to his speech even when they don't understand. He nods toward them and raises his eyebrows.

"I understand," he says and turns away again.

"Yes. I am moving forward," Jawad says.

"I see your point. Yes, an important statement.

"May you be rewarded as well.

"Thank you, brothers. Peace be on you."

Jawad turns toward the car. He removes the SIM card from the burner phone as he gets in. "Let's go," he says.

In the car he breaks the SIM card and smashes the phone. As they drive he throws pieces out of his window.

Before they turn south, Jawad says to the driver, "There is a view of the city you must all see. No turning back now. Head for the Taksin Bridge."

CHAPTER 17

Patch sends Tallis and Brick to BKK airport. They welcome the Webbers to Bangkok and drive them to their new home, which is a condo on the eleventh floor of a residential high-rise in the Ruamrudee district. Tallis and Brick share a two-bedroom apartment on the third floor. Patch bunks alone on the sixth. This is not a luxurious building, but access to the Don Mueang Tollway, and multiple forms of public transportation nearby, makes it a responsible choice. A natural-born salesman, Web goes out of his way to show Sam the BTS boarding station at one end of the block. He knows being near the transit system is a must.

Inside, she first inspects the kitchen of their condo, running a finger across older model appliances and touching a cracked white wall tile. The refrigerator is fully stocked, as are the cupboards. "I like the balcony," she says. It spans the full width of a spacious living room. At Web's request, Patch has seen to it that the balcony is equipped with deck furniture and a treadmill.

Web heads into the bedroom and calls for Sam to join him.

"I've seen a bed before, cowboy. Let's at least wait for the sun to go down."

"Very funny," Web says. He shows her a walk-in closet.

"To be honest," she says, a mischievous smile emerging as she speaks. "I imagined something with a water feature, a view of the river, fitness room and nude butler. A steam bath would be nice."

"I've disappointed you."

"Stop it," Sam says, and goes to him. They embrace and she says, "This will be fine. It's actually perfect. I can get on the rail anytime I want. Besides, I feel safer with our guys in the building."

Web knows Sam will bring home paintings and sculptures, decorate a wall or two, get new furniture and have the carpet replaced. Actually, if she doesn't replace the furniture he will, but soon enough the place will feel right to both of them.

They each enjoy a small glass of wine before bed.

When his wife falls asleep, Web walks to the balcony. He fills a pipe with a custom mixture of Captain's Mate and Cherry Hill tobaccos, then leans on the railing. The scale of his obligation weighs heavily on his mind. "Just another gateway," he mumbles—one of his favorite sayings. Every challenge is a gateway to the next adventure.

Halfway through a bowl of tobacco, plumes of smoke merging with the Bangkok skyline, Web hears tapping behind him and turns. Sam is on the other side of the sliding glass door, moonlight illuminating her supple body from the waist down. She removes her pajamas and undergarments then slowly comes closer to the glass. Now the light shines on all but her eyes and forehead. She presses softly against the glass. Web smiles. He puts his pipe on the table, ember still glowing, and places his hands against hers, the glass between them.

Sam slides the door open and steps to him. She pulls his arms around her waist. "It's going to be all right, cowboy, and thank you."

"For what?"

"For this place, the time together, for everything."

Web's first workday in Bangkok starts with sudden driving rain. It pounds their balcony, the deck furniture and the fitted slip cover that protects their new treadmill.

Patch stops in for coffee, and to deliver an update. He describes how his team already started installing cameras at critical junctures in their grid. The op center build is ahead of schedule, which surprises Web. Patch says, "I have a handle on our crew now, too. Pushed them hard for a while then turned them loose. Turned into a real cluster, but at least we know what we're dealing with. They went to see the apes fight."

"Seriously? That's hilarious."

"Not hilarious. Things got out of hand, monkeys running down the street or some mess. Police grabbed up a few of our people. Choochai had to get the general involved. I apologized for both of us and assured them it will never happen again."

Web is more amused than upset, but he understands the gravity of the situation. "Did they start something or were they just in the wrong place at the wrong time?"

"They didn't start anything, but they also didn't get the hell out of there in time. Not sure what's worse. Brick says they'd have been all right except one of the crew members can't hold his juice."

Sam is in the kitchen stretching her legs, resting them on the kitchen counter one at a time and touching the floor with the palms of her hands. She calls to them. "If you guys don't hustle, I'll have to leave without you."

"Sorry. Didn't realize you were waiting for us. Take off anytime you want," Web says. "We're heading in different directions anyway."

Sam steps into the living room, grabs a few thousand bhat

from a short stack of cash in Web's bag, and slings her Louis Vuitton handbag over one shoulder. She puts on a wide-brimmed hat. "Patch, you take care of this guy today. After riding him the way I did on the balcony last night, he's weak in the knees." She smiles and leaves for the BTS, umbrella in hand, anxious to reunite with the city.

Web grabs his leather bag filled with paperwork and cigars. Patch always carries a laptop. Whether in the US or in Bangkok, they both wear holstered and concealed Glocks.

Patch calls Tallis and Brick on their way to the lobby and then they wait under the building's awning at street level. The rain stops nearly as suddenly as it began.

When their operatives arrive, Brick especially, looks as if he just woke up. But he trots off to fetch one of the Range Rovers. Tallis surprises Web with his attentiveness, head on a swivel, asking Web to take a few steps back inside until Brick returns. Web wonders if Patch had a talk with Tallis or if it's just his style.

Brick drives. Patch and Web sit in the back seat of their armored limo, where Patch occasionally points out landmarks. It's a ten-minute sprint from the condos to their rail yard warehouse. Today they take the second of four routes Patch has identified and will use at random.

As they ride, Patch says, "You might recall from maps and the photos I sent, but the warehouse sits on Chaturathit Road at the intersection of Sirat and Maha Nakhon expressways. Location of the warehouse and the operation center are both great. As to status, we're ahead of schedule except for launchers. Ginger can't get the bigger birds in the air without them. The sensor packages are outstanding, by the way. You're going to like what you see."

"What's the hang-up? Have you had any of the birds in the air?"

"We flew hand-held units on a twenty-mile run. Data links held up great. The Thais don't expect our bigger units to come online for a while though, right? We're still good?"

"On paper we are very good, but in reality, they probably want us in the air yesterday. I'd like to talk with Tshua today. Is he around?"

Tshua Vang is one of Web's dearest friends and a leader of a Hmong clan Web has worked with in Asia and the US. Tshua has a perspective that few understand. He is welcomed widely in Hmong communities, including rural Thailand and areas of Laos. He is embedded in both modern technology and the old ways. Tshua's connections in electronics manufacturing throughout Southeast Asia, and a family connection with intelligence agencies, make him one of the most valuable assets Web has. Web sometimes calls him the Hmong from UNCLE. It's all in fun, but everyone knows Tshua is no joke.

Patch says he hasn't seen him for a while because he's been conducting training. He says, "Tshua's guys want to stay in the warehouse, so I parked trailers in there. They seem comfortable."

"What the hell, Patch? Move them to an apartment complex. It's an insult."

"No. It was Tshua's idea. It's done. His guys are from up north somewhere and don't want apartments. They fell in love with the big open space of the warehouse. We went around and around on this."

"Does Choochai know? Rail yard security comes sniffing around in the middle of the night, we're exposed. Either that or they'll think they found squatters."

"We took care of all that. Local police and security guards won't be an issue. To them we're just another crew hired by the government to run wire and set up traffic cameras."

Brick catches Web's eye in the rearview mirror. "They roasted half a pig yesterday on a spit. Them little fuckers really know how to grill, I'll tell you that."

"I believe it," Web says. "But we never want to call them little fuckers."

"I didn't mean nothing by it, boss," Brick says. He looks flustered. "I like them."

"Term of endearment," Tallis says, turning his face toward the back seat. "It's like saying get the hell over here, fuck stick."

No one says anything for a few seconds, but Web laughs first. "You know what I mean. Watch your language and be respectful. They deserve it."

"Yeah," Patch says. "Watch your freaking language." He slaps Brick on the back of the head.

"Didn't mean nothing," Brick says.

"I believe you. How is the Hmong crew working out, Patch?" Web asks.

"The Hmong are a hell of a team. They install cameras like there's no tomorrow. Waterways are a bigger problem than we imagined, but Rich has a plan mapped out. His team is studying water landings across the entire basin. We'll be putting up cameras on the Chao Praya and Tha Chin rivers forever, and still just scratching the surface."

"It's called job security, Patch."

"Call it whatever you want, it's a pain in the ass."

Web looks out the window at the crowded highways of Bangkok, cars racing by, an endless churning cityscape. He thinks again about retiring here one day. "Maybe I'm wrong about accommodations. Wouldn't be the first time. Sounds like they've made the place into a home."

Brick goes on, "They're real interesting. Hard workers."

"Now he's trying to make up to you," Tallis says. "Hold out for a happy ending."

Web is only partially amused. "Patch knows their story, but you young guys may not. We owe them. The nation owes them."

Brick nods his head in agreement. "I read up on what happened after Vietnam. Tears your heart out."

Web brings the conversation back to operations. He asks if the crew has installed anything on Highway 4 to the south, or along roads leading east to the Cambodian border. General Phang's keen interest in these roads, especially thoroughfares connecting Bangkok with the southern districts and Malaysia, is top of mind for him.

"Not yet, but Choochai got us feeds from the Border Patrol. They have a fifty-mile buffer of coverage, more in some places. It's hilly down there, massive areas of nothing but trees. Thai Navy still isn't on board about the shoreline, but we've gotten promises," Patch says.

"I'll talk to the general."

"Did I tell you?" Patch continues, "The op center is only about a five iron from the telecommunications station at the air base."

"With your swing that would be, what, fifty yards?"

"Funny. You can see doorknobs on the building from our lobby. How's that?

"By the way, Choochai dropped off new orders yesterday. Remember how we hoped to avoid the Maeklong railway market and the Damnoen Saduak floating market in our proposal? They're back. Direct orders from top staff. It's tight as packed sardines in there. I don't see us getting that online for years."

Patch calls ahead as the Range Rover pulls into the industrial train yard. Warehouses in this park manually load and unload trucks and rail cars. The huge doors at one end of their warehouse swing open and they drive into the spacious interior.

An installation truck parked inside catches Web's attention. The logo on the doors reads Sunrise Telecommunications in both Thai and English. Patch says there are three more trucks just like it in the field.

"It would be best if this is the last time we drive Range Rovers to this destination. Do you agree? Could call attention," Web says. "I thought we had beaters."

Patch nods toward trailers at the far end of the warehouse. "We parked them behind Hmong town," he says, smiling. Five small trailers sit in a Gypsy circle at the far end of the warehouse.

Web can make out chairs and a half-barrel fire pit in the center of the circle of trailers. Three port-a-potties stand against one wall. Not far away, on a raised concrete platform normally used for loading trucks, he sees two refrigerators and a freezer. His tone approaches disappointment, but he holds his tongue. "All the amenities of home. You sure they don't want apartments?"

"They like it right here," Patch says, apparently tired of defending his decision. "If it will make you feel better, let's raise salaries since we're saving on apartments."

"Sure. And we don't have to pay for extra security. That should be worth something. Is that a cot on the roof of that trailer?"

"It is. One of their guys sleeps up there. Says it gives him a better vantage point."

"Vantage point for what?"

"Hell if I know. Just likes to be up off the ground, I guess."

The warehouse functions as a staging area for trucks and workers charged with wiring dead spots in the city and surrounding areas. Web wants more workbenches installed. Knowing he has members of the team sleeping there, he asks Patch to hunt down an entertainment center and wire the place for television. "Maybe find a couple sofas, chairs and a big table.

They review installation maps tacked to one of the walls. Color-coded pushpins dot roads and estuaries indicating the location of recently installations. Other markers show areas still to come. Web says corkboard would work better, but Patch says the walls work just fine.

"Whatever," Web says. "You do good work, Patch. I'll catch up with Tshua later, maybe visit his office downtown tomorrow. Let's keep moving."

They leave the warehouse and head north on Highway 31, Don Mueang Tollway, to the Don Mueang International Airport and the adjacent industrial and military complex. General Phang found a hangar near the Directorate of Air Operations Control and the Thai Air Force Civil Engineering Department.

Web laughs as they enter the parking lot next to their converted hangar.

"What?" Patch asks.

Web points to the small sign on the front entrance. "Air Traffic Repair Center. I forgot we named it that. The picture of the plane over a rice paddy is a nice touch." They park and enter the building.

"How do you like your office?" Patch asks. He smiles as they walk through a tiny lobby with three worn chairs and a stained wooden reception desk. The room has a musty and unused smell. Web laughs at the thought. "You went all out," he says, knowing full well that it's all just part of their cover. Even so, he wants the carpet changed.

A small hallway leads past four tired offices. Patch points out features. "Your office. My office. Shared office space. Of course, we won't be using these much, but it helps with appearances."

"This last office is our conference room. Table and six chairs. The presentation monitor doesn't work, but we'll never turn it on anyway. As long as we don't take guests into the back, we look exactly like we're supposed to look."

"That's genius," Web says, pointing to repair manuals and parts posters on the wall.

Patch smiles. "Did that for you. Glad you like it."

"You put up repair posters for me, but where are the pinup girls for you?"

"Very funny. Can we continue now?"

At the end of the short hall Patch punches numbers into a keypad hidden behind a hanging calendar. He opens the door and they step into a large control room shaped like an amphitheater. Technicians look in their direction.

Web's eyes immediately go to the massive video wall to their left—eight large connected monitors form a single wall of moving images. Every square inch is visible, because the pilot stations and technical booths between them and the wall are terraced down and away from the entrance.

"Reminds me of a college lecture hall except it's so high-tech," Web says. He's surprised at how deeply the terraces are carved into the floor. "You dig all this out, or was it this way when we took occupancy?"

"Pick and ax," Patch says, clearly kidding around.

"Jerk."

"The general sent us jackhammers and a backhoe. Concrete was nearly cured when we arrived. That smell we get right now is carpet tile adhesive. Went down four days ago."

Each tier of the op center has several multi-monitor workstations and instrument panels, and each comfortable-looking workstation supports two team members with reclining chairs. One is the pilot, the other manages sensor packages and flight controls. Two of the pilots are actually flying, or so it seems. Patch says no, they are using simulators.

Five server racks stand inside a locked, glassed-in room to their right. Twenty or more meters in front of the entrance, Web climbs four stairs onto a large raised rectangular platform built into the center of the back wall. It features an operations control station and a long conference table with a smaller control panel inlaid into the surface. The plush seating surrounding the table faces the video wall and operations area.

A square section of the raised flooring is cut away. Web walks to it and leans over a steel railing, rising from a kick-wall that surrounds the opening of that cutaway on four sides. A few feet below the surface of the riser, he sees another grid of monitors. They are inactive at the moment, displaying only a signal-not-found alert.

"NASA would be jealous," Web says. He turns to Patch.

"Where's Rich? I'd like to see some of this stuff in action."

Patch yells. Rich crawls out from under a row of desks. His hair is mussed and dirty. He apparently hasn't shaved in a week. His clothes are covered in dust and paint splatters.

As Rich approaches them, Web calls out. "Love it. I see those can-lights in the ceiling, or maybe those are pin spots? Get the effect you wanted?

"I did," Rich says, and steps onto the riser. He gestures for Web and Patch to take seats at the command table. "We're getting closer every day. Let me show you some of the latest stuff."

"Show Web the street-cam demonstration I saw yesterday," Patch says.

Rich taps the touchscreen and drags his fingers across switch sliders. The room lights dim and Web sees, for the first time, how the special lighting Rich wanted creates pools of light in an otherwise dark space. The strategically placed pin spots send narrow shafts of light down onto pilot stations. It was an inexpensive solution to the kind of futuristic feel Web wanted Rich to achieve.

The video wall comes to life with a massive image of a Google map. The default is a pointer set at their location. The BTS aboveground and the MRT underground lines are currently highlighted. Rich taps keys to reveal a visually impenetrable number of colored dots. "There are around three thousand street views available to us so far, more coming in every day. All those dots you see are cameras."

Web gives Patch a high-five as Rich zooms in on a neighborhood. The closer he zooms into the map, the farther the dots separate. When viewed very closely, Web sees they are actually more like triangles than circles. Rich continues. "Green indicates full function. The wide side of the pie pieces indicate angle of view.

The pointy part is the actual street location of the device.

"I can access any of these cameras with a single click, or call up groups of them at once by dragging a selector over an area. Of course we have dozens of other views geocoded against data sets. You get to them through the dropdown lists we built into the interface. Technically, we have no limit to how many cameras we can attempt to show at any one time, but I've found that a grid of twelve is about all we can see clearly on the monitors. We're still comparing camera views with Google Earth, and sometimes eyes on the ground, to make sure we have everything configured properly."

"Do we? Have it configured properly, I mean?" Web asks.

"I think so. Red dots mean a camera is not working. The camera has failed or our connection to that camera has failed; either way, red means we have to send someone to that location to investigate. I'm thinking of another color in the legend to show cameras that work, but have poor resolution. If we go there you'll see half the map will be blue."

The map changes. The dots give way to patches of dark gray. "I created this so we'd have a better idea of where we are still dark. It can mean there are no cameras available, or that we just haven't gotten the feeds yet. It's going to take a while to get everything online but the bigger issue is resolution. Many of the CCTV installations just don't have what we need to reach the general's vision."

Web crosses his arms and stares at the video wall for a while. "I take it we haven't yet done much with object recognition or biometrics."

"The project is coming along, but no," Rich says. "Joe and Anish ran tests in the hangar using cameras with various resolutions. Good cameras give us good results. We all knew resolution would be an issue, but I still don't know what we do about that. I don't see us upgrading thousands of private cameras."

"Why not?" Web asks and laughs. He steps to the edge of the riser platform and looks out at the pilot stations. "I'd like to meet the team."

Rich calls for Anish, Lee and Joe to meet the big boss, a term Web doesn't particularly like, but allows for the moment. He insists that he be on a first-name basis with his crews and that they feel comfortable talking with him about anything.

Web steps down from the riser and joins Anish and Lee. They are slight in build and act like they've consumed far too much coffee. Web remembers Anish very clearly because of his conflated accent. Hindi-sounding subtext in a Texas drawl makes him smile every time. The man's father was in-sourced from Pune to Houston, and the family never went back.

"Patch tells me you're a hell of a systems administrator, Anish. We're glad to have you on board."

"I try," Anish says. "Thank you for the training allowances you gave us. Maintaining certifications is expensive these days."

As Web talks to Lee, other technicians approach. Lee's features are unmistakably Vietnamese, but he sounds like he's from the Mid-South Delta region, possibly Mississippi. Web makes a mental note to follow up on that in the future—interesting kid, funny, self-deprecating at moments.

In contrast, Joe is physically and mentally hardened. He is the perfect stereotype of a former professional light-heavyweight boxer. As expected, when they shake hands, Web is locked in a vise. Joe's face tells stories even when he isn't speaking. Scar tissue puffs and glistens around both eyes and his chin. His nose is bent and flattened on one side. From the sound of his voice, Web knows his nasal passages are obstructed. He empathizes, thinking about those days in summer when his allergies rear up and he can't breathe. Though Joe's fighting years are long over, Web notices that one eye socket and his right cheekbone are freshly bruised.

"You've been in a lot of fights, Joe. Spar recently?"

"You could say that, sir," Joe says.

After talking with everyone in the control room, Web and Patch excuse themselves and head for the hangar.

"I told you we don't have our launchers, right?" Patch asks. They walk through another hardened door into a small fabrication shop. Tools are stored with precision. Workbenches are immaculate. Hot spares and assorted parts rest in well-marked bins. Web says, "I can tell we're using top-flight military mechanics. Either that or the shop hasn't been used."

"Shop is used every day. She's worth every penny," Patch says.

Patch taps a button on the back wall. An up-and-over garage door rattles and rises, exposing a forty-five-thousand-square-foot hangar. Web sees free weights and a squat rack in the corner to his left, but the only avionics equipment in the hangar sits on a large steel deck-over shelving mezzanine at the far end. The hangar is equipped with two sets of massive doors, one set partially open. Two assembled UAVs rest on mobile racks in front of the mezzanine. Web sees a dozen storage crates on the racks and assumes that most have birds still in them, unassembled.

"Think we have enough room?" Patch says with a smile. He opens his arms in a gesture of expanse. The ceiling rises fifty feet above their heads. A couple basketball courts and ample seating could have been built into the space and still there would be room to park his fleet of collectable automobiles.

Web sticks his index fingers in his mouth and whistles something like a catcall. The sound echoes off the barren walls. "Perfect!"

A woman's voice calls out from a small tool shed hidden in the center of the storage structure. Inge Rush steps out from behind a wall of UAV storage containers. "What?" she shouts.

"Sorry," Web calls out, laughing. He feels embarrassed for using that particular whistle. "I whistled to make a point. The room is empty. We need launchers."

"Don't be whistling at the employees," Patch whispers as they walk in Inge's direction.

"Too late. Hope she has a sense of humor."

"Not for that shit, dickweed."

They meet Inge in the center of the floor. She is taller than Web imagined and younger looking than her true age, which he knows to be thirty-three. Patch introduces her as Ginger.

Ginger got her name for the ample red hair beneath her Tiger baseball cap. Her commanding presence isn't lost on Web. She stands proudly, yet her gestures are completely at ease. She smiles a lot. Nothing inauthentic or overly enthusiastic about her. She shows no discomfort approaching authority.

"I'm glad you two can finally meet," Patch says.

"Pleased to meet you, Mister Webber. Patch talks about you all the time."

"Call me Web. Are you good with Ginger, or would you prefer Inge? Sometimes people get stuck with a handle they would rather get away from."

"I've lived with Ginger so long, my real name sounds foreign."

"Ginger it is. I'd like to inspect the UAVs, but we're all having lunch in a few minutes. Are you going to join us?"

"In a minute. Just wrapping up a few things," Ginger says and excuses herself.

As she walks away, she calls out, "Hot as hell in here, Patch."

"Working on it, Ging. We'll have the air moving in a few days."

"I like her," Web says as they head back toward the control room. "What's the other story you were going to tell me."

"Don't let that pretty face fool you. The woman's tough as boot leather. I didn't get this from her directly, but it came up twice in conversations with references. The captain of her unit could have been called Cap'n A-hole. He hit on all the gals. That isn't unusual, but some guys go too far. Got written up three or four times as a possible rapist, but nothing came of it. Anyway, Ginger takes it upstairs for her friends and gets nowhere," Patch says.

"What'd she do?"

"She gets with some of the other women and a few sympathetic men. They form a team and study this captain's behavior. He's the kind of loser that gets drunk then walks the compound.

"Long story short, he's drunk on his ass one night and comes on to her. She says to back off. He gets in her face, like she owes him. She runs and this yahoo follows her into some building or other. She tells him to get the hell out and things get out of hand.

"The whole thing is captured on night vision video."

CHAPTER 18

After lunch, Patch and Web return to the hangar to find Brick and Tallis both sweating profusely in the improvised gym. Tallis is punishing the heavy bag with wrapped hands and quick feet. Brick, as usual, is lifting massive free weights.

Web calls to Tallis as he and Patch cross the room. "What did that bag ever do to you?"

Tallis turns toward Web and Patch and performs something like a light bow.

Patch whispers to Web. "You should stop in earlier sometime and see him go through his Chinese forms. Pretty cool stuff."

Tallis unwraps his hands. Brick throws him a towel and the four men meet just off of the thick dense interlocking rubber mats, an area used for lifting, sparring and hand-to-hand drills.

"Show me something, Tallis," Web says.

"What do you mean?"

"I told him to come in early sometime and watch you practice the forms," Patch says.

"I never asked. How long have you trained?" Web says.

Tallis drapes his towel around his neck. "Not today."

"How long have you been at it?" Web asks.

"I started when I was a kid. The old man enrolled me in Tae Kwon Do, but I followed the art back in time."

"Why?" Web asks.

"Lynette," Tallis says. He doesn't even smile, but Patch laughs.

"And?" Web asks. "I've got to hear this one."

"Yeah. I met her at a party. She invited me to go with her to a Tai Chi deal. Couldn't turn her down."

Web is confused. "So that's what you do, Tai Chi? You were nailing that bag like a master. Didn't look like any Tai Chi I ever saw."

Tallis finally smiles. "Instructor grew up in Taiwan. I spent a summer back there with him as a kid and I've been at it ever since. He has students all across Europe and the US studying Chinese systems."

Brick, towering above all of them, veins popping out of his arms and neck, says, "Don't let him get one of them joint locks on you. Hate that shit."

"I bet," Web says. He turns back to Tallis. "Patch and I would like the two of you to have dinner with us tonight."

Hemingway's is among Web's favorite restaurants in Bangkok. The golden teakwood structure is over a hundred years old, an icon of Southeast Asian history. The French ambassador lived here, as did other dignitaries.

At Brick's request they are seated outdoors facing the entrance. The terrace is enclosed in a brick half-wall surrounded by tall, broadleaf foliage. When frustration and pressure build, Web and Sam dream about selling everything and retiring to a place like this, maybe in Bangkok or Pattaya—halfhearted dream for Web, but very real for Sam.

They all want the tenderloin for their entrée, but order Parma ham, Calypso prawns, ceviche and breads as starters. Web begins with Tallis. "You speak Latvian and Russian, right? Your resume said three languages."

"English," Tallis says. "Actually, I can get by in Romanian and Lithuanian. I know some Serbian, but I'm not great with either one."

Web smiles at himself for missing the obvious. He says. "We don't have anything pending right now, but there are ways I think you could be helpful in other kinds of projects. Things we haven't talked about. Your Russian especially might be of use to me."

Tallis glances toward Patch then back to Web. "Whatever you decide is good with me."

"Good attitude," Web says.

Patch finishes off a prawn and leans into his operators so he can speak quietly. "We're having this conversation away from the rest of the crew for a reason. Like Web says, there's nothing right now, but we sometimes do projects for various agencies. Tallis will work directly with the boss and Brick will work with me."

"Anything you want, boss," Tallis says, clearly pleased.

CHAPTER 19

Motorcycles, and riding them, are as important to Brick as having toilet paper. He gets a substantial advance from Patch and joins his Uncle Gunner at Harley-Davidson Bangkok. The two of them have a long history on two wheels. Gunner and a few other vets formed a motorcycle club after 'Nam and they still do their best to live off-grid, even in Bangkok.

It takes Brick less than an hour to select his bike and close the deal. He wants custom pipes installed. By noon he is cruising on his new cherry-red Wide Glide, a sun-dried cigar in his teeth. Near dusk Gunner heads home and Brick makes a call. Within a few minutes he rumbles up to the front door of Ginger's apartment.

Ginger throws a few items into his saddle bags, climbs on, and wraps her arms around Brick's torso. They ride for an hour then pull into the lot of a hotel halfway to Pattaya.

Around midnight, wearing only a towel, Ginger steps out of their bathroom. Brick is overheated and sweaty in his boxers. The room's two queen-sized beds are a mess. One mattress is nearly on the floor. Covers from both are strewn about in unlikely places. The lampshade is tipped to one side and undergarments circulate on the ceiling fan above them. Ginger can't find her blouse.

"You know we're breaking all the rules," Brick says.

Ginger gives up the search for her clothes then springs onto the bed and bounces with excitement. "Ready for round three?"

Ginger undoes the towel. She springs at Brick, wrapping her

scarred legs around his torso.

Brick arrives at his apartment near dawn, road-weary, grinning from ear to ear, hoping to get a few hours of rest before Patch arrives. As he drifts into sleep he savors the lingering scent of Ginger's perfume, her touch, the way she opened up to him, memories that will last a lifetime.

At 0630, Tallis sits in the kitchen of their apartment. If Patch hadn't already gotten on him for stretching Saran Wrap over the toilet bowl and gluing coins to the floor, he'd staple Brick's pant legs shut for not telling him where he was all night.

When Brick came in earlier, failing miserably to be quiet, all he said was that he couldn't stop riding. Tallis knew better, but promised not to say anything.

Earlier in the week, Patch ran into the man who packed his first parachute and taught him to jump. His name is Proctor, and Proctor left the states five years earlier to run a skydiving club in Bangkok. Over the years the two men stayed in touch, mostly on holidays, but when Patch ran into him it was like they'd never said goodbye.

The plan is to skydive in the morning and ravage the town through the afternoon and into the night. According to Patch, it will be impossible to set the bar too low on this one, which is why no one but Brick and Tallis are invited. At least that's what Tallis thought until he got a call the night before.

Three unopened boxes of cereal sit on their kitchen counter. Tallis stares at them for a few minutes then turns them upside down and cuts the bottoms out of each one. Before he turns them upright he presses a paper bag to the open bottoms and carefully slides them into a cupboard.

Patch texts his men that he's on his way. After running cold water on his neck, Brick comes into the kitchen. He grabs a coffee and sits heavily at the table, blurry eyed.

"Sam is coming to the jump," Tallis says.

"Whatever," Brick says. He downs a few aspirin with a bag of juice.

"The pilot is some guy named Proctor. Taught Patch to jump when he was just a kid. Did you know that by the time the boss showed up at jump school he had a 48-hour free-fall badge?"

"Sound about right for Patch. You should put those empties in the trash."

"Patch doesn't drink?"

"Pick them up anyway."

"I'm Latvian. I drink." Tallis collects empty beer bottles as Brick gulps coffee and soaks his eyes in Visine.

Patch knocks on the door and lets himself in. He grabs a cup of coffee and sits. "You guys eat?" he asks.

"I had cereal," Tallis says. "Brick might want a bowl before we take off. You want one? Cereal is in the cupboard."

"Thinking of something more substantial," Patch says.

Brick grabs a spoon and bowl. "Do I have time?"

Patch checks his watch. "It's going to be a long day. What do you burn, a couple thousand calories an hour?"

"Tall says Sam is coming?" Brick asks.

"Been on me to jump for a year. I figure, what the hell. After the jump we drop her off and the rest of the day is ours. First thirty drinks are on me."

Brick laughs. He takes a container of milk out of the refrigerator and grabs a box of granola from the cupboard. Cereal pours onto the counter and floor.

Neither Patch nor Tallis react.

"Really? Very mature, Tallis. Help me clean this shit up."

"You poured cereal on the floor," Patch says.

"Boss makes a good point," Tallis says.

Patch sips coffee while the guys clean up and then he says to Brick, "Let me show you how this works." He grabs an empty bowl and steps to the cupboard. He holds it under a box of bran flakes and slides the box out slowly. Cereal falls into the bowl as if a mechanical dispenser has provisioned it.

"Bachelor cut, right, Tall?"

Tallis doesn't crack a smile. "Common practice."

"Screw you guys," Brick says. If an operative isn't ready for pranks, he will be miserable every day of his life. He takes the bowl from Patch, pours milk and devours the cereal using a large serving spoon. He says, "Where are we headed after the jump?"

"Tuk tuks, cigars, drinks, maybe you get a lap dance down by the river, a quick dip in the canal, usual stuff," Patch says.

"You'll never catch me in one of those canals," Brick says. "This one guy I read about fell in and died a week later from a lung infection."

"Wimp," Patch says. "Okay, we pass on swimming, but for God's sake. Try to keep an open mind. We've got a badass city to take on."

Brick gets the job of being Sam's jump instructor. He gives instructions in the car all the way to the jump site. Instruction continues there, while Patch and Proctor exchange notes on where life has carried them.

Soon they stand at the open door of a DHC-3, the Gulf of Thailand in the distance, Pattaya and Bangkok both visible from their altitude.

Two jumps later Sam is hooked for life. Says she wants to get her USPA license and replays video of their jumps all the way back to Bangkok, stressing how she can't wait to show Web what he missed.

CHAPTER 20

Fifteen information technology and avionics specialists arrive in vans at the rail yard warehouse. Most of them enter the building for the first and last time. Waiting for them are seven Hmong workers and nine linemen.

No one knows why they are there. They are jovial. Groups of three and four talk and laugh together. Everyone has something to add about places to visit, restaurants and grocery stores.

As the crew talks, Web tacks photos and newspaper clippings onto a wall. The team grows silent. A few of them move closer to study images of bloody corpses, exploded automobiles and damaged buildings.

"Photos come courtesy of the Thai military," Web says. He stands in front of his crew with his arms on his hips. "This job comes with a set of risks and responsibilities. As I've said a hundred times, we can't afford to lose our anonymity.

"The other night had to have been a lot of fun, messing with Sasquatch and all, but it ended with public drunkenness, fights and the police. Pulled a lot of strings to put all that monkey business, behind us. Pun intended." Chuckling ripples through the group until Patch walks a particularly gruesome photo of bodies in pieces through the group.

As he shows the photo, Web says, "Those pictures are of a guy who worked for the same people we do. Difference is, he wound up in the news marked as an advisor to the military. That explosion took his life two weeks after the story broke. He was sipping tea.

The bad guys left a package under the next table. IED shredded him into what you see there in the picture."

The Hmong team stands off to one side and listens carefully while Tshua translates as Web continues. "Part of our job is to help hunt the bad guys. Guess what? They are hunting us, too. They are highly motivated and have deep resources." Web pauses for effect, scuffs the ground with a shoe, and turns toward Lee in particular.

"I don't mean to alarm you all unnecessarily, but it's imperative we not draw attention to ourselves. Does everyone understand what's at stake?"

People nod. Some repeat aloud that they understand. "Bangkok is still among the safest big cities in the world. Stick with the protocol Patch gave you, and no one need worry about losing privileges."

The room remains quiet. A few of the IT staff ask to see the photo again, and Patch obliges them.

Rich speaks in an uncharacteristically defiant tone. "Sorry, boss, but I don't see us sitting in apartments for a year. I don't see the harm in a little jogging, shopping, heading out for dinner or visiting shrines. Some of the crew go to church. I lived here a couple of years and never once thought about security. It's a big, anonymous, friendly city."

Before Web can react, Patch scowls and takes a step in Rich's direction. He nearly snarls. "I don't give a damn how vital you think you are, Rich. Web will back me up on this. We're all replaceable." He takes a step back and addresses the group, finger pointing at all of them. "That goes for everyone. Understood?"

Silence.

"That's not a rhetorical question, people," Patch barks.

"Understood," Anish says aloud.

"All right, then," Patch adds. "Stick with the protocol. Don't travel alone at night unless you're stranded. If you're stranded, you call for help. Don't attract the attention of the media. We never, ever talk about the project. Anyone asks, we're here to make street traffic safer. It's that easy. Any questions?"

Web is unnerved by how intense Patch seems to be, but decides to use the energy to positive effect. He says, "Since you're on a roll, say a word or two about drinking."

"Happy to," Patch says. He takes a step in Lee's direction, but addresses the group in general. "You all signed a contract. If you can't hold your liquor, either cut it out of your life or go home. Better not be any questions about that one. Fastest way to get on my bad side is to let drinking speak for you. Any questions?"

No questions.

"Thanks, everyone," Web says. Wanting to end on a positive note he adds, "Sorry it came to this. Like Patch says, it's part of the job."

The session is over. Web asks Patch for a word and they step a few yards away. "You all right? You dressed Rich down pretty good."

"He was in on it. His idea to get everyone's attention."

"Rich came up with that?" Web asks.

"Yeah. His idea. Have we gotten any more feedback from the Thais? I haven't heard from Choochai for a while now. We have a lot to discuss."

"We will see him tonight. General Phang has something for us, says it's urgent. You can fill him in then."

CHAPTER 21

Brick drives Web and Patch to the Intercontinental Hotel, downtown Bangkok. The rush of traffic and thousands of people milling about on foot, confirms Web's faith in human nature. He's heard that the number of people visiting the Erawan Shrine since the senseless bombing there has nearly doubled.

For this visit with General Phang, there are no military vehicles or armored limos, just the hustle of bellmen among the ebb and flow of tourists and businessmen.

Brick, an unlit cigar in his teeth, asks if he should wait. Patch says no, he'll text when they need a ride, then he and Web step onto the brightly lit front-entrance drive. The bellman approaches, but Web waves him off.

Choochai comes out of the building carrying a large blue envelope. "I apologize for General Phang. We can get started now."

The lobby bustles with customers. They mill about under the massive crystal chandelier, or lounge at the railing of the second floor balcony. Clusters of three and four sit in chairs near ornate floral arrangements, some of which stand two and three meters tall, contributing to the lobby's timeless grace.

As they ascend stairs toward the cigar lounge, Web asks if everything is all right and whether there are issues with his work or crew.

"No problems," Choochai says. "Your progress very good. The general is very pleased that you are ready to go."

"Ready to go is probably an overstatement. Does he really think that?"

They pause outside the door to the lounge. Choochai says, "This was my understanding. I apologize."

"Interesting. We're close, just not fully operational. Is that what the meeting is about?" Web asks.

The men enter the lounge, and stand just inside the door. "We have new information on insurgency leaders. The general wants help from your eyes in the sky," Choochai says, smiling and pointing toward the ceiling.

Web has doubts his crew can take on any mission yet. The long-range units have not arrived, nor have the pneumatic launchers been configured or tested for mid-range UAVs. He decides not to voice his concern until he understands what will be asked of his team.

Web and Patch order drinks and select cigars from an impressive selection. As the three men settle into leather chairs, Choochai hands Web the envelope. It contains seemingly random photocopies of documents and articles, and a dozen or more photographs.

"Jawad?" Web studies grainy surveillance photos evenly divided between two locations. The subject of the surveillance wears a green brimless Kufi cap and *thobe*, a full-length, robelike garment common in the Middle East. Two of the clandestine photographs are out of focus. Web guesses they were taken through a long lens or possibly through a vehicle's window. In the first photo, the subject stands near a restaurant's entrance. In the second instance he stands with a group of young men.

"Where did the pictures come from?" Web asks.

Choochai's phone buzzes. "Excuse me," Choochai says and walks toward the entrance.

Web turns to Patch and whispers. "Not good if Choochai over-stated our capabilities."

"You think?" Patch says cynically.

"Who has he been talking to?"

"Me, I suppose, but I've never said we are ready," Patch says.

"We'll deal with it. You've run high-profile manhunts before. These photos trigger any memories?"

Patch picks up the folder again and draws on his cigar. He smiles. "The one big difference I see is that I won't be sitting in a hide."

Choochai returns with General Phang. The general wears casual clothes, but walks with purpose. His face is resolute as he enters the room, but softens when he sees Web and Patch.

An unopened bottle of Sullivan's Cove Scotch is brought to the table, along with an assortment of aged cigars handpicked by the tobacconist. General Phang chooses a Cuban Cohiba Behike. The tobacconist cuts the cap and offers a light.

The general picks up the folder.

Choochai fills in the general on their discussion thus far. "Web just asked how we got the photos."

"They came from an unexpected source," the general says, and sighs his approval of the Scotch. He takes another moment to enjoy the cigar, gazing as a cloud of dense, creamy smoke wafts into the air. "They cannot keep up with demand. Your country's embargo created a mystique."

"Nicaragua also makes an excellent cigar these days," Web says.

The general smiles. "The seed is not the soil. But we did not come to discuss cigars." He pulls a photo of Jawad from the folder and drops it on the table. "This one is ruthless. In February his group, Ja, parked a van loaded with explosives at the back wall of a police station. Seven died. His own people were the target, presumably to keep them from talking."

"How did he know where they were?" Patch asks.

"We don't know. One week later Ja bombed the entrance of a movie theatre. Maybe it was retaliation, or maybe just a random attack on a soft target. We do know the strikes come more often.

"In March there were three—two in the south and one near a BTS station here in Bangkok. The most recent was the most violent. Border Patrol personnel were the targets. I need you to help us find and stop this man."

"How can we help?" Web asks.

The general edges forward in his chair and rests his elbows on his knees. He is intentional in his speech. "There is going to be a funeral. You don't read Thai, but I gave you a newspaper clipping."

Patch digs out the clipping and hands it to Web.

The general continues. "The insurgents attack, someone retaliates, more attacks, more retaliation. This funeral is for a prominent insurgency spokesman. He died at the hands of a simple farmer who lost his son. Many insurgents will be there, possibly disguised. If Jawad shows his face, we want to be ready. I will send our team to your operations center to coordinate.

"I need you to observe from the air. Three years we have waited for this capability. Now it is here!"

The general's exuberance fades quickly when neither Patch nor Web seem to join him in the moment of triumph, but Web recovers quickly. "Get time and coordinates to us and we'll be ready, even if we have to use hand-launched units. By the way, we are very near to testing facial recognition in some locations."

Choochai speaks enthusiastically about the video wall, and how innovative the sky deck is. He describes standing at the railing in order to see what the sensors see, and encourages the general to visit the new operations center as soon as possible.

Web appreciates every minute he can get with the general, and hopes to continue their conversation deep into the night. He offers to buy a second round of cigars, but too soon a military aide appears at the door, escorted by two of the general's day wives.

"It is time for me to go," the general says. "May I offer a ride, gentlemen?"

Web thanks him, saying it won't be necessary. Choochai leaves with the general. When alone, Patch texts Brick that it's time to be picked up.

"If the launchers don't get here in time, we're screwed," Patch says.

"Can we use the hand-held units? We just have to get crews in place. Should work."

"How do we get close enough to manage operations?" Patch thumbs through the general's photographs one last time and stuffs them into the envelope. He hands the envelope to Web.

"I'm not in the mood to consider failure. We burn a little midnight oil and come up with a solution."

"If you say so."

Web downs the last of his Scotch and drops his spent cigar into a snuffer. "I saw you looking at those pictures. Jawad is their problem, right? All we have to focus on is getting birds in the air over that funeral. Ready to go? I need some air."

They leave a healthy tip for the waiter, who acknowledges their generosity with a bow. They bow back and head toward the lobby and front entrance. "Do you ever tire of lugging that thing around?" Web asks, as they open the door and head toward the stairway in the lobby. He refers to the heavy seventeen-inch MacBook Pro over Patch's shoulder. Web rarely sees him without it.

"Nope."

Halfway down the stairs leading to the lobby, Patch grabs Web's arm. "Hold up a sec," he says. He nods toward men just outside the entrance climbing out of Humvees.

Web adjusts his glasses. "What do you see?"

"Volkov. He has four men with him. What do you want to do?"

Kuzma Volkov, Russian expatriate and fierce competitor, often tries to muscle in on Web's deals. Over the years they've taken millions in business from each other. Their most recent personal encounter was at an arms expo in Dubai. A quiet argument over a shipment of mortars quickly deteriorated to yelling, verbal threats and a fistfight. Security guards escorted both of them to the door.

"Public building," Web says. "Take this." Web removes his Glock, holster and all. He hands it to Patch, who clips it to the back of his laptop case. Patch knows the drill. Web's strategy is always to hand his weapon to a man that knows better how to use it and then rely on him to deal with whatever happens next. Web calculates that nothing will require a gun.

"You're awfully brave all of a sudden," Patch says.

"Scotch will do that," Web says, and hustles down the stairs. He walks briskly toward the Russians as they enter the lobby.

Patch adjusts the strap on his laptop case, opens the flap and tucks it behind his MacBook. As they cross the lobby floor, he says, "Try to remember how old you are."

"Nothing is going to happen," Web says. He feels emboldened by the sound of Patch's steady gait at his side. With each step his anger grows. He imagines punching Volkov in the face and how good that will feel. His fists tighten. Then he thinks better of it—two against five.

Volkov and Web lock eyes. Volkov says something to his men and they close ranks around him. "Look what the cat dragged in," Volkov shouts across the lobby. Hotel customers and a bellman glance in their direction.

"Your face has healed up nicely, Kuzma," Web says.

"You too, my friend." Within a few meters of each other, Kuzma glances at the envelope Web holds in his hand. A curious look crosses his face.

"Cigar bar is all yours," Web says.

"We appreciate this. Join us for vodka and a stick so we can talk about old times. Maybe do some business. Maybe we talk about what you carry in your hand."

Web hands the envelope to Patch. "Put this away," he says quietly.

"Maybe that is mine," Kuzma says. "Maybe you are meeting with General Phang and cutting into my wallet."

"It's not your envelope," Web says. And then, putting things together in his mind, knowing he should keep his mouth shut, he adds, "At least not anymore."

Volkov lurches forward and punches Web straight in the mouth.

Fists and elbows fly. Web, not a small man, fights hard. He pushes forward for about six seconds. To make sure Volkov regrets throwing the first blow, he returns three of his own.

Patch bashes Russians with his MacBook. Web and Patch hold their own, at least as far as Web knows, until he is taken to the ground by behemoths. He takes blows to the jaw, throat and eyes. The room seems to spin. His arms go slack as one of the men on top of him knocks his lights out.

Web's ears ring. He gazes at brilliant swirling lights and realizes he is on his back. It takes a second to recognize the light as being a crystal chandelier suspended above him. He thinks, *Man. That is a really big chandelier.*

Brick leans over him to ask if he is all right. "What?" Web asks.

Brick helps Web to his feet and sits him in a chair. Patch stands nearby, shaking his head. His broken laptop rests on the floor a few feet away. The hinge is snapped. Two Russians help Volkov stand, but he wobbles. They support him.

Then Web hears Tallis speaking in Russian or Latvian, he's not sure which. He is yammering with one of the Russian operatives as if they are old friends. He turns to Brick. "What the hell?"

Tallis hears the question. "Truce," he says. "This guy was born in Riga, like me!" The Russian waves hello.

Web is flummoxed. He feels for damage on his face then rubs his head before trying to stand. Brick grabs his arm again. The room still turns. "I don't think I can walk just yet, Brick. What'd I miss?" He sits.

"We seen the shit hit the fan just as we pulled up. You missed Tallis go all Ninja and what-not. Fuck, that guy can fight. Remember Patch smashing the hell out of these guys with that laptop? Freaking hilarious. I don't think he has a scratch on him."

"Weapons?" Web asks.

"Everybody is armed, boss. You know that. But fighting between you and that one guy over there ended with both of you on the ground. Once you were out of it, things settled down pretty fast. You okay?"

"Vodka!" Volkov shouts.

"Do I need stitches?" Web asks.

Brick looks him over. "Ice, mostly."

"Everyone else OK?"

"That one Russian is leaking pretty good, but everyone is going to be all right."

Web decides he feels better, at least for the moment. The pride in him gets him to his feet. He calls out to Tallis, "Ask the bleeder if he wants stitches. We have a med kit in the Rover if anyone needs it."

Customers of the hotel stare from the security of the balcony and from behind counters and columns. The bellman looks relieved that things have calmed down, that he doesn't have to get involved. The bleeding Russian keeps one hand on his nasty scalp wound. Blood runs down his face and arm. The concierge calls first for a towel, then a mop and bucket.

Tallis talks to the injured and tells Web the Russians will take care of their own.

"What the hell!" Patch barks. "If you boys are finished playing nice, we need to get out of here."

When they have cleared the front doors and stand next to their Range Rover, Web opens his phone. He dials the general. "We ran into Kuzma Volkov here in the lobby," he says, forearms resting on the roof of the SUV, head pounding now. "He punched me. I punched him back. Things got a little out of hand and the police are probably on their way. Maybe you should send someone down here to talk to management."

The Russians come out of the hotel. The bleeder yells over to Tallis in Latvian. Tallis yells back and laughs.

"What'd he say?" Web asks.

"He says next time we should have a drink instead of fight. I agreed."

Brick asks again if Web needs an assist. Web says no, even though he isn't sure. He's been knocked out enough times to know what could happen during the night. He considers having Patch take him in.

"We came in two cars," Brick says. "Tallis and I are going out to eat. You can come along for a nightcap if you want."

Web is about to say sure when Patch says no for both of them. "We're through," he says. "Have a good time."

"Keep your powder dry," Tallis says. He and Brick turn to leave.

When they are a few meters away, Patch calls them back. He opens his wallet and pulls out a condom. He hands it to Brick. "Thanks for showing up when you did. My daddy gave me this back in high school. I want you to have it."

Brick, Tallis and Web all laugh. Brick tucks the condom into his pocket and starts to walk away again. Patch calls out, "That's for you too, Tallis. You need to share."

"Now, that was funny," Web says. "Sure you don't want to join them? Could be fun."

Patch gets behind the wheel. He puts the keys in the ignition and starts the SUV, but doesn't yet put the vehicle in gear. He looks Web over and says, "I'm only going to say this once. Next time you ask me to dress down the crew for getting into fights, remember what just happened."

"Point taken."

CHAPTER 22

Two trucks park by cell towers in southern Thailand, near the junction of highways 4 and 42. Hmong workers exit the trucks. They climb towers and appear to work on roadside equipment. But inside the trucks, technicians unpack and assemble UAVs. The pilots assigned to the mission set up ground controls and prepare for aerial surveillance of a farmhouse less than a mile away.

A separate clandestine listening post, under the direction of the Internal Security Operations Command, is hidden in a wooded area less than four hundred meters from the farmhouse.

At the op center in Bangkok, Thai officials receive a short tour of the facilities from Web and Patch, then take seats at the command table where they will coordinate the efforts of multiple teams involved in the operation.

The lead intelligence officer assigned to the operation is named Farid. He briefs the Americans using succinct English. "We know that weapons and money are coming into the country from somewhere here in Southeast Asia, possibly the Middle East. We aggressively disrupt attempts to establish training camps and strongholds, but insurgents have trained in the Philippines and Indonesia, possibly other locations. Hopefully today we will gain insight into the funding sources. The insurgency raises money from their own membership, but is different."

"How so?" Patch asks.

"When people are angry enough, on both sides, they will pay almost anything to get revenge. But we also hear crazy things. Soup sold by street vendors is a source of funding. Ask for it by name and the purchase funds the cause. It's difficult to believe selling soup to poor countrymen can account for expensive weapons we face now. That's why we are here."

"What ever came of the negotiations? I read about sessions in Kuala Lumpur a while back," Web says.

"Someone is always negotiating, but hardliners refuse and disrupt. City officials, the police and our military regiments are all targets, as are some of the negotiators. Our methods have not always been successful. The people are tired. Very few participate in violence, but many are affected. Muslims are victims of extremism like everyone else."

Rich asks if the operation is a fact-finding mission or a tactical maneuver.

"It will only become tactical if we identify one of the men on our list," Farid says.

Patch receives a text, shows Web the message and excuses himself from the table. As he heads for the hangar, Web tells the Thais that they are preparing to launch the larger UAVs, an announcement that excites him a great deal. It means that the launchers have arrived.

When Patch enters the hangar he discovers a problem. Ginger and her team are frantically troubleshooting a pneumatic component.

"I spoke too soon," Ginger says. Patch stands with them, arms folded, as the crew retraces steps leading to the failure. They modify a few things, check fittings and attempt a dry launch. The last thing the team wants is to fire with inadequate pressure and drop a six-figure UAV on the concrete in front of them.

Ten minutes later, the team is out of ideas. Ginger calls the launch a no-go and apologizes to Patch. Patch turns away from his crew, barks a few choice words, and walks toward the control room with the devastating news.

Before he reaches the exit, the youngest member of Ginger's team calls him back. He has opened a Skype connection with a tech at the manufacturer's facility. The young man holds his iPad up to the stubborn launcher. Within minutes they switch to a different release valve and conduct a successful dry-fire.

They retract the gimbal on a UAV and mount the unit on the rail. Ginger notifies pilots in the op center to prepare for launch, then Ginger crosses her fingers and presses the release button. The release of pressure sends the UAV into the air. Ginger congratulates her crew as Patch returns to the command room ready to inform the Thais that longer-range birds are on their way to the site, ready to augment the shorter-range hand-held units already in the field.

Rich dims the lights in the control room. The video wall flickers. Moments later, the first hand-held UAV of the day is thrown into the air from a semi-concealed area behind two parked trucks near the home where the funeral will be conducted. Images stream from its sensors and are projected onto the video wall.

Simultaneously, the larger UAV leaves the hangar and heads south. Pictures from both units are displayed side by side.

"Amazing," Web says.

"Do you have images from our informant?" Farid asks. "She's

been on location all morning."

"The informant is a woman?" Web asks.

Farid pulls a photo from his briefcase and hands it to Web. "Some secessionists are violent to their wives and daughters. One of these women now helps us. She'll record activities around her with surveillance eyewear. We sent you a pair. Like Google Glass," Farid says and smiles.

Rich hands Web a pair of the glasses. Pinhole-sized indentations, with micro-lenses, are set amid a cluster of rhinestones on both sides of the frames. Web hands the frames to Patch.

Patch demonstrates their use. "There's a pressure plate behind the right ear. Bluetooth sends still images and video to a micro transmitter in her belt. The range of the data link maxes out at about a quarter mile. Right, Rich?"

"We're getting the signal through a stationary relay, but we tested from the air in the case she leaves the building. We don't have any performance issues exactly, but there are some serious limitations. We don't have audio. Any substantial obstruction in line-of-sight hurts transmission. Maybe the programmers worried about battery life, but when the device is turned on, it only sends images every fifteen seconds."

"What about image resolution?" Web asks.

"Reasonable for close work—six megapixels is my guess. Excuse me a second. I think we're about ready." Rich holds up a finger as he listens to someone through his headset. He brings up a series of still images. They show the crowded interior of the home under surveillance and verify that the funeral is in progress.

Farid is visibly excited. Rich moves one of the photos to the right end of the video wall. He cycles through images of the casket and distraught mourners every few seconds. Aerial views of the home and surrounding neighborhood are displayed on the left. They show cars parked in the drive and along the road.

"The interior shots were collected over the past hour. I'll show recorded video in a minute or two and then we'll go live."

"It is against our religion to take photos or make recordings at a funeral, but in this case it is the woman herself who takes the photos. It is her idea."

"You're a Muslim?" Web asks.

"You shouldn't be that surprised. I am Thai, first, then Muslim." Farid steps to the side and stares at the video wall. The deceased's body faces Mecca. An Imam sits next to the body, reading from the holy text. He's there to keep watch and to offer spiritual guidance.

Farid describes the proceedings. "Four men will take the body to the graveyard," he says, but his words trail off. His attention is riveted to the monitors as he sees a stream of recorded video.

"We're live now," Rich says. He enlarges the video feed and positions the stream in the center of the wall. The video pans right, then left, then goes black. One of the techs loudly asks what went wrong, but Rich waves at him to be silent. He turns to the command table. "This is one of the limitations I talked about. When she's not recording video, we're stuck with fifteen-second intervals. I'll replay the video, but until she sends more that's all I have."

Rich replays the video for Farid. Farid asks to pause on a frame of three men standing near the entryway door. Two of the subjects look out of place. They are tall and wear thick beards. They are also very muscular and are dressed in a different style of thobe.

"The collar!" Farid says, referring to the band cloth around the necks of the three men. "That design is not common here."

Rich sends a copy of the video to Anish with instructs to grab and enhance stills of the men. Anish replies that the low-resolution images, taken in dim light, will likely not yield much. Rich replies that he understands the challenge. Just do it, he says.

Farid asks for a third replay and points to another figure, back turned, wearing a green kufi. He says, "Jawad wears this cap. We need more pictures." His enthusiasm is infectious. Web and Patch tap knuckles, but then they are all forced to wait. Between new images that only cycle every fifteen seconds, Farid says other informants located Jawad a week earlier, or so they thought. But as with earlier attempts, he was gone when the counterterrorism team arrived. "He's like a ghost," Farid concludes and returns concentration to the video wall, leaning forward with each new photograph, then leaning back to wait for the next. There are no more images of the green cap or the mysterious visitors, only images of the family, the casket, the backs of heads. Enthusiasm gives way to enervation.

One hour into the operation, men carry the casket out of the building. Farid becomes excited when the man in the green cap, possibly Jawad, joins the three foreigners in a white SUV. One of the hand-held units follows them to the burial grounds. A second unit is launched so that the first can be retrieved and refueled.

"Will you send in a team?" Web asks Farid.

"Even if this is Jawad, we will not send men until the proceedings are over. Now, with your capabilities, we can afford to wait. Can we also follow the foreigners?"

"If you could communicate with the informant, we could have verified already whether the one guy is Jawad," Patch says.

Farid agrees but says simply that the informant is not familiar with technology and could get caught. He asks again if they will be able to follow the foreigners.

As the funeral procession returns to the family home, UAVs cycle in and out of the area for refueling. Still images from the informant show the transition from somber funeral to a warm celebration of a life. They gain little of strategic value from the informant's photos. It is frustrating Farid to see snapshots every fifteen seconds—people at a punch bowl, images of women in the kitchen, images of children playing, numerous photographs of the informant's husband eating. A few times the men of interest appear in the background, but are often out of focus. Farid sits stoically at the command table.

When people begin to leave, Farid is intent on pursuing both the foreign visitors and the man he believes to be Jawad. Thirty minutes later, he watches as a man walks to a red pickup truck with a black bed cover. The man puts a box in the back of the truck.

Pilots tag his vehicle. A hand-held unit follows, as do the technicians in the truck that launched it.

Ten minutes later, the foreigners leave the building and travel south. Rich passes images to the border patrol, along with orders from Farid. Web apologizes for flight limitations and reminds Farid that long-distance units are scheduled for delivery early in the coming year. When in place they will be able to observe from a much higher flight path, wherever the target might go. But for now the mid-sized UAV can only follow for a few miles. After that, the foreigners are not seen again until they drive beneath a video camera on the side of Highway 4, twenty kilometers south. Within minutes of that new sighting, the border patrol picks up the vehicle and follows it to the southern border with Malaysia.

Meanwhile, the red pickup truck turns off Highway 4 onto 35

and heads east toward the center of Bangkok. Farid directs activities from the command table in the operations center. An undercover surveillance vehicle intercepts the truck and rides parallel to the suspect for nearly a kilometer. Farid paces as images of the red truck are gathered from the pursuit vehicle. Both vehicles are tagged by the software.

"This could be it," Web says to Patch.

"Maybe," Patch says, but Farid gets a call. The man in the truck is not Jawad.

Photos from the tactical unit show the license plate, make and model of the vehicle, as well as the passenger's face. Within a few minutes they determine that the driver is a cousin of the deceased.

Farid consults with General Phang via phone and they decide against any overt action. Instead, just west of the Rama Frontage Road loop, a police car stops the truck under the pretense of random drug inspections. As the truck undergoes the inspection another police car pulls over a second random vehicle just ahead to throw off suspicion.

Policemen use a dog to sniff the truck. The driver is told that the dog is looking for drugs. He is not. This dog is trained to identify explosives. The driver allows them to rummage through the only box under the bed cover, a box of fruit. The dog finds nothing, and the smiling policemen send the dead man's cousin on his way, an electronic device tacked to the undercarriage.

Within the hour, Thai Border Patrol videos show close-ups of the driver and passengers of the white SUV at the border crossing. They photocopy the passengers' passports and licenses. The Border Patrol asks if General Phang wants the men detained. He declines. There is nothing illegal about attending a funeral.

CHAPTER 23

Web returns to the condominium late, as usual. He grabs a pipe and fills the bowl with a blend of tobaccos that Roger from the Perfect Ash back home put together for him. He's learned the smell of a pipe is more tolerable to the people around him than a full-bodied cigar, especially for Sam, especially in the evening. Especially this evening. He joins her on the balcony.

"The air was off," he says. He slides the door closed behind him.

Sam smiles and steps to the railing to gaze out at the city.

He tamps his tobacco into the bowl, lights his pipe and moves to the rail. Sam leaves the rail and sits, a clear sign that she's unhappy.

"You still upset about the trip?" Earlier in the day, as they had lunch together, he'd gotten a call from General Hines. During that conversation he committed to an open-ended trip to Dubai. The announcement hadn't gone over well with Sam.

Ensconced in her lounge chair, arms folded across her chest, legs crossed, Sam says, "We should have purchased a high-rise with a view of the river."

"We can talk about that anytime you want, but you're avoiding the issue."

She slides her fingers up the side of her tea glass, collecting moisture on them, and then flicks water his way. "I thought we'd have more time together, is all." She's smiling, but Web knows her better.

"Come on. We share dinner most nights. We took a day trip to Sai Thong national park, right? Went to Wat Arun together, lit incense and all that." It sounds good as he says it, but he knows she's right. He puts down his pipe and takes her hand. "I'm sorry I have to go. When I get back I'll move us to the River condominium complex. Patch can just deal with it."

Sam tugs at him to sit with her and then snuggles against him. "Forget that. I just needed to vent. I get that restless feeling sometimes and want a companion. You know? The timing of your trip sucks."

"I'm serious. We can move if you want."

"Knock it off. I'm over it."

They rest together, Sam half on top of Web in the narrow lounge chair. "At least tell me where you're going."

"I'm honestly not sure. I was told to be in Dubai next week for a meeting. After that, I don't have a clue. Won't be dangerous."

Sam sits up and lovingly punches him in the chest. "If it's not dangerous, why did you say that? Why even mention danger?"

Web laughs. "Because I don't want you to worry."

"Then don't say it?" She settles back into his arms and continues. "How long? A couple days, a week?"

Web senses something new in her tone. He says, "I'll be gone as little as possible."

She doesn't reply. They rest together in silence. He considers not going, but dismisses the thought. He has no choice.

Soon the sight of stars and sounds of the city below carry them both toward sleep. Every few minutes Web opens his eyes and realizes he's dozed again. Eventually, Sam asks if he is ready for bed.

"Just about," he says, stirring. "Are we good? I need to know we're good, and I need a word with Patch. If we're not good, let's pick up the conversation when I get back."

They stand. Sam touches him on the cheek and releases the top buttons of her blouse. She steps to the edge of the balcony and leans her back on the railing. "If you take too long I'll have to start without you."

Web laughs. He kisses Sam and apologizes again for the way he handled lunch.

Web calls ahead to Patch as he rides the elevator. He's offered a beer but declines. As they take seats at the kitchen table, Web says, "Hines crawled up my ass again about that deal on the Turkish border. Says he went around us to Dyna, so now the agency is pissed at both of us. I told him that could happen, but he doesn't listen. Short version, I'm headed to Dubai for a sit-down."

"We never had a chance at that contract to begin with. He knows it. We shouldn't have even bid."

"Didn't bid. That's the point. I said we weren't interested. Pointed out the conflicts of interest and thought it was all behind us, but he tacked our name onto his damn RFP."

Patch's back stiffens. "Every time he does something like this, a lot of people get their bowels in a bundle and the puddle ends up on us, Web. Not him." When he's spoken his mind, he stands and leans against the kitchen counter. His teeth grind together.

"Want my recommendation?" Web asks.

"No."

Web chuckles. "Let it go. I'll only be gone for a few days."

"You're being manipulated."

"It's called capitalism, Patch. He can manipulate us all he wants as long as the deals keep coming. Look. Hines is a rude bastard sometimes, but he's our rude bastard. Anyway, that's not the only reason I came down. I'm going to take Tallis on this one."

Patch paces sits, resigned. "Whatever. You'll still be here for the wedding?"

"Sam and I both. You?"

"I'm bringing the guys, but we can't stay long. Back on this agency thing. If you're going to be in Dubai anyway, I'll fly Bayhas to meet you. He probably needs a hug by now."

"I thought Bayhas was doing all right over there. Are the Kenyans giving him trouble?"

"What do you think? He's from the Sudan. They don't trust him."

"They have to trust him. I hired him to represent us there, precisely because of what he knows. They want to know how to handle people coming across the border, why not work with someone who knows that area. Fly him up. We'll figure something out. Book us all at the Ritz."

Web stands to leave. Patch opens the door and asks if General Hines will be at the meeting. "Not sure," Web says. "All I care about is that Dyna will be there. We straighten things out with her and we're good to go."

"If he is there, get in his fucking face for me, would you? Give him a Volkov."

Web laughs and heads for the elevator, then turns around. "How is Anish working out? Seems pretty bright. Maybe we should promote him, incentivize him to stick around a while."

"I'll give it some thought. Travel safely."

Sam is still on the balcony when Web returns. Her blouse and sweat pants rest on the table. She lounges in her chair wearing only undergarments. The straps of her bra hang loosely from her shoulders and she feigns sleep. Twitching toes, a horrible imitation of snoring, and a curious smile undercut her feigned disinterest.

As Web kicks off his shoes, Sam opens her eyes and asks, "What took you so long, cowboy?"

CHAPTER 24

Jawad knows the power of money. Preying on human greed suits him. In that regard, Thais are no different than anyone else.

Jawad solicits insider confidantes to probe government and military officials for their loyalties and weaknesses. They stumble upon a man who underestimates the situation. It is easy to get him to share secrets his superiors. He thinks he is trading away innocent information, never once believing he is helping insurgents.

Akara is driven to the Ratchadamri BTS station in Bangkok. He climbs stairs to the Saphan Taksin rail platform, checks the schedule and waits. Twelve minutes later, he gets on the Silom line train and travels southward past Sala Daeng and Chong Nonsi stations. At the Surasak stop a man in uniform boards. The officer carries a folded newspaper under his left arm. Akara struggles through the crowded car until he stands next to the man. He asks if the man has ever eaten at the Blue Elephant. The man says their green curry is the best in Bangkok.

Akara asks if he can see the man's paper. The officer hands it to him. Akara opens it, and removes a sheet of paper, tucking it into a pocket. He pretends to look at articles. During the bustle of people boarding and leaving, he slips an envelope into the paper and hands it back to the officer. He thanks the man and steps away.

The officer exits the BTS at Krung Thon Buri. Akara exits at the end of the line, and walks to a waiting car. He gets in.

"It's done?" Jawad asks.

Akara hands the slip of paper to Jawad, and says, "It's done."

CHAPTER 25

Tshua's nephew, Boon, returns to Thailand after a decade in Orange County, California. Boon is in his mid-thirties. He has needs. He has money, money enough to attract a bride.

He tells his uncle that traditional Hmong women are different from westernized Hmong women. Tshua empathizes with him and together they consult Boon's father and others on the *Tshoob Kos*, procedures for marriage.

Through meetings set up by leaders in the clan, he soon finds himself attracted to a much younger woman of another clan. Her name is Kaliah. Boon's uncle and father both feel she will serve him well. Boon promises to treat his wife with respect and negotiations begin. Tshua helps with the bride price. Boon offers jewelry equivalent in value to what Kaliah's father makes in a year. She accepts the gift, which means she accepts his proposal for marriage. Soon the whole clan is involved in planning the traditional wedding celebration that Web and his crew are invited to attend.

Keeping with tradition, Kaliah stays with Boon's family for a few days. Boon's father consults the shaman and performs a blessing ritual, asking his ancestors to treat Kaliah as their own. The family and their guiding spirits receive her.

Wedding feasts take place at other family homes, leading to an extravagant party at the Renaissance Bangkok Ratchaprasong Hotel, a premier wedding venue.

Families from both clans are present. Web and Sam arrive with

Patch, Brick and Tallis just in time to see dozens of family members performing a traditional dance. They wear ornate clothing in the style of their birth families. Complicated and ornate images embroidered onto their garments tell their history and the difficulties they have overcome.

Some of Kaliah's family who have adopted Buddhist ways engage a bhikkhuni to perform a blessing. At the request of Tshua's brother-in-law, a Catholic priest also blesses the newlyweds.

Patch, Brick and Tallis cannot stay long, but Web and Sam remain to enjoy the evening. Tshua joins them with a bottle of 18-year-old Macallan Scotch. Web comments on Tshua's black tux and white bowtie, joking that he should wear that every day.

"I'm so happy, Tshua," Sam says. "Thank you for inviting us. It's too bad you all had to leave Laos."

Tshua bows slightly. "Thank you. We miss our home. Today brings back memories."

"And cigars, my friend." Web pulls a pocket humidor out of his tux. He places two sticks on the table.

When they light up, Sam waves a hand in front of her face. "Tshua, there's so much to Hmong history and culture that I don't understand. Educate us."

Tshua looks around the room at his family and friends. "In the beginning of time the human and spirit worlds were one. All beings, human, animal and spirit, lived in harmony. It was good for us to interact with the spirits. They cooperated with us, trained us and watched after us. The world was in balance.

"In that time a spirit couple, the Dab Pog, trained us in marriage. You saw that today. We learned from them how to find our spouse and raise our children. The lessons survive among the Hmong and are preserved by the elders so much that when we lose our way the *txiv neeb*—you know them as shamen—help us find our souls and return them to our bodies. In the West, people have mostly lost their way. Some of them, like Boon, come back."

"That was beautiful, Tshua. It sounds similar in other religions, in different ways of course, but it makes sense. In Christianity angels used to visit believers. The Buddha talked with Devas. My ancestors thought of us as being possessed by daemons and demons."

"I didn't know you were so up on this stuff," Web says to her. He's constantly amazed by what he's learned simply by being married to Sam.

"Well, maybe I am," she says. "I find it interesting. I'm interested in the bride, too. If you gentlemen will excuse me, I haven't had a chance to congratulate her." Sam excuses herself and leaves.

As Tshua and Web smoke and reminisce, a disturbance breaks out near the ballroom entrance. Both men stand. A hotel manager has blundered in, leading a contingent of Caucasian men and women. Sam is confronting the group, arms flailing, motioning toward the door. Web and Tshua quickly head for the commotion. Hmong men jump up and rush toward the group as well. Fighting breaks out. Web and Tshua land in the middle of it. When Web hears Russian spoken, he instantly understands what happened.

Hmong elders fight viciously with six or seven Russians. The wedding planner runs out of the room. Two Russians try to calm their more aggressive family members and break up the fight, but it's too late. Within seconds, they too are fighting for their lives.

Frenzy takes over. Sam stands her ground between the bride and the Russians. She plants a kick on the face of her opponent, a hefty woman wearing an inordinate amount of makeup and swinging a bag. Seeing this, Web breaks out laughing almost as hard as he's fighting. Tshua proves, with his fists, why he is so revered in his clan. The fight ends with Hmong elders chasing broken, bleeding, overwhelmed Russians out the door and into the street.

Sam turns to Web. "We tried to explain to that jerk that Hmong and Russians don't mix."

"The manager should've known better, baby. Are you all right?"

"Fine. I think. Wow! That was actually fun!"

Web smiles, still learning from and about her. "You cracked that woman's makeup pretty good. Her face practically fell onto the floor. Sure you're all right? I see blood on your chin."

"I'm fine, but your lip is bleeding, cowboy," Sam says.

When they get back to the condo Web and Sam go to the bathroom to treat each other's wounds. Web dabs at the blood on Sam's chin and discovers it isn't hers. Sam presses ice into Web's fat lip. Their faces come closer to each other and they kiss. It is a moment Web will remember for as long as life allows.

CHAPTER 26

Patch hires a river taxi for the day. He and Rich travel the estuaries annotating maps and taking photographs.

Twelve million people live within the Chao Phraya River watershed. Rivers and a latticework of canals cover thirty-five percent of Thailand, making these waters one of the busiest thoroughfares in the world. Millions travel in hand-carved canoes, long-tail boats, river taxis and express boats. Yachts, fishing vessels, barges and ocean liners cruise Bangkok's rivers around the clock.

Web's team inundates the riverbanks with cameras. They wire river taxis and position sensors near express boat docks. Patch wonders aloud how many boats are on the river. He adds, "It's not even rush hour."

"I don't care how many," Rich says. "The question is, how many red-hulled long-tail boats do you see with three passengers? Our systems play I-Spy really well."

"I never thought of it that way. They can't do much to slip us until they hit land."

Rich takes a few more photos. "That's why having cameras in the right spots is so important. We get them leaving shore and it's all bits and bytes until they land."

As they continue up the river, Patch suggests that Rich look up. Skyscrapers rise at infrequent intervals, offering incredible views of city streets and open water. "Do we have the feeds from those rooftops?"

Rich closes his laptop and sets his maps aside. "I asked weeks ago, but somebody is dragging their feet. Maybe you can get the general to make it a priority."

"I'll have Web call them before he leaves, but it's just an AFI."

"AFI?"

"Another fucking inconvenience. Didn't they teach you anything in kindergarten?"

CHAPTER 27

Jawad tells his followers that he has business in the Middle East, and will be away for a week. While he is gone they are to continue preparations. He flies to Kuwait City on his native passport, as Sarab Najjar.

Jawad's younger brother Ibrahim meets him at Kuwait International with a limousine. He wears the traditional white thobe. Once calm and funny, Ibrahim is now sullen and anxious. His fingers twitch.

"Thank you for coming. Things are falling apart here, brother," he says. They ride together in a limousine headed for their family villa. "Did you hear? We are banned from the Olympics. Everything has changed. Life is worthless. I'm going to move my money to London, maybe live there."

Jawad is furious. "No, brother. Not London. Forget the Olympics, cars, women and parties. Join the faithful. We are fighting for the soul of Islam!"

Ibrahim recoils. His face twists in anger. "What happened? You sound just like them now. Everyone wants to fight. It's tearing us apart. I have lived by the five pillars all my life and they dare call me a rejectionist? Father has gone to Morocco, Sarab. I'm going to London."

Taken aback by his brother's rant, Jawad says, "Let us prove our faith, you and I."

Ibrahim turns his head and mumbles. "You haven't been here."

"My apologies," Jawad says. "You are right."

They ride in silence for several minutes.

"Why not London?" Ibrahim asks.

"Brother, you have been misled by the West. They will seize your money when the time comes. Let me protect your future by investing in Southeast Asia—Malaysia or Indonesia. Invest in an Islamic country, not the West. I don't have the wealth that you do, but this is what I have done and the rates of return are just as good. I can help you. There are business opportunities there."

"You are doing well?"

Jawad smiles. "Doing very well. Invest with me. I can manage your funds and keep them safe."

The limousine turns into their estate. Attendants carry Jawad's bags. The brothers stand in the grand entrance of the family palace where Ibrahim points to the elegance of the room and sighs. "I don't want to leave this life, but it is time. I'm curious about your ideas. Tonight you can tell me more about your investment strategy."

"Good. Tomorrow I meet an investor then fly back to Thailand."

In the evening Jawad convinces Ibrahim to put fifteen billion Kuwaiti dinar, fifty million dollars US, into accounts that Jawad will manage. They arrange the SWIFT transfer to Kuala Lumpur.

In the morning, Jawad wakes up elated by the capital he now controls, but nervous about the men he is to meet. As he drives toward a city park he checks his rearview mirror often.

At the park, he waits. His intuition and training says he is watched, but he is patient. He knows the protocol. Twenty minutes after arriving, a horn sounds. He walks to a parked van, gets in and is driven away.

CHAPTER 28

Web and Tallis wait in Suvarnabhumi Airport terminal for their dawn flight to Dubai. Tallis has no electronic gadgets grabbing at his attention on this trip. He is quiet, scanning nearby passengers. Web interprets this more focused demeanor as nerves, a man unsure of what is expected of him. He checks messages on an encrypted app and finds one from Bayhas. His friend and contractor has arrived in the UAE and will meet them for dinner.

Web turns to Tallis. "Spend any time in Kenya? We have a project there. Our manager is Sudanese. You'll like him."

Tallis displays the mischievous grin Web has learned to recognize. He says, "I've never been there, but I hear it's the bomb. You?"

Web shakes his head. "You're going to use that word in an airport?"

Tallis laughs.

"Anyway, yes. I've been to Kenya a few times. Sam and I spent a week near Diani a while back. Before that I went on safari. That was back when even an American could drive around without worry, but things have changed. Border-crossing clansmen have ruined the tourist trade. It's a shame."

"Economic terrorism. Welcome to the future. You're talking about the mall attack, right?"

"The attack of 2012? That and later incidents, sure. It takes a special kind of sickness to walk through the mall firing into women and children. They took down sixty-seven people that day. Brits still won't authorize travel along the coast, or anywhere within sixty kilometers of Kenya's northern border with Somalia. Bayhas says the western areas of the country are hot too now, over by Mount Elgon and Uganda, that area. I hope they can work things out."

"Bayhas the guy we're meeting?"

"He is. You'll like him."

They sit in silence for a while. Web needs rest. He closes his eyes to recall white sandy beaches and the sway of grass on the savannas. A strange thought runs through his mind, a line from a song maybe. "How long it takes, how many years to save the world."

Bayhas is waiting for Web and Tallis at DXB airport, Dubai. He's as tall and muscular as Web remembers him to be, one of the very smartest operatives he's ever had the privilege of working with—informed, insightful and resourceful. He speaks intelligently about everything from geopolitics to French cuisine.

Within an hour the trio enjoys cigars and conversation on the terrace at No. 5 Lounge and Bar, Ritz-Carlton Hotel.

"Is the world at war, Bayhas?" Web asks over dinner. "I say yes. The world is at war. Every time I walk by a newsstand, the front page is about one or another conflict zone."

"Conflict and celebrity divorce," Bayhas laughs. "Am I right? Your newspapers are the worst."

"There is that, but you know what I'm saying. These days I fill orders from parts of the world that should be peaceful. Kenya, for example. Makes you wonder why. It's clear the world is at war."

Bayhas has lived in the Middle East much of his life, but he also has extensive experience in central and northern Africa. He considers himself to be a historian. "No," Bayhas says. "The Internet shows us every little thing across the globe. It may seem the world is at war, but look at the numbers."

Bayhas speaks with his whole body. "Death by violence, as a percent of the total population, is less and less over time. That's what research tells us. Don't listen to everything you see in the papers, my friend, especially US papers. Get a good paper."

Tallis grins like a mischievous tween, but doesn't join the conversation.

"Tell that to your clansmen, the Somalis, that bit about numbers going down. Actually, I don't think anyone in Africa would agree with you," Web says.

"Anyone in Africa? Not so. CAR or Nigeria maybe, but not all of Africa." Bayhas says. "No way. Areas are at war, but the world is not. The world is a big place and grows more peaceful every day."

"The Central African Republic is the most dangerous," Web argues. "Car and Dar both. What about Chad, Rhodesia and Mali? The entire Sahel is moving toward genocide. Ask the French. Africa is at war, Bayhas. Those are the numbers. Let's check off the continent of Africa. Africa is at war. Move on to Latin America and you get more bad news. Not as intense, but at war." Web has fun pressing his point, escalating the debate, playing loose with the facts.

Bayhas laughs. "You're a crazy man. There are displaced peoples in Africa and the Middle East. Okay, parts of Africa, yes. Sudan is a fragile state. But you are crazy to say Latin America. No way."

"Yes way," Web says, egging on his friend. "Thousands are killed every year over drug money. Know how to stop it? No one does. Check off Central and South America."

Bayhas can barely control his enthusiasm. He says, "Now. If some despot explodes a nuclear device or some other WMD, that would change the math, but death by violence is going down, down, down. Look it up, my friend."

Web points his finger at Bayhas then at Tallis. "Africa, the Middle East, former Russian Bloc countries. Tallis can tell you, man. He spent time there. If we're not at war, or soon at war, what's the arms race about?"

Bayhas slaps the table and points right back at Web. "The arms race is at your door, my friend. The US."

Web turns to Tallis. "Can you believe this guy? We're having a cigar, philosophizing about whether the world is at war, and he changes the subject to an arms race. What the hell is that?"

And then directly to Bayhas, he says, "You could bring up anything, ocean fishing, but look where you took us. I'm cutting you off. No more tea, or maybe we need another round."

Web motions to their waiter. "Another round over here quickly, before we cut ourselves off."

Bayhas laughs. "You brought up the arms race, my friend. And if not the US, then who?"

"Russia," Tallis says.

Bayhas slaps his forehead in disbelief. He can barely contain himself. "OK. Let me explain the arms trade to the arms dealers. We are here now, in the United Arab Emirates. I'll use this place as one of many examples.

"Years ago the US sold eighty F-16s to the UAE. Do you remember that?"

"Vaguely," Web says, "Fifteen billion dollar deal."

"Yes, yes. What the hell? F-16s? Look what happened. All across the Middle East they turn oil into weapons." He speaks with grand sweeping gestures. "Everyone wants everything. Look at Afghanistan, Turkey and Iran. Count the countries. Do you see where this goes? Consider Yemen and Pakistan." Bayhas counts on his fingers and becomes even more animated, bending at the waist with each country. "It started with US jets and missiles. Now look. Everyone wants drones. Who started that? Iran is crazy for the bomb. Everyone is crazy. Why? Because years ago someone wanted to make money on jet fighters."

Web waves his hands in the air, a sign to stop. "You don't know what you're talking about, Bayhas. No one spends fifteen billion dollars on something they don't need."

The waiter arrives. Web drops his spent cigar into a snuffer and lights another.

Bayhas continues, "You are too close to it, my friend. Yes. Someone wanted F-16s here, but whom, and for what purpose? Ask yourself that?"

"Web has a point, Bayhas. Think of Myanmar, the Philippines, Malaysia, Indonesia, Western China and Chechnya. I think you're right, boss. The world is at war," Tallis says.

Web gives Tallis a high-five. "We haven't even touched on Syria, Yemen or the Sinai Peninsula."

Tallis adds to the list. "What about Russian annexation. They try to move the boundaries in Georgia almost every night."

"I heard something about that. Really?" Web says.

"Yeah. True story," Tallis says, crossing his heart. "At night a farmer's pasture is on the Georgian side of the border. In the morning his cows speak Russian. Someone moved the sign. It's so bad people park dead cars on the border to make it harder to change. Seriously. You go there and see rusted out Toyotas, Mitsubishis and Opels parked in the fields."

"That's hilarious. Well, actually shameless is a better word for it, but still funny."

"We should do that with Canada, annex the Bakken oil range," Tallis says, which prompts even more laughter.

"So what do you think, Bayhas?" Web says, returning to the subject at hand. "The world is at war, right? I can give you more proof if you want."

"Please don't," Bayhas says. He holds up his hands in surrender. "Let's smoke our Mohebis and not talk about war any more. Depressing! We talk about how peaceful the world is."

Web laughs and checks his watch. "To be serious for a moment, do you have everything you need in Kenya? Are we getting you the financials on time? The better question is, do you feel safe there?"

Bayhas sobers slightly. He pushes his tea aside. "The government is responsive. I've had an escort wherever I need to go, but if you come use Mombasa Road to get from Jomo airport into the city, and don't go into the Eastleigh area."

"I'll keep that in mind," Web says. He wasn't aware that things had gotten to that state. "General Mburu promised to look out for you. If that changes in any way, you let me know. I can hire more personal protection. How long will you be in Dubai?"

"Only tonight. How about the two of you?"

Web shrugs his shoulders. "Not sure. I hope to meet with another group later this evening. If that happens maybe, we all fly out tomorrow."

Bayhas looks confused. "You flew in just to conduct one quick meeting?"

"Long story," Web says.

Web and Tallis listen for the next half hour to a detailed report of activities in Kenya, how Bayhas met with officials at the Chief of Defence Forces and closed the deal Web started back in Washington, DC, how Musa and Umoja are his greatest obstacles in the military, less interested in doing business than are the local businessmen. Bayhas assesses them to be pragmatists, but lacking in the technical background to fully understand the value of an ISR network.

Web suggests he arrange a tour for the Kenyans of the Bangkok op center. Bayhas agrees that a hands-on demonstration is exactly what is needed.

Nearing 2200 hours, Web gets a text. He and Tallis excuse themselves and head for the lobby.

"Who are we meeting?" Tallis asks.

"We are meeting whoever shows up," Web says. He marches through the lobby and out the front door. A limo waits for them near the entrance. The back passenger-side door swings open. Web climbs in the back, Tallis in the front.

"I'm glad it's you," Web says.

The woman seated in the back asks, "What is he doing here?"

"Tallis Sverns, meet Dyna Stavros. Among other things, Dyna is liaison between the Romanov Agency and the International Atomic Energy Agency. Dyna monitors the fringe of the nuclear security community. And Dyna, Tallis is an employee of mine, multi-lingual operative."

Dyna is a slight woman, but tall. She appears to be in her late thirties, dark hair and wickedly dark lipstick. She speaks with a mild Eastern European accent as she says, "That's who is here, I'm asking why."

Web laughs. "Let's just say Tallis is someone I want you to meet."

Dyna studies Tallis's face for a moment and speaks in Russian. She asks Tallis how it is that he fell into bed with Web.

Tallis answers in Russian. "Pure luck."

Dyna smiles. The driver of the limo pulls into traffic. Dyna speaks directly to Web. "If you want him here, there must be a good reason. Tell me what's going on in Turkey that has Hines so damn upset. And while you're at it, why did you make that proposal?"

"I didn't. Hines put our names on the damn thing. I said no, but he went ahead anyway."

"Why in the world would you say no?"

Web looks at Dyna curiously. "You don't know, do you. He didn't tell you?"

"Tell me what?"

"The buyer wanted to pay in oil, for Christ's sake. I told Hines all about it. Oil in Southern Turkey? Has ISIS written all over it. Even if it were legit, what the hell am I supposed to do with trucks of oil? Lube my car? Get serious, Dyna."

"He didn't set up the sale, we set up this sale. I need you to go through with it."

Web curls his brow and shakes his head. "Not going to happen."

The limo travels slowly along Al Sufouh Road, past Knowledge Village and Dubai College. Dyna says, "We need this sale to go through, Web. I don't care what they want to pay with, or how you negotiate the deal, but it has to go through. We've been working on this for eighteen months."

Web sees the determination on Dyna's face. The fact that they both flew to have this discussion underscores just how serious she is. "What's so important about the sale of a few hundred rifles? I don't get it."

Dyna glances at Tallis, as if considering what to say next then says something to the driver in Arabic. She turns to Web and says, "The rifles are insignificant. Half of them won't work anyway. What is important are the homing devices we've embedded in the stocks. I don't care how you get paid, just make the sale. We need a handle on how materials are crossing the border."

As she speaks, the driver turns a corner and heads back toward the hotel. They ride in silence for nearly a mile.

"Oil?" Web says. "I trade in commodities, but not in that part of the world. You find a suitable buyer and I'll consider it. Otherwise, no deal."

CHAPTER 29

The op center day shift turns over the control room at 1900 hours every evening. This is not a drinking group. They spend most weekend evenings at Thailand's sprawling thirty-acre JJ Market. Its formal name is Chatuchak Weekend Market. Two hundred thousand visitors pass through the maze of chaos, as Joe calls it.

This evening, Ginger, Anish, Lee, Picasso and Joe revive their escalating food challenge. Ginger says it builds character to challenge each other with sampling from hundreds of Thai dishes, recipes for which sometimes date back in centuries. Tonight, Ginger dares her companions to eat cooked insects and parts of animals that Westerners discard or grind into hot dogs. Anish bravely tries Goong Ten, miniature shrimp still alive and dancing. Picasso goes for Larb Leuat Neua, raw beef with mint. Ginger says the mantis prawns, Gong Chae Nam Pla, are fine cooked in fish sauce. All five adventurers decline the raw version. Black duck egg salad disgusts Lee. Black feathers in a boiled egg? No thanks. Joe says Baak Bpet, barbecued duck face, which he holds by the bill, is fantastic.

All five techs are pretty sure that locals don't themselves eat half of what is there, but they don't care. The crew ends this evening's challenge when Ginger, the most adventurous of them, throws up a stomach of crickets, water beetles and silk worms soaked in pepper sauce. She recovers by devouring a fistful of mints.

After several hours, the team goes hunting for jewelry, shoes and other gifts to send home to friends and family. Shopping for electronics, clothing and oddities is the main reason anyone goes to the market.

As the team passes a booth crammed with electronics, phones and electronic tablets, a loud and aggressive salesman follows them. "Low price! Everything must go!" He won't stop his banter. "Come look! Wide selection! Low prices!" Anish and Joe become annoyed as the man becomes more aggressive.

"What do you think, guys?" Ginger asks. "I'd like to send a cheap tablet back to the States, video chat with my grandmother." She asks Joe if the bank is open. He is the one who always carries a wad of cash.

"Everything must go," the salesman repeats. He jumps in front of them now, arms spread wide blocking their path. "Yes. Tablets. For the pretty lady, sixty percent off—sixty-two percent off."

Joe voices a bad feeling about the guy, but as often happens, Joe does anything he can to please Ginger. He hands over a wad of cash. Following protocol, they return as a group to the electronics booth. Joe enters the back room first.

CHAPTER 30

Approaching 0500 hours, Patch wakes to the sound of loud pounding at his door. He pulls on a pair of pants and arms himself. Choochai practically leaps into the room when Patch opens to him.

"Please forgive," Choochai says. He pulls out his phone, punches a few buttons and holds it up to Patch. "The general's office got this message one hour ago. I will bring you both to our command center as soon as possible. Web doesn't answer his door."

Patch hears a disturbing recording. In broken English the recording says, "Stop the drones. We have your pilots. CIA dogs go home or we kill them all."

"This came in the last hour?" Patch asks. "Only the one message?"

Choochai nods. His face says they need to hurry. "Wait here, Colonel," Patch says. He leaves the apartment and calls Brick as he waits near the elevator. Brick answers, "We're hot. You and Tall, twenty-second floor, on the double."

As he rides the elevator upward he speed-dials Sam. She doesn't answer her phone. He pounds on the Webbers' door and calls her name. No response. Patch bangs louder and yells for her again. Cursing, Patch drives all his weight into the door. It cracks. A second thrust and he's in.

It takes only moments to verify that Sam isn't in the condo. Brick arrives and steps through the broken door, pistol drawn. He helps Patch search for clues to where Sam might have gone. There is no sign of struggle. The coffee maker is cool. The bed has been recently made or was never slept in.

As they search the apartment, Patch gets a call from the op center. A young, anxious tech says they've received a call. It's probably nothing, he says, then starts apologizing for calling so early.

"Get to the point right now," Patch barks.

"The caller said we have to destroy the 'X26s' and leave Thailand or they're going to kill everybody. Freaked me out."

Patch takes a deep breath. His voice slows. He says, "Forward the message to my cell. I need you to be cool with what I'm going to say. Find the key hidden on top of the uppermost blade of the left server rack in the data center. Break out the weapons and don't let anyone leave the building. I'll have extra security there as soon as possible."

"What's going on?"

"You did the right thing by calling. Is Rich there?"

"He comes in at 0800."

"Call him in. Call everyone. Don't let anyone travel alone, but get them to the center. And then I need every scrap of video that shows Samantha Webber leaving her condo. Find out is she alone or with someone, and where she went.

"I also want you to scrub video of the day shift from the exit door last night to wherever the hell they went. We think they've been taken. You're the best and brightest techs in the business. Work directly with Brick on this one, you got all that?"

The tech says yes and the call ends.

"What the hell is going on?" Brick asks.

Patch puts his phone into his pocket. "Somebody claims to have our people. Choochai is driving me to the Thai command center in a minute to work on this thing with General Phang."

"You think they got Sam? Which people?"

"Haven't verified a damn thing, but we have to assume the worst."

As they leave the Webbers' condo Brick asks about the door. Patch says, "Grab the one off my apartment. Replace this one then head over to the crew members' apartment complex. If we're lucky, This will all turn out to be some sick bastard's hoax."

They ride the elevator down to the fifteenth floor. As they ride, Brick says, "After the door, then what?"

"Find Sam. That's your mission. Use any resources you can muster. The op center will probably come up with something soon, just keep me informed."

"On it," Brick says. As they leave he pulls out his phone.

Choochai looks anxious. "Did you wake Web?" he asks.

"Web is out of the country. Until he returns, I'm in charge."

"I understand," Choochai says.

Patch grabs his new laptop and a weapon. He pulls on a shirt and turns to Choochai. "Get me to the general."

They leave for the elevator. Brick calls after him from the open doorway of Patch's apartment. "What about your door?" he asks. "Your stuff will be exposed."

"Think I give a damn? Get on with your mission."

Choochai is a madman behind the wheel. He races the general's personal McLaren Coupe at full throttle whenever possible, weaving in and out of traffic.

"We should contact Web," Choochai says.

"I'll call when we have better information."

Choochai is forced to slow down behind two delivery trucks. Patch says, "We need a security team at the op center."

"The general already arranged that," Choochai says, and stomps on the gas.

CHAPTER 31

Web is asleep when a phone call jerks him to consciousness. He looks through blurred eyes at the display, sees it's Patch, and answers the call. "Better be good," he says gruffly.

"Where would Sam be at six in the morning?" Patch asks.

Web sits up straight and slides his feet to the floor. "What's going on?"

"Just answer the question, Web. I'm trying to locate her."

"If she's not in the condo she's at the health club or maybe running. Sonny is in town. They're probably training somewhere. Actually, hold on," Web says. He switches apps, rubs his eyes and checks his calendar. "Patch? They're at a bike race. What the hell is going on?"

Web hears Patch sigh. "Didn't think to check for her bike."

"You're killing me here! Why the hell are you concerned so early in the morning?"

"People may have been taken, Web. Choochai is driving me to the Thai command center now, to help coordinate a response."

Web leans forward and rests his elbows on bare knees. His phone, in speaker mode now, hangs loosely in his right hand. He wants to yell into the phone, find out what the hell went wrong, but he doesn't. Quietly he says, "Find her, Patch. Who all was taken?"

"We think they got the day shift. No one knows who or why. Working on all that now."

Web checks the time. "Tallis and I will be there as soon as we can catch a flight."

An hour later, Web's mind races ahead of the taxi, ahead of the plane that will carry them to Bangkok, and forward to decisions he will have to make in the coming hours. He pulls out this phone and taps in a number. Dyna answers. "I need your help," he says.

"This is not a secure line."

"We'll just have to deal with that later. Have you ever heard the name Kuzma Volkov?"

CHAPTER 32

Ginger's flashbacks are unrelenting. Images from the moments before their capture at JJ Market overlap memories of her patrol under fire in Iraq. Friends and coworkers fight for their lives in unforgiving sand and dust at the side of a road. Then they are in the back room of an electronics shop, then in military barracks. She remembers being pulled from a box and thrown against a block wall. There are moments when she recalls climbing endless stairs in the dark. She is still in the dark, cuffed along with her friends, sitting in the stifling heat and stench of a small room.

Neither she nor her fellow prisoners can focus on much of anything for more than a minute or two. If she's asked a question, half the time nothing comes to mind before they move on to the next topic. She wants to scream, or cry, or kick the shit out of Joe, but people are counting on her.

"Oh!" Joe says. The surprise in his voice is the same surprise he had the last time he said it. He thinks they are still at the market.

Ginger smelled something back then, ether maybe. "They are drugging us!" she says. "Don't eat the food."

"Oh," Joe says again, lying in the dark next to her. He is sandwiched between Ginger and Anish. "My name is Joe, not Joseph."

"No one called you Joseph. We always call you Joe."

"Oh," he says.

"Did they beat you up?" Joe asks. "I'll kick their ass if they touch you."

"Not me, Joe. You. They beat the shit out of you when they dragged us down the hall. You have a concussion or worse. Try to rest."

"When we made the movie?"

"Then too, probably. What movie?"

"I didn't tell them anything," Joe says. "Can't break the champ."

"That's because they already know everything," Anish says. "They know our names, where we live, where we came from. You just have to read the paper."

"There's something wrong with Picasso," Lee says. "I can hear him messing with the shit can again."

"He'll be OK," Ginger says. "He's making art. You had to make a movie, too, Anish?"

"Yeah," Anish says. "Just read the paper and they won't mess with you. He's doing it again, Ginger. Jimmy! Leave the shit can alone. You'll get typhoid."

Ginger barks for everyone to just leave him alone. "There's something wrong with him. Flashback or something. He'll work it out. You'll work it out, won't you, Jimmy? You're an artist, right? Artists always work it out."

Jimmy doesn't answer at first, but then, from somewhere in the dark on the other side of the room, he says, "I know what I'm doing. When we make our stand I'm going to fling shit. We can attack then."

"That's actually smart," Ginger says. "But when they come for you just go along. Just do what they ask. Heroes get the shit beat out of them."

They rest in the dark. Occasionally men talk beyond the door that holds them hostage. A guard outside the door shifts his chair and speaks in angry muffled Thai.

"It's like poetry when you talk," Jimmy says finally. "I'd like to paint you someday."

"Are you talking to me?" Ginger asks. "Sure. As long as you don't paint on me."

Anish laughs cynically. "His art is shit anyway."

"Next time they come I'm going to rush them," Lee says.

"Fuck yes," Joe says. "I'll kick their ass."

"You tried that," Ginger says. "Shut up a minute. You have a concussion, and no one is rushing the guards. Fuck's sake, gentlemen. Use your heads. If they try to move us, then you throw shit and we all fight for our lives, but not yet. If we do fight you have to get them on the ground so we can use our feet. Can't fight worth a damn with your hands tied behind your back.

"You want to do something, figure out how to get your cuffs off. Sharpen the edge of the shit can or something. It probably won't work but it's worth a try."

"Get them all the time. It's nothing," Joe says.

"What the hell are you talking about? What do you get, Joe?" Ginger asks.

"Headaches."

"This is different," Ginger says. "Your speech is messed up. Take it easy."

"Oh."

"I can't feel my fingers," Lee says. He yells at the thin dim crack of light beneath the door. "Let us loose!"

The response, the same one as last time he yelled, is a loud pounding on the other side of the door.

"Don't struggle against the cuffs," Ginger says. "The swelling gets worse. None of us can feel our fingers. Please. Shut up and color."

"What?"

"Just an expression. Stop your complaining and man up."

"Was I in a fight?" Joe asks. "Somebody should turn the lights on. I feel sick."

"You have a concussion. When you puke, turn the other way this time."

"Oh. Sure thing. I'll turn."

Silence.

"Ginger?"

"What, Joe."

"I think someone is sitting there."

"That's me, asshole," Anish says, but before Joe can react, the door bursts open and three guards rush in. They grab Lee by the hair and drag him from the room, kicking Joe twice in the head before they leave.

CHAPTER 33

Twenty minutes pass in nearly dead silence. The door bursts open. Lee is thrown into the room and the guards grab Ginger. Joe and Anish both kick wildly, but despite their protests, she is taken away in violence.

Two minutes later she sits on a chair, hands still bound behind her back, a rope around her neck. Armed men stand to either side of her. She faces a video camera on a tripod. A small table sits in front of the tripod, laptop open, Skype turned on, the face of a bearded man fills the frame of the laptop. Jawad stares at her with a sadistic smile.

He speaks to her by name. "Inge Rush," he says. "War hero for the crusaders. You've changed since your high school picture. How is that limp coming along? Please state your name."

Ginger doesn't reply. The crew members dragged away before her were right. The insurgents have done their homework. She studies the man's face, memorizing every pore. She looks to the men at her right and left. She says, "My name is Jawad."

A man strikes her in the back of the head with the palm of his hand.

Jawad seems angry that Ginger knows his face, which gives Ginger a fleeting moment of satisfaction. "Your name!"

"Jawad the masturbator," she says. The man behind her strikes again, hard. She fights to retain consciousness and then to get free, but it's no use. The rope at her neck is jerked tight. She feels her veins swell and fights for breath. "Suck my big dick," she manages to say.

She is hit again, the rope loosens, and Jawad laughs. "I expect nothing less from such an honored veteran. Unfortunately for you, we have all day. Please be a hero. How does it go? Name, rank and serial number? What is your name, Inge Rush?"

CHAPTER 34

P atch joins General Phang at the Thai command center. Men sit at small desks in front of multi-monitored terminals. Each member of the general's team is absorbed in his task.

Greetings are short. The atmosphere is busy, crowded and tense. The general waves for Patch to join him. "What do we have so far?" Patch asks.

The general holds up a finger then beckons to one of his colonels to come forward. They speak in Thai then step away to discuss something with another man. A translator steps up to Patch and speaks in reasonable English.

"We are getting close? The call is from a cell tower in Ratchawin Village. We have tracked three insurgents, maybe four, to that neighborhood six month ago. Soldiers has been sent to look for your friends."

"Can I assume the Border Patrol has been notified?" Patch asks. "We can't let them cross the border."

The colonel answers. "Border patrol doing good job."

The general returns. A heated discussion with one of his advisors ensues. Patch doesn't understand Thai, but the word Ratchawin is used often. He steps away from the general and calls the op center.

Rich answers the call.

"Glad you're at the controls, Rich. Anything I can pass on to

General Phang? They're planning something. I'm not sure it's the right action to take."

"Cameras picked up our team getting off the BTS last night. We see them entering JJ Market, but we can't find them leaving. We've scrubbed every frame of video we can find. If they left, it wasn't as a group and they sure as hell didn't use public transportation."

"You saying they're still at the market?" Patch asks. The general waves for him to return to the conversation. "Stick with it, Rich. I have to go."

"There's more," Rich says.

"Quickly."

"I don't trust one of the general's guys."

"What is that supposed to mean?"

"He took calls last week while he was here. Looked nervous."

"Don't get paranoid on me, buddy. There's no room for speculation. The general looks like he's going to move on a neighborhood. I have to go."

"Maybe we can help."

"You have birds in the air?"

"Working on it."

"Ratchawin neighborhood. Keep an eye on the market, too. I'll get back with you."

Patch ends the call and joins the general's conversation to relay what he's just learned, that it's possible their crew never made it out of the market. The general seems interested, but is undeterred. In front of Patch, the general signs an order to move on Ratchawin. Patch is not in a position to question that order.

Meanwhile, when Sam and Sonny cross the finish line of her duathlon, Brick is there waiting. Sam is out of breath and exhausted, but finds the energy to jump up and down in excitement. Sonny congratulates her on a great performance as Brick approaches.

"Brick. You made it! What a race. Did you see much of it?" she asks.

Brick smiles. "Congratulations. We have to go," he says. "You're both coming with me. This way."

"What's going on?" Sonny asks. "I have a rental in the parking lot."

"We'll take care of it. I'm sorry, but it's time to go."

"Do what he asks," Sam says, responding to Brick's intensity.

"We need to get our bikes," Sonny says.

Brick says he will take care of it later, but Sonny protests. Sonny's racing bike, it turns out, is worth more than Brick's new Harley.

Brick calls Patch to say that Sam is all right and under his protection.

Hearing his call, Sam becomes even more anxious. As they drive toward the bike racks she demands to know what is going on and whether Web is all right."

"Web's just fine," Brick says. "He's on his way back from Dubai. Some of our crew is missing, maybe taken. You guys are probably no longer in danger, but you know the protocol."

"When?" Sam asks.

"Where are you staying, Sonny?" Brick asks.

"Royal Hotel. It's just up the street."

"During the night sometime, Sam. I'm moving you both to

the Intercontinental. I'll bring clothes and what-not to you. Patch doesn't want you at the condo until we get a handle on things," Brick says.

At the Intercontinental Hotel Brick asks for Sonny's keycard. When they are safely tucked away in a room, he hands Sonny a sidearm and leaves for the Royal Hotel.

CHAPTER 35

Following a tactical discussion with Patch, Rich and the op center team launch two UAVs and ready six more for flight. He tasks pilots with observing the Ratchawin Village area, the neighborhood General Phang's team has targeted. They also pull up feeds from the BTS and other cameras in that neighborhood.

The techs have never seen a military action like the one unfolding before them on the video monitors. They watch a convoy of military vehicles converge on Rama 3 near Lumphini Park Riverside. The convoy turns into the Ratchawin Village area. As it does, people scurry from the streets.

Members of Thai tactical units swarm like ants through the maze of narrow streets. They cordon off traffic moving in or out of the area, then rush into Sathu Pradit 57 Alley and quickly disperse. The crew watches with amazement as tactical units move through every square inch of the neighborhood. Chaos ensues at the leading edge of their advance. Everyone living in the neighborhood is pushed and prodded into the streets, where families either sit or stand on the pavement. Hundreds of people are driven from their homes and apartments. A wide view of the action shows traffic beyond the roadblocks has backed up for ten kilometers.

Meanwhile, techs in the op center focus on the perimeters. From the air they are able to track multiple individuals, kids as it turns out, who flee or attempt to flee the scene. In the process, leaning over the rail of the sky deck watching the action unfold below him, Rich is able to see new opportunities for technical improvement.

But he also questions something else. How did the early morning caller know to use the precise name for the X26? The jets haven't yet arrived. No one would have seen them in transit or on the tarmac. The possibility, even if remote, that this failure in operational security might lead back to him bores wormholes in his consciousness.

When the tactical action in Ratchawin slows, he hands control to the operations manager and steps away to focus on the question. Like any accomplished information technology systems administrator with a good budget, Rich has numerous forensic tools at his disposal. For an hour he reviews settings and traffic at the firewall, hoping that he doesn't find a hole. When he feels confident they have not been breached, he turns to the ominous possibility of an insider. Rich sits at an isolated workstation and enters information into mind-mapping software.

To the public, the op center building should appear to be nothing more than an airframe repair shop. The repair shop phone number is never used; no one has ever called them on the public number, and information about their relations with General Phang and the Thai Military is closely guarded. The general hasn't even been to the center yet out of concern not to draw attention. So how did an insurgent get an internal number? And they used the precise name for jets that are still on order.

Rich types observations and ideas into mind-mapping software then pushes his chair back from the desk. His suspicions crystalize into a workable hypothesis. No one in the center uses the jets' actual name. He calls them the big dogs, a phrase established well before Web knew which vendor and model they would buy.

Digital devices attached to a computer or server are uniquely identifiable, if not by the user, then by the code that sits behind the interface. USB devices are no different. If a user attaches two or twenty devices, the system differentiates between them and can give the operator names, even icons, that identify each device, uniquely. Through event logs and specialized software, Rich traces devices across the network, back in time. It doesn't take long for him to see that unauthorized devices had been used.

USB ports are disabled in the data center, standard operating procedure for a highly secure operation. In fact, there are no keyboards or monitors allowed near the racks by anyone except for senior administrators, and even then they must be unlocked and rolled into place to be used. But in the op center, where users access data during daily routines, and often swap out specialized peripherals, this is not the case. Security relies in part on policies and procedures which include roles-based access controls and multi-factor authentication.

When Rich opens the intrusion detection activity history, his mind collapses into panic. The system shows intrusions, but isn't forwarding alerts to his phone. He pops a thumb drive into a USB port. Nothing happens. His phone doesn't vibrate. No messages follow. Horrifying as this is, he restores the functionality quickly. But the larger issue cannot be fixed.

Rich takes deep breaths and shakes his head. Security personnel often lose their jobs for less. In his world this is a firing offense, but he does what he has to do. He places a call to Patch. When Patch answers, he says, "Are you alone? We need to talk?"

Patch, still at General Phang's command and control center, excuses himself from the action. He steps to the back of the room.

Rich asks if the general's men have found anything.

"Goose chase. What's up?"

"Explanations and apologies will come later, Patch, but I discovered a security breach. It may have come from one of the general's techs. I can connect the breach to the kidnapping."

"Hold on," Patch says. He walks briskly out of the busy control room into a less busy hallway. "Better be goddamn sure, Rich. What's the evidence?"

"When we did the orientation last month someone stuck a thumb drive into a pilot's USB port. I should have been alerted right then, but our system wasn't forwarding. They took documents."

"You have measures in place. Why didn't you say something right then? This is a goddamn RGE. You know that, don't you."

"It gets worse. They have the staff directory—names, locations, roles and responsibilities."

"I'm pulling your frigging guru card, Rich. Seriously. This is a resume-generating event if I ever saw one. We have people missing! And don't you dare say you're fucking sorry. Not just yet. I don't want to hear it."

"But I am, Patch."

Silence. Rich moves his phone an inch or two away from his ear, hand shaking, and rests his forehead in the palm of his hand, elbow on the table, spirits on the floor.

In a calmer voice, Patch says, "At least you told me."

Rich doesn't reply.

Patch cusses again into the phone and then calms down. "Don't tell anyone what you found until we talk. I'll be there in half an hour."

"Someone should tell Web about the screw-up. Are you going to talk to him?"

"Me? Hell no. You're going to tell him your damn self. He'll be back in a few hours."

CHAPTER 36

W eb and Tallis rush back to the operations center. Web takes up a position next to Patch at the command table and gets a briefing. He lays out his plan and hands a phone number for Kuzma Volkov to Rich. He requests that the call be recorded.

"You don't need to record anything Volkov says. I know you. Neither of us will forget a word of the conversation," Patch says.

Web wants the call recorded anyway, and asks that the room be cleared of all but Rich and active pilots. Rich would have been sent out, too, if Web felt comfortable with the technology.

When the room is cleared, he turns on Rich. "Patch is ready to fire your ass. What the hell happened?"

Rich's eyes flood as he looks back and forth between Patch and Web. A childlike innocence washes across his face, broken, a man without defenses. He says, "It was a setting, is all. Stupid mistake. During the configuration stage, I got pinged every three minutes. Every time someone plugged in this or that I got a text, so I turned off my notifications alert and forgot all about it. It's totally on me, guys. I feel like shit."

"But we're good now, right?" Web asks. His mind is already moving ahead to action steps, to things they can actually do about their situation, to the phone call he will place to the Russian arms dealer.

"Yes. We're good now. I apologize."

"I'm not the one to apologize to," Web says dismissively. "You can take care of all that when we get our people back. As far as I'm concerned, that's the end of it. We won't talk about it again until your compensation review. You good with that, Patch?"

Patch speaks to Web as if Rich were not present in the conversation. He says, "If he does a good job from here on out, I'll never bring it up again. Water under the bridge. Now get on with it. Make the call."

Rich slides a headset into place and adjusts settings on the command table's control panel.

Web holds up a finger indicating to wait. He turns to Patch. "You act like this is a bad idea. Out with it."

Patch throws up his hands. "Kuzma probably doesn't know squat about where our people are. You know that, right? But I get the logic. His damn logo is on the rail of every AK the general's men have confiscated in the past month. I saw a couple of them this morning. And we both know photos in that envelope came from him, right? I don't have an issue with making the call, I have an issue with time. Call already. It's all we have."

Web closes his eyes and rubs his face. He tries to visualize Kuzma Volkov giving him what they need, knowing that if he can't see the call working in his own mind, there is little chance Volkov will make a deal.

He asks Patch one more time for the dossier on Volkov's whereabouts. Patch pulls the printout from his laptop case. Following Dyna's research and using her contacts, the Israelis came through for him.

Web opens the printout of the dossier. He hands a second slip of paper to Rich. "According to Israeli intelligence, Volkov is at that address right now. See if we can get something off of Google Earth."

Rich enters a street address in Sharm El-Sheikh, Egypt. He warns that the image won't be as clean as what they see back in the States, nor are they likely to get a street view.

Patch taps his fingers on the table top. "You're stalling, Web."

Web gives Patch a look. Patch raises his palms in surrender. "Just saying."

When Web sees the Google satellite view he realizes it won't help.

"Wait," Rich says. He types as he speaks. "A friend of mine owes me big favors. How much time do we have?"

"We don't have any time," Patch says. "What have I been saying?"

Web waves at Patch to knock it off. "How much time do you need?"

"I'll tell you in a minute," Rich says, and types madly.

Web turns to Patch. "What is he doing?"

Patch shrugs his shoulders and shakes his head. He checks his watch and rests his face in the palms of his hands.

"I'm going to have a damn anxiety attack. The stress is killing me," Web says. He stands to pace and says he needs a Scotch.

Patch leaves the control room for the office and comes back momentarily with one glass, a bottle, and a box of cigars.

Patch puts the bottle on the table. "This how you stay sharp these days?"

"You're a buzz kill, know that?" Web says and pushes the bottle away. He clips and lights a cigar.

"Not in here, fellas," Rich says.

The words "shove it" rise in his throat, but Web stops himself. He takes a defiant pull on the stick and sets it aside. He mutters. "Can't catch a break. How long, Rich? Patch is right. We need to get this over with."

Rich nearly jumps out of his seat with excitement. "I want my guru card back! You're going to love this. Head to the sky deck."

Web and Patch leave their chairs at the command table and lean on the sky deck railing. They look down onto four blank monitors. Web is about to complain when a view of Egypt appears in high resolution.

"You want eyes? We have eyes," Rich says. "Chip can only give us the satellite feed for thirteen minutes. We need to dial the Russian's number like right now."

Web takes in the view and chuckles. "Seriously? How'd you pull this off?"

"I worked in Stuttgart, remember? Are you ready?" The view zooms toward the sprawling compound where Volkov presumably resides.

"In a second," Web says. He and Patch study the live satellite feed. Two Humvees and four or five other expensive cars are parked in the driveway. Guards mill about in front of the buildings. Nearly a dozen people lounge near the swimming pool at the back. Most of them are women in bikinis.

"Volkov has as many cars as you do," Patch says.

"Not even close. Do we have zoom, Rich? Give us the pool. He'll be near women."

Rich makes a few keystrokes and the satellite's field of view rapidly narrows. "That could be him right there," Web says. He points to a group of three men standing near a liquor bar.

"Let's see who answers the phone. Make the call," Patch says.

"This is real time?" Web asks. "There's no delay?"

"Best optics and data links available," Rich says. "Fiber all the way. There's lag but it's insignificant. Dialing now."

Rich pushes the call to command room speakers. They hear two ringtones. The man Web suspects to be Volkov pulls a phone from his pocket.

"Tuck Webber," Web says. "We need to talk."

Volkov steps away from the men he is with. Web points toward him and swirls his finger, looking at Rich. The image zooms forward and centers on Volkov.

"This is big surprise!" Volkov says, the sound of his voice pulsing through the speakers. "How you got this number?"

"Five of our people were taken in Bangkok, Kuzma. I need to know what you know," Web says.

"Be careful, my friend," Volkov says. "I'm knowing nothing about some kidnappings."

"We know you're supplying insurgents. Your weapons have shown up all through the south."

"Is just business," Volkov insists. "I recall your weapons are also all over south."

"I understand business," Web says, feeling his temperature rise, but this time remaining in control. "This is personal. You have information. I need it. What will it take?"

Web watches a woman approach Volkov. He pushes her away and begins to pace. "I sell weapons here and there. I have no knowledge of Thailand."

"Let's not fuck each other, Kuzma. What's it going to take to get my people back? You know I'm going to get my hands on someone eventually, Thai intelligence or me. Save us time and make some money. What's it going to take?"

"Maybe this conversation is finished."

Rich holds up his hands, signaling that eight minutes remain in the satellite feed.

"You are a hell of a businessman. What is your Thai trade worth to you?"

"What is Kenya worth to you?"

"You've done your homework."

"I may know buyers, maybe not. But I know nothing about your problem."

Web watches Kuzma pace. He begins to do the same thing. He tells Volkov, "Kenya is a five-million-dollar package. Our cut at most will be ten percent and I have expenses. For starters let's say you deliver the right people, beginning with names, locations and backgrounds. The guys in photos you gave to General Phang would be a great start. You also pull out of Thailand for a year or more. Do that for me and my take in Kenya is yours."

Patch shakes his head and throws up his arms. Web waves him off.

"Maybe I take the Kenya deal anyway," Volkov says.

"If you could, you would have done it already."

Volkov laughs. "Is true."

"Look, Kuzma. Except for punching me in the mouth I have no problem with you. Just business, as you say."

Patch shakes his head in disgust, turns and steps a few feet away. Rich snaps his fingers to get Web's attention and holds up one hand.

Five minutes remain.

"What's it going to be? $450,000 is a hell of a lot more than you're going to make from insurgents here in Thailand," Web says.

"You punch like a girl," Volkov says. "But you're a funny guy."

"So we have a deal?"

"Perhaps. There is more to offer. One millions cash, I give you everything. I am not a difficult man."

Web counters Volkov's offer. "$550,000 for everything, and it better be good. I'll even sweeten the deal if you act right now."

"What is this sweetener?" Volkov asks.

"Get me all the information for your buyers in under an hour—names, addresses, what they purchased, everything—and I'll park a third Hummer in your driveway. Get it to me in under twenty minutes, I'll throw in a GTO muscle car. If I were you, I'd park it right next to the red Mercedes. Do we have a deal? Half down when we get your information, and half after we verify its validity."

Volkov looks to the sky, nearly directly into the satellite feed. "You are a man of surprises, Mr. Webber. You'll get a call within one hours."

"Done. Now what is the additional information I paid for?"

"I may have heard something about explosives. These explosives are not from me. Remember this, and tell your General Phang is not me if something big goes boom."

The negotiation with Volkov ends. Web asks Rich to call the team back into the room and they discuss next steps. His young crew is enthusiastic, yet afraid at the moment, willing to do whatever it takes to get their friends back. They could never make operatives out of technicians, but the thought crosses Web's mind. Tonight, he says to himself, anything goes.

CHAPTER 37

Patch drives. Web looks out the window, deep in thought. He says, "With or without information from Volkov, do we call General Phang? What if there really is a mole?"

"Let's see what Volkov comes up with. If it's actionable, maybe we find local talent and keep this to ourselves."

Web pulls out his phone.

"What are you thinking?" Patch asks.

"I'm thinking that Tshua knows a hell of a lot of people in this area of the world."

At the warehouse, Hmong linemen eat seared black pig. The workers, oblivious to the situation, invite Web and Patch to eat with them. Web has other ideas. He calls for Brick and Tallis to join them then meets with Tshua.

"People are missing?" Tshua asks.

Web nods. "Not just missing, taken. I wouldn't have asked you to come here, but we're desperate."

Tshua's calm and reflective persona shifts. Years of his family struggling to keep people safe during the Secret War made Tshua one of the most cunning and fearless men Web has ever known. He needs that Tshua now.

"We have been friends for many years," Tshua says. "I count you as my brother. How many were taken?"

"We can account for all but five crew members. One is a woman. She's the only one with combat experience. The rest are simple technicians."

"The red hair," Tshua says.

"Yes. I can't take this to the general just yet."

Tshua clears his throat and speaks slowly, as if breaking bad news to Web and Patch. "Thailand is a big place. Do you know where your people are?"

Web turns to Patch. He says, "Call Rich for an update. I need a minute alone with Tshua."

Patch hesitates for a moment, then stands to leave.

"How many men will be needed?"

Web waits until Patch shuts the door behind him. He says, "I'm waiting for a call. When it comes, I hope to have names and locations for people high up in the insurgency. That's what I paid for. Hopefully one of them knows where our people are, or will tell us who does.

"We'll have to grab insurgents from wherever they are. It could be as simple as breaching huts, but you know what I'm saying. If we have to storm a hardened complex I'll have no choice, but to bring in the Thai military. I came to you because I can't have six foot-whatever Caucasians running around in the bad guys' neighborhood. We'll get nowhere."

Tshua smiles broadly.

"Oh, you think that's funny?" Web says, but he also laughs. "There's a Russian dealer supplying insurgents with small arms. I made a very expensive deal for information. We should be hearing back within the hour."

"Russians can't be trusted," Tshua says. Antagonism between

the Hmong and Russians is universally recognized. The end of the US involvement in Vietnam in 1975 led to the Secret War. Pathet Lao hunted and killed the Hmong in unforgivable numbers. The unthinkable is known as the Hmong Genocide. Russians aided the communists with supplies and logistics during that dark period in history, and it will never be forgotten.

"I understand the trust issue, but right now I will try anything. Whatever it takes. Like I said, we're desperate," Web says.

Tshua quietly accepts Web's argument. Web goes on. "So now you know why I'm here. Can we leverage your connections? I need experienced operatives to run missions."

Tshua stiffens. "Web. The Hmong are with you." The statement confuses Web. He hopes Tshua has grasped the reality of what he is saying and is not thinking about the young linemen outside the trailer, eating pig. "Thank you, but I have to say, this is not a night for young minds."

Tshua nods in agreement.

Patch knocks on the trailer door and comes in. Web's immediate reaction is to request more time, but Patch raises his eyebrows and smiles. Web says, "That was quick."

"Volkov's message came through. Rich already has birds in the air. We have three names and three locations." Patch hands an iPad to Web.

Web swipes and zooms in on three dots on the map then hands the iPad to Tshua.

"Nothing fortified though, right?" he asks Patch.

"Too soon to say. We'll have intel in an hour or less. Maybe some of Tshua's guys could do a walk-by. Just an idea."

"We're well beyond that," Web says. "Tshua's in."

"Are you sure, Tshua?" Patch asks. "Recon could be dangerous."

"You have done much for our people. I am sure," Tshua says.

"Thank you. You are also a brother to us," Web says.

Then Tshua places his hands on his knees. "So it begins. What resources do you need?"

Patch closes the trailer door behind him and sits. "Three locations adds up to three teams. SOP suggests five men at each location, maybe more. I'll pull the equipment list together as soon as we know what we are up against."

"I'm guessing weapons, night vision goggles. Anything else?" Web asks.

"Don't know yet. Whatever the case, some of these locations are a long haul. We need to roll as soon as possible."

The complexity and danger they face becomes apparent to Web. "Let's think this thing through for a second, guys. Tshua has to round up at least, what, fifteen guys? According to Rich's map we have a lot of road to cover. Looks like one of these spots is smack-dab in the middle of a crowded city street. Question. Is it even possible that we do this ourselves?"

Tshua stands. He points toward the door. "I said the Hmong are with you! We will do our part. You do yours. Excuse me."

Web is startled by Tshua's decisiveness. Patch stands, smiling. He opens the trailer door and before they are even out of the trailer, Tshua is engaged in his first call. Tshua shuts the door behind them.

Web smiles at Patch. "Now you see the other side of Tshua. Point of fact, we'll have to rely on him for just about everything. We've supplied thousands of assault rifles and millions of rounds of ammunition to Thai military and paramilitary units and here we are. I'm not even sure we can scrape together enough stuff for the operation."

Patch reassures him that somehow things will come together. They just need to stay focused and be resourceful.

"How? I can't even send someone out to buy the weapons we need, not our guys anyway. It's illegal for foreigners to purchase guns in Thailand."

"We have linemen. Just stay cool. This is what we do."

Two Hmong warriors enter the warehouse within a half hour. More arrive every few minutes. The older men come in work clothes, some in camouflage; all carry themselves as if going into battle. Within the hour twenty-three men arrive. They talk solemnly. Some carry weapons they've hidden away for decades. These are older, hardened men, ready for anything their leader asks of them.

Tshua organizes three squads based upon his knowledge of skills, physical attributes and ferocity. He sends some men home for reasons that are not apparent to Web, and then personally meets with each squad. His motions are deliberate. His words, though indecipherable to Web and Patch, are short and to the point. Every gesture says there is no turning back.

Until this moment, the Hmong's warrior spirit was for Brick a footnote in history books and Special Forces training manuals. They've worked with the grandchildren and nephews of fighting men and assessed them to be agile, hard workers. But linemen are not warriors. The men who show up for the missions wear the scars of battle and carry themselves honorably.

A shaman arrives. A Buddhist priest blesses the men.

Brick pins infrared Glo Patches to the shoulders of the Hmong. Infrared tape is applied to the roof of the cars and vans. If they must rush into the insurgents' dwellings to rescue their team, night vision goggles will help distinguish the Hmong. Two riflemen are assigned to each team. All the men have, or are given, pistols. At Web's request, Tshua raises his voice during final instructions. He emphasizes the importance of taking captives alive.

Tallis downloads a custom app onto iPads so they can receive images and other communications sent from the op center. Patch reviews his checklists. Brick and Patch demonstrate the door- and window-breaching techniques they want the Hmong to use, and soon three teams are ready for action.

Web and Patch shake hands with each of the men and say, through a translator, how grateful they are and how much they respect their courage. Everyone leaves the warehouse for one or another of three destinations.

Brick and Tallis are assigned to one of the rural locations, Patch and Web the other. Tshua is in charge of the more challenging urban setting, where it is most imperative that their operatives blend into the environment during the approach.

Web is behind the wheel of a worse-for-wear late-nineties pick-up. A van carrying five Hmong warriors follows them. He is nervous and wonders if he is naïve in trusting Volkov, but it's too late to change direction. He studies Patch, riding shotgun. Each of them has strengths in the partnership, but when it comes to the threat of violence, or the execution of a mission, Web surrenders leadership to Patch every time.

Patch opens his app and watches a live feed from birds following overhead. Icons give him access to all the UAVs' sensors and soon he is swiping between views, enlarging and reducing the images with a squeeze gesture. He calls Rich. "I want the tactical teams to only see the targets they are working with." Rich confirm that that is the case. Patch is the only one who can see all three video streams. What he sees and describes to Web as they drive are two small rural homes and a densely populated neighborhood laced with narrow streets and alleyways.

"I don't like this," Patch says. "Streets are congested. We don't know how many people are in that building. We should beef up Tshua's numbers.

"You're in charge," Web says. Before he can say anything else, Patch has the op center connect him with Tshua.

"I'm sending Brick to your location. Five men won't cut it if things get out of hand."

"I've taken care of this," Tshua says.

"What does that mean?" Patch asks.

"It's taken care of. We know the neighborhood, and I have more men joining the party."

Patch shakes his head and looks at Web. Web speaks loudly to be heard. "You should have told us. Have everything you need?"

Silence.

"Tshua?" Web says.

"You have to trust me. I can't talk right now."

Patch looks straight at Web for a moment then pulls the phone closer. "We trust you, Tshua. Good luck. See you on the other side."

Patch ends the call. "Dogs are out of the barn. Pull over up here."

Web pulls to the side of the road and turns off the engine. The farmhouse they are headed toward is roughly a thousand meters away. Patch gets out of the vehicle and gives last-minute instructions to Hmong warriors behind them, before sending them ahead to conduct surveillance.

Patch and Web sit in the cab of the pickup truck in the dim light of the iPad. "Bag of snakes. We should have called the general," Patch says.

Web knows that Tshua's decision bothers Patch. "I have faith in these guys. It will be all right. It's better this way."

"For all we know Volkov is laughing his ass off. Tshua could be charging into a journalist's home or something."

"Anything is possible," Web says. His temper rises. "It was a calculation, all right? I made a decision. Sure as hell not going to second-guess the move now."

They don't speak for a long moment. Patch stares straight ahead, but says, "I think I was wrong about Volkov and I'm probably wrong about Tshua. It is what it is."

"Thanks for that. We play the hand that was dealt us."

"You should get some rest," Patch says. Web agrees. He's wearier now than he's been in years, but sleep is impossible. They watch video feeds of marked vehicles approach and pass targeted buildings. They see men walk along the street in the city. They see the faint glow of infrared patches on the shoulders of their men as they race across country roads to positions behind sheds.

A small car visits the farmhouse they will attack. When it leaves, they choose not to follow, but Rich manages to obtain the make and a partial on the license plate. He puts a tech to work tracing the car's owner.

Web tries again to sleep. Each time he closes his eyes an uneasy feeling comes over him. He stares blankly at the sun visor, the steering wheel, out the window into the darkness. There is a possibility, remote but reassuring, that his crew members could be in one of the locations. He dismisses the thought.

"Where do we go from here?" Web says.

"We capture the bad guys," Patch says. "Are you mental?"

Web chuckles. "Not this operation. I mean in general. Why the hell do we do what we do? When you called me in Africa the first thing that went through my mind was Sam's safety and the safety of our crew. I don't know what I'll do if we can't get them back. Know what I'm saying?"

Patch takes a long while to answer. "I could give you a lot of crap right now, but it's not the time. Sam is safe, for starters. We're doing what we can to rescue everyone else."

"I suppose."

"You asked why we do what we do. I know why I'm here. Things haven't changed much and it's not very noble. I want to retire comfortably. I'm going to own a place on a golf course somewhere in Georgia."

"When are you going to have time to play? You're addicted to the trade."

"Look who's talking. I tell you something else. I like to travel in the freaking winters."

"You know what I've always wanted?"

"Money."

Web laughs. "Since you mention it, yes. I want stacks of money, big houses, lots of cars to talk about, celebrity connections, the good life. Sam says I already have all that, but I keep pressing for some reason."

"You do have all that."

"So what is it?" Web asks absentmindedly.

"Cigars."

Web laughs aloud. "It has to be the cigars. If we'd been thinking, I'd have a box in the truck. The money is good, don't get me wrong, but it's her, you, all my friends. That's what keeps me going."

Patch sets the iPad aside. "Let me unfuck your thinking on this one. I've known you for a hell of a long time, Web. You're a pressure-sucking adrenaline junkie just like me. If we're not on the hunt, whether it's a deal in the hand or a war in the bush, you're a miserable SOB. Ninety years old, you'll be selling laser bots and camo underwear."

Web realized he has reached the giddy stage. "I could sell the shit out of camo underwear in Eastern Europe right now. They're going to get their asses handed to them if they don't pay attention."

Web's phone rings. "Shit!" Web barks.

"What?" Patch asks.

"Startled me, is all." Web looks at his phone, taps a button and puts Tshua on speaker. "What's up?"

"Three minutes," Tshua says.

The rush of the moment chases sleepiness out of every fiber of Web's body. "Any last advice, Patch?"

"Bring your people home from the party in one piece. That's the most important thing."

"Good luck, my friend," Web says, and ends the call.

Web connects with Rich through the iPad to find that additional UAVs were sent. Two now circle each area of operation, ready to tag and follow anyone who might escape the assaults. Patch and Web cycle through the video streams on their tablet and Web unconsciously rocks in place as the action begins.

As the Hmong approach the farmhouse door, Web speeds toward their location so he and Patch can bring additional firepower if needed. But even though they arrive within seconds, the action is over. The Hmong drag captives from the building and give Patch a thumbs-up. The threat of violence is over. All the same, Web brakes to a stop and Patch runs inside. He and the Hmong rummage through the building hunting for computers, cell phones, journals—anything that might be of use during the pending interrogation. Minutes pass.

"Get out of there," Web mumbles. He watches anxiously from the cab of the idling pickup truck, glancing often at video feeds from other locations. He incessantly checks his rearview mirrors.

Patch and the Hmong emerge on the run. They hustle bags and boxes into the trucks and all leave. Rich announces to Web that actions at both rural locations ended successfully. As Web drives, Patch reports on video feeds of the urban setting.

A dozen Hmong warriors swarm a multi-story structure one of the busiest neighborhoods in Bangkok. Lights come on in adjacent buildings as flashes of light spark in the windows. Vehicles race to the front door. Men pour into and out of the building. Most disturbing, a man is carried to one of the vans.

Web and Patch maintain a live encrypted audio connection with the op center. "Sirens," Rich says of the urban site. Web hears him tell Tshua that his men have just minutes.

Tshua issues sharp commands in Hmong. Web wishes he understood the language, but the intonation in Tshua's voice is enough to know it is not good. "Pulling over. I have to see this."

Patch backs up the video for Web to see what has happened so far. As he does, Rich reports that Tshua's men have finally left the neighborhood.

"Rich! This is Web. I have to know if the man carried out wore Glo Patches."

"He's one of ours," Rich says.

"Repeat!"

"We double-checked, boss. The man carried out is one of ours."

CHAPTER 38

Based upon the word of a Russian arms dealer, Web and a team of Hmong elders snatched people from their homes in the middle of the night. There was gunplay at one of the sites. Now that the operation is over, Web prays that Volkov didn't lie to him.

During the raids two farmhouses were taken without resistance. When the Hmong crashed the door of a large urban home, they quickly cleared the ground floor. As they raced up a set of stairs at the back of the building, however, a man carrying a bolt-action small caliber rifle fired down the stairs, hitting the first Hmong warrior in line. The bullet entered the elder's chest and lodged in his spine. His friends showed incredible restraint, limiting return fire to the shoulder of the insurgent who fired on them. When they did, the wounded householder collapsed to one knee and fell forward, tumbling downstairs onto the man he had just killed. Three other men, two women and a child in the building, did not resist.

Now, at the warehouse, prisoners rest on the ground against interior walls. The captured men sit blindfolded, hands cuffed behind their backs, meters apart. Hmong guards walk in front of their captives barking orders, ratcheting up tension. Chaos subsides within minutes of securing their prisoners and the warehouse becomes eerily quiet.

The women and child are placed, under guard, in one of the trailers. They are fed, mostly to comfort them and allay their fears. Lessons learned during his days in special forces are put in play by Patch. The women and children are questioned in the first hours by a nurturing Thai-speaking Hmong woman brought in for the purpose.

Meanwhile, warriors sit stoically or pace nervously near the makeshift fire pit in the center of Hmongtown. They openly mourn the death of their friend, saying how he died quickly, and with honor, retelling stories of his bravery in Laos and his role in the horrific migration. He survived so much, they say, and all agree that the ancestors will receive him with pride.

Web and Patch stand with Tshua near the fallen warrior's body. The deceased rests on a table, covered by a blanket, his journey over. Tshua describes in detail how the shooting happened and asks Web to remember the man's family. Then he turns toward the prisoners, points an angry finger, and says their work has just begun. He says, "Lives depend upon us getting information."

"We will," Patch says, and leads Web and Tshua to a table covered in laptops, cell phones and file folders taken during the raids. Everything is organized by the building it came from and by media type. Patch says, "Rich will have to go through the electronics. One of his guys is pretty good at hacking and they are on the way. It will be your job, Web, to manage this process. Tshua, I need you to provide interpreters."

"We got information during the drive. I'll begin with those two," Tshua says, and points to a pair of bruised prisoners. He goes on to talk about interrogation techniques, recalling in vulgar detail and visceral clarity some of what was used on his people.

Web interrupts. He says pointedly that Patch will run the interrogations. "We talked about this earlier and I feel confident in his approach," Web says.

"You don't have time for that," Tshua says, referring to the techniques Patch outlined earlier. "We have experience in these matters. We know better than you, what it takes to break a man." Tshua seems anxious to show what he and his men can do, but Web insists that he take his lead from Patch.

"At some point," Web argues, "I will hand these men over to General Phang. As angry as we all are right now, we can't allow things to get out of hand. Patch, I need you to weigh in here, please. Is Tshua right?"

"All due respect, Tshua. Web is right, but I'm with you in part. If you can get your men to create the proper atmosphere, I'll do the rest. I need you to represent a persistent threat, even if that threat is never acted upon. Do you understand? The key is not in direct confrontation. The key is leveraging what Rich and Web find to trap them. If there's a connection to our people, to Ja and Jawad, we'll find it."

"Don't forget, gentlemen," Web says. "We may be wrong about them. It's possible they don't know a damn thing, in which case I've committed us to an unthinkable list of crimes. We need to maintain discipline."

Tshua looks at the tables, the prisoners and his men. His face shows disappointment, but he agrees. "Your crew, your approach," he says, and walks away. Web hears Tshua order two of his men to meet him at the workbench.

"That didn't go the way I thought it would. Are we doing the right thing?" Web asks Patch.

"Now? You're going to ask that now?" Patch shakes his head and barks at Brick to set up chairs in the center of the floor. And then Patch walks away, leaving Web to work through his conflicted thoughts.

Patch, Brick and Tallis meet in the center of the room. "Let's see how they like the hot seat. Give me someone new every four or five minutes. You don't have to talk to any of them, just let them feel your strength, all right? Especially you, Brick. You get your hands on them, they'll realize instantly how futile it would be to attempt escape. Okay guys, let's get busy. You both know what to do," Patch says.

Tallis finds and arranges chairs as Brick literally grabs the first prisoner off the floor and drops him on his feet. His massive hands wrap around the back of the prisoner's neck and arm. "That's how you do it," Patch calls out before rejoining Web at the table.

"You all right, big guy?" Patch asks.

"As long as I don't get ahead of myself. What if they hold out or just don't know anything?"

Patch folds his arms. The two men look into each other's faces for a long moment. "I've been here before, Web. Trust me. Between the interrogations and the intel we took, if they have anything useful at all, we'll get it. We good? Stay on task and we'll be fine. Find something. I'm going get this thing started."

As Web goes through documents, prisoners are rotated into a lone chair surrounded by angry Hmong and towering ex-special forces operatives. The constant sound of blades being sharpened at the workbench has a gnawing effect on everyone in the warehouse, including Web.

As they arrive at the chair, prisoners' blindfolds are removed. The Hmong drink, angry scarred warriors all of them, men with no apparent limit to what they might do if left unchecked.

Patch questions each prisoner for five minutes at a time. He sits knee-to-knee asking the same questions, over and over again, the interpreter often raising his voice for emphasis. He wants to know where his friends are. He needs to know who took them. Brick towers over the seated prisoner but doesn't speak. Tshua's men become more vocal with each prisoner, and in the near distance, blade sharpening continues.

Rich and one of his systems administrators arrive with disks of digital forensics tools. The room is tense, ramped up, violent in tone and dimly lit, except for the bright lights over the chair in the center of the room. Prisoners rest at intervals against the walls. When Rich experiences this fear, repulsion consumes him. Rich wants nothing to do with the interrogations, and says so. Web takes him aside and talks him down.

Reluctantly the system admins turn their backs to ongoing interrogations and take seats at the table. In front of them, two laptops and an older model desktop computer. Bilingual linemen assist with translation, both for Web's efforts with document discovery, and with interpreting the results of numerous hacks.

Web leads the team by calling out what to look for and what to set aside. It takes an hour to sort out and separate family photos, bills, correspondence and digital mail from potentially relevant bits of information, and that information resides in browser histories, sent mail files, deleted images and even in what apps are loaded. Anything not deemed immediately relevant is marked or otherwise loaded into discard folders for later review.

Meanwhile, prisoners cycle into the hot seat and back to the wall. The process unnerves many of them to their core. They ask what will happen to them and plead. Some cry. Brick and Tallis take notes on each captive's behavior in isolation, in transit, and in the chair.

Interrogation is a horrible art, steeped in centuries of the most brutal human behavior imaginable, but as Patch predicted, the intelligence gathered at the sites gives the crew their first breakthrough.

Rich connects two of the captives through email exchanges. The threads they explore lead to new names and compromising language, a calendar entry with curious language and corresponding journal entries for the basis of eventual questioning. Each thread carries them deeper into the insurgent's network and closer to damning information about Ja.

The most promising captives are two young men named Satra and Tariq. Satra is a thin, foulmouthed young man, brave at first but fading fast. Tariq, a heavyset coarse individual with a muscular frame, is resolute in his silence.

Web calls Brick, Tallis and Patch into a conference about the evidence he and his system admins have uncovered thus far. After describing connections between Satra and Tariq, Web says, "Tariq is our guy."

"I agree," Patch says. "It's only a matter of time before we trap him in a lie. After that, who knows. My gut says he'll break. Satra, for sure. Will break. Is that your assessment, guys?"

Brick and Tallis agree but suggest they work on Satra first.

"Give me about ten minutes, Web, then walk over with your information."

Satra is brought to the center of the room for the fourth time. Patch once again takes a chair in front of him. Their knees touch. Before the blindfold is removed this trip, Patch places his hand on Satra's thigh and waits. The man jolts at the touch. Patch presses his weight on Satra's knee and has the interpreter repeat slowly what he says. "This is the fourth trip, Satra. There won't be more. If I don't get what you know, there won't be another chance. I'll hand you over to the next men in line, and they are not anything like me."

Web watches from a distance. Brick stands over the captive, his bulk dwarfing the slightly built young man. The Thai insurgent sits in soiled pale blue boxers and a dirty T-shirt. His hands are tied behind him. Web looks away.

Patch removes the blindfold. Brick's imposing figure, even in line at McDonald's stateside, makes people nervous. The presence of Patch and Brick together, along with increasingly angry Hmong men all around, has created an obvious effect.

Patch speaks through a translator. "I'm out of patience with you, Satra. You know why you're here?"

Satra repeats what he's said a dozen times before, that he does not. He doesn't know where Patch's friends are.

"Untie this man," Patch says. Brick removes the cuffs. Satra rubs his wrists.

"Sorry about that," Patch says, and asks again. "Do you know why you are here?"

Satra shakes his head. Patch says, "When I ask a question, answer with words." He repeats the question, waiting for the translator.

"No. I don't know why I am here," Satra says. He complains of being snatched up for no reason. He is a good man with a family. He is a simple farmer.

Patch interrupts with a hard slap to the young man's shoulder and a finger pointed directly at his face. He leans forward, inches from Satra's eyes. "I don't care. You're here because your comrades kidnapped my friends. We want them back."

Satra nearly goes into shock. He stammers. "I don't know like this," he says in broken English. "I swear to All-Merciful."

"Yes you do. Tell me about your friends," Patch says. He holds up a sheet of paper and reads twelve names, among them the names of the other prisoners, including Tariq, the man with whom he has shared emails. Some of the names are simply pulled from the air. Satra squirms, looking to his right and left, for anyone to comfort him or take his side.

Patch accuses him of knowing three names he knows Satra does not. In the mix he adds Tariq.

As with the other names, Satra says no. He doesn't know Tariq. But as he says it he twitches horribly.

Web approaches and points directly in Satra's face. He hands over a piece of paper and Patch has the interpreter read two emails connecting him to Tariq. Then he says, "Tariq is working with the Russians. You are working with the Russians." At the mention of the word Russians, the Hmong become agitated. "Wow," Patch says. "These guys hate Russians and this is your fourth trip to the chair. The Russians say you know where our friends are. They gave us your name and address. That is why you are here. The Russians turned you over to us. Tell us where our friends are."

Satra doesn't speak. He looks at the Hmong, and at Brick.

"Satra!" Patch barks. "I asked you a question. Reply with words. Where are our friends?"

"I don't know."

"You know someone who does. Who? Does Tariq know?"

Satra doesn't answer. He appears confused.

"Words! You aren't going home until we have our friends. Tell me what you know. These guys hate Russians like you."

The Hmong grow louder.

"I am not Russian," Satra says loudly. His face mirrors how crazy the accusation is.

"Doesn't matter to me. The Russians sold you weapons. You use those weapons on us. Did you think we wouldn't find you?"

Satra denies any knowledge of weapons, Tariq, or anything else. A broken man, he sometimes stutters.

Speaking louder, Patch demands to know where his friends have been taken. Satra trembles, but says nothing.

"Words!" Patch yells, agitated. Brick grabs the back of Satra's neck.

Patch shows incredible anger. He practically spits out the words, "Cuff him. Bag him. Set up another chair and bring Tariq."

Brick cuffs and blindfolds Satra but leaves him in the chair. Tallis brings a second chair into the circle as Brick wrestles Tariq into the spotlight. Tariq is helpless against Brick's strength and soon Tariq sits quietly. When he is calm, Patch sits in front of him and the blindfold is removed.

Patch leans forward. "Within an hour you will tell me where our friends are, or give me the names of people who know. Why? You are out of time. Tariq! Do you know this man? His name is Satra."

Tariq glances at the cuffed, blindfolded little man next to him. He doesn't speak at first, then denies knowing, Satra. Patch has the emails read to him aloud, as he touches the man's legs, arms, chest and face. It's a bizarre thing to do in any circumstance, but has a profound effect on the prisoner.

As the emails are read, Rich lets out a whoop and walks through the crowd of Hmong. "This guy," he says, looking at Tariq and pointing. "You have to see this."

Tariq looks as if his life just ended. His face shows a mixture of defiance and utter collapse. His shoulders sag. He looks at Satra, as if asking for help, as if he will get answers about what Satra may have said or not thus far, but Satra is oblivious, locked in fear, blindfolded and in shock.

Patch nods toward Brick. "Keep his undivided attention," he says. As he leaves, Brick wraps his massive hands around Tariq's face, blinding him to where Patch goes.

Rich and the systems administrator have breached the hard drives of two computers. The system admin sits in front of one of the laptops, smiling about his accomplishment. "Check this out," Rich says. The admin rotates Tariq's laptop so Patch can see what they've found. "The guy has a folder packed with interior photographs of the Sathorn Unique Tower, that abandoned skyscraper downtown. Ghost tower, they call it."

"And?" Patch asks.

"And the idiot has another folder with the same name, but it's encrypted. In my world that means something. This one was in the trash. It's unencrypted. We'll possibly crack the encrypted version later, but who cares. We have enough right now to make an incriminating connection."

"Connection to what?" Patch asks.

"You're going to love this," Web says.

The admin opens the folder and cycles through photos as Rich continues his description of the find. "These photos don't have people in them, nor are there any balcony shots. The building is huge, something like fifty stories tall, right? You go on the Internet and every urban adventurer that has climbed it takes at least four or five shots of the city from up there. But this guy doesn't take one. Why is that?

"Once you're above the area where shopping and restaurants were supposed to have been built, you have something like forty floors of residential space with open sculpted balconies all the way to the top. Who climbs all that way without taking a pic of the city? It got us thinking. We dug deeper and discovered this."

"What are we looking at?" Patch asks. He sounds impatient now, taken away from his moment with Tariq.

"Look closer," Rich says. He zooms in on the corner of one of the photographs and points to two figures in an adjacent room, one writing on a clipboard while the other points upward, toward the ceiling. The photo is dark and slightly blurred, but clear enough to show men amid the broken drywall and loose sections of ceiling that was once to become the most luxurious condominium complex in Bangkok.

Web encourages Patch to take a closer look. As Patch inspects the photos, Web says, "Good work, guys. Fantastic. I want you to take all this intel back to the op center, keep a team on it, but start surveillance of that building."

"I'll be damned," Patch says. He touches the laptop display with a pointed finger, the tip of which covers an image of Jawad's face. "Imagine that," he says, and heads toward the center of the warehouse.

CHAPTER 39

Hours after Patch confronts Tariq with evidence linking him to Jawad and the Sathorn Unique Tower, Tariq breaks.

"I am nothing to Jawad. I am an outsider," Tariq insists. "A friend of a friend asked me to help. That is all."

Patch presses Tariq and verifies that Jawad knows names of his staff. He knows that jets will soon arrive and that there is a connection between Web's team and the Thai military.

Tariq describes Jawad as a man of great ideas, international connections, and deep resources. "Jawad is smart," Tariq insists. "He will never be caught."

Later in the interrogation, Tariq admits he was once in a warehouse where men speaking Russian delivered rifles.

As the Hmong overhear talk of a direct connection to Russians, Web grows concerned that he'll end up with decapitated prisoners. At Web's insistence, Tshua sends some of the more vocal warriors home to sober up, rest and reflect on their fallen clansman.

Tariq claims he doesn't know where the kidnapped crew members are. "Jawad researched several sites," he says. Sathorn Unique Tower was among them, but Tariq holds his ground on not knowing more. He insists he was never included in those discussions.

At 0600 hours Web gets a call from Rich. He is practically giddy on the phone, convinced that he has verified the location of taken crew members. Tshua appoints a respected elder to help Brick and Tallis guard and protect the captives so that Web, Patch and he can leave for the op center.

In transit, Tshua humbly acknowledges that Patch was correct about his plans.

"It could have gone another direction," Patch says, acknowledging that if things had not turned out with digital forensics it would have been very difficult to get any of the captives to talk.

"What have you got?" Web asks as they enter the control room. They step onto the command deck and take seats at the table. Lack of sleep has caught up with Web. He feels woozy and weak to the core. He asks for coffee—lots of it.

Rich sends images to the video wall. "Our people are in the tower. I don't know why they picked that location, but the evidence is pretty clear, at least to me.

"It starts at JJ Market." Rich cycles through street-level videos of the crew leaving the op center, then getting on the BTS and exiting at the market. Video shows them chatting and horsing around as they hustle down the BTS stairs and walk toward the market entrance. It's emotional for Web, to see them so oblivious to what is about to happen.

Rich continues. "They're all still together at 2015 hours, right? Nothing unusual. Backup tapes verified that they do the same thing very often—op center, BTS, market, then home.

"They always leave together, perfectly aligned with protocols. This time that didn't happen. We scrubbed all public transit loading docks and taxi stands. No evidence of them leaving. Without the info from Tariq, I might assume they are still in the market. Actually that was our assumption. Until an hour ago we monitored every possible exit path."

"Maybe they are still there," Patch says.

"Stick with me," Rich says, impatience in his voice. "Point of fact, we did get that lead from Tariq and that begged a question. If they are in the tower, how did they get there? Working backwards, we scrubbed video for vehicles large enough to transport our crew." He shows images of delivery trucks coming and going until he settles on a step van.

"There's nothing unusual about other deliveries. We don't see people being pushed around or anything. Delivery trucks show up, they wheel items into the market and bring out empty dollies. All deliveries. No pickups. No large containers leaving until this."

Rich plays a video of three large wooden boxes being hauled out of the market on dollies. They are wheeled, one at a time, up a ramp into the van. "This video shows boxes coming out of the market, not in. They moved three containers, went back and then hauled two more. Five crates in all were moved into the van."

Web is excited. Patch says, "I need a hell of a lot more than that."

"I agree," Rich says. "Could be nothing. But this is where it gets really fucking interesting. Scrubbing backward from the tower, we picked up the exact same van on Kamphaeng Phet Rd, the Sirat

Tollway a couple times, and South Sathorn Rd. Check this out," he says, and shows a new video of the step van idling through narrow streets near the river.

"We have them on Charoen Krung, two blocks from the front of the tower. Thing is, it takes eighteen minutes for them to get to the next camera a half mile up the street. My guess, they took our people out of the van and into the tower."

"Impressive work," Web says. For the first time since hearing of the kidnapping nearly thirty-five hours earlier, he believes they have a realistic chance of getting their people back. "What do you think, Patch?"

Patch appears to choose his words carefully. "It's convincing enough to commit to recon, but that's all. Everything I know about the structure says it's going to be a nightmare getting intelligence, but we have to find a way."

Rich sends more images to the video wall. He says, "I expected as much. We've gathered as much information as we can. Photos of the building on the left of the video wall were obviously taken from the air.

"Everything on the right is straight off the Internet. Some images are lo-res, might be a year or two old, but all potentially helpful." The still images show jagged rebar on the roof, cluttered stairwells, junk-strewn concrete. The tower's interior is a maze of open stairwells, unprotected elevator shafts, and cluttered and deteriorating condominium spaces in various states of completion and decay. Rich says, "You look at this stuff long enough, you can practically smell the dust and mold. Building has been open to the elements for years."

"Like I said, it warrants recon. We need eyes inside to verify if our people are really there. Open to ideas, gentlemen," Patch says.

"I say they are there," Rich says, a note of defiance in his voice. "Call the military."

Patch gives him a look. "And what if they're in that frigging apartment building behind the tower? Or one of the storefronts, or maybe the van still has our people in it and they've taken their hostages south. They might have stopped in an alley so someone could take a piss, right? We need intelligence, not conjecture."

Rich cues up live video from 4,000 feet and then surprises everyone with a replay of a single UAV pass around the structure taken at daybreak. He'd ordered the pilot to fly close to the structure. The camera angle is low, aligned approximately with the mid-point of the building tower's height.

Patch rests his knuckles on the table. "That shows a lot of initiative, Rich. But don't ever do something like that again without orders." As he speaks his phone sounds. He checks an incoming text.

"It was still pretty dark," Rich says in his own defense. "That one UAV is silent as a bat, but I get your point. I risked tipping them off."

"Look, guys," Patch says. "Our element of surprise, if we even have one any longer, will fade quickly. We snatched the insurgents eight hours ago. It's going to be midmorning soon. We need a plan."

"What are you thinking?" Web asks. He knows Patch is right. They can only hope that no one shows up at the places they raided the night before and finds broken doors and missing people. "You're the guy with all the experience. Whatever you come up with."

Patch leans over the sky-deck rail and studies aerial images of the building. "Anyone comes or goes at that site I want to know, immediately. I also want ground-level human intelligence, at least cameras, on all four corners. That tower is set back from the street. The street will be crowded soon. It would be easiest for Tshua to send a few men and women, pedestrians, to keep an eye on things."

"There's a shrine and a 7-Eleven down the block, shops all over the place. I can work observers into the landscape. No problem," Tshua says.

Patch continues. "Let's start here. Our birds will keep an eye on the back and sides of the tower, but there's a parking ramp. We'll need eyes in that structure." He points to a ramp that is separated from the building by a narrow alley. A walkway extends from a level near the top of the parking ramp to one side of the tower.

"Abandoned buildings have squatters," Web says. "Maybe we send squatters in to look around?"

Rich offers a suggestion. "I have another idea. Maybe I can get us close without walking the halls."

He pulls up photos from Tariq's computer and cycles through them until he finds the graffiti he's looking for—a gorilla face illuminated by a shaft of light. He then shows the same graffiti on the video pass of the UAV. "This is on the west side of the building, close to the twentieth floor. Maybe we fly micro-drones into the building."

Rich picks up a black case that's been waiting at his feet, evidence that he's been plotting something of the kind all along. Inside are five small containers. Each holds a controller and a miniature SUAV that looks like an insect. The largest is a dragonfly. He says, "Today's military versions are exponentially better in every way. The optics, speed, range, silence and other features are really sweet, but this is what we have.

"Only thing is, if we try to fly them up from the ground, or even from the top of the parking ramp, I think their batteries will puke."

Web asks to see them. Rich describes how three of the insects have single-button homing. "This little mosquito-like dude is probably our best option. Even up close I can barely hear it. Looks just like a bug humming along. The cool thing is, we can switch all of them from constant video feed to intermittent images. The bad thing, no infrared. We're limited to ambient light and what I see of that interior is often dark."

"Flight instructions?" Patch asks.

"Can't be more than a quarter of a mile away."

Tshua has an idea. "How close do we have to get to the twentieth floor? Can they fly up two floors, how about three?"

Rich calls up visuals of the building's side and replies with a question of his own. "If we can get someone to walk them up to, say, the sixteenth floor? Eighteen would be better, and if it isn't windy or raining, we can fly them the rest of the way."

They brainstorm ways to get into the building as Rich checks the forecast for weather conditions. "No rain," he reports. "Minimal wind. High humidity, which will actually help us."

Web turns to Tshua. "You're the only guy who can get people that high in the building, if it's even possible."

Tshua smiles and rubs his shaved skull. He says, "We need a family hunting for shelter—mother, father and child. They climb stairways until someone tells them to stop. They turn around, go back down a floor, and release the little insects."

Web adds. "The idea is genius, but no kids. How about a doll in a blanket?"

"No," Tshua says. "It has to be the real thing, a family. Let me worry about this." He steps away from the command table to make calls.

At 0930 Rich and his pilots capture images of the building taken from high above. They verify that the gorilla-head graffiti is on the twentieth floor. Everyone leans forward in their seats as a family of three walks casually up the narrow Soi Charoen Krung 51 Alley, between the tower and parking structure, pushing a shopping cart full of old clothing, boxes and food containers. The family wears stained clothing. They are wired for sound. The woman wears the trial pair of video-enabled glasses from the funeral operation.

Among their possessions, divided into several pockets, the family carries a few thousand bhat to bribe lookouts and other squatters. The video feed from the glasses transmits to the op center via a van parked a block away. Pilots in the van stand ready to control the flight of insect SUAVs, and to keep an eye on the alley entrance.

The woman's glasses show that a rusted cyclone fence runs the length of the alley to her right. The couple follows that fence to an opening that squatters or urban adventurers have cut into the links. They make a show of attempting to get their shopping cart through the fence, but end up hiding it as best as they can in the rubble and trash left by vagrants. They enter with only their backpacks and a few plastic shopping bags.

In the op center Web and his team watch the couple and child climb one of two partially assembled escalators in the vast, cluttered space that was to be a palatial upscale shopping mall. Neither escalator has rails, which makes the ascent look incredibly dangerous, especially with a child.

As the family nears the top of the escalator a woman dressed in a loose-fitting white sarong confronts them. A bearded man sits under a blanket on a mattress a few meters away—jerky footage, grainy quality, a serious situation. Behind the male guard stands a shiny new chain-link fence with a chained and padlocked gate. It blocks the only stairway upward into the tower.

Tshua translates as the family begs and bribes. There is nowhere else to go, they argue. Their child is tired and maybe ill. As negotiations drag on, the woman in the white sarong makes a call. The video glasses transmit intermittent photos. Combined with the audio receivers, the entire conversation is transmitted to the op center. The family appears to be winning the negotiation, and the op center personnel, spellbound by what is unfolding before their eyes, quietly cheer them on.

But for no apparent reason, the man throws off his blanket. He stands and aggressively waves a pistol, shouting, "Go! Go now!"

The family turns back and rushes down the static escalator.

In the op center, Web throws up his hands. "Plan B, anyone?"

The room is silent. Web paces. Patch pulls out his laptop and mumbles something Web doesn't catch.

Rich is undeterred. "We use a quadcopter to drop the insects from above. Falling uses almost no battery power. We drop three or four, they fall ten or fifteen stories, we stabilize them, hunt for the right openings and we're in. What do you think?"

"Other than the fact that we don't have a quadcopter and it's never been attempted, it's brilliant," Patch says. The cynicism in his voice is palpable.

"HobbyThai," one of the techs calls out, referring to a business popular with UAV enthusiasts. Rich taps the name into a web browser search engine and displays the website on the video wall. He yells toward the pilots. "Someone give me specs."

Web interrupts. "Wait a minute. Screw that," he says. He pulls out a credit card and hands it to Rich. "Have someone go buy one of each quadcopter in stock. Put a rush on it."

Rich sends a man then pulls out the insect drones. He meets

with pilots, demonstrates each flight system, and sends them into the hangar to practice. There, they walk behind the flying insects until they drain the batteries. They recharge and repeat, this time flying the insects outside as well to get an idea of how they handle in a breeze. In the process they learn that landing will be the most difficult aspect of the flight.

A tech returns to the op center with a dozen quadcopters and related equipment. Tallis practices flying them in the hangar as Web fabricates a carriage and remote release. Patch grows impatient with lost time, but by mid-afternoon, using tools at their disposal and Web's knowledge of metal fabrication, they stand in the hanger, ready for testing.

Tallis flies the quadcopter in and among rafters in the hangar. Upon command he presses a button of the remote taped to his controller and ping-pong balls fall to the ground. Convinced they are ready for the mission, Tallis and the insect pilots leave in a step van for the Sathorn Unique Tower.

When the pilots are in place, the op center gives the command. They release the quadcopter from the top of a parking ramp five blocks from the tower. The crew drives the van to a position near the block where the Sathorn Unique Tower rises above the Bangkok skyline.

In the op center, Web watches video feeds with anxious anticipation. He warns Rich that if the pilots can't gain flight control of his little buggers after the drop he may never find them.

"I won't get them back even if we do gain control," Rich says.

The jagged top of the building is laced with exposed rebar and weatherworn concrete. Rich taps a button on the side of his headset. "Pilots get ready for drop."

Rich verifies that all systems are streaming video and that communications channels are open. Web sees the maneuver from two perspectives. A fixed-wing camera sensor locks onto the quadcopter from a distance. The video wall shows a small red circle in the air. It descends toward the top of the tower. The other point of view comes from the quadcopter itself. Rich projects it to the observation deck. That view moves to a point directly above the tower, then flies to one side, the angle immediately shifting from a fifty-foot drop to the roof, to what appears to be hundreds of feet to the alley surface below.

Rich directs Tallis to fly the quadcopter to ten or twelve meters above the tower and twenty meters to the western side.

Rich taps his headset again. "Pilots one, two and three, are you set?" he asks. U-one, U-two, and U-three all respond from the van where they will report control of their respective insects.

"You know your number," Rich says. "On my count. Drop in three, two, one, drop." And then he counts off the fall. "Fifteen, fourteen, thirteen," he says, counting off the seconds before the pilots are to take control of the free-fall.

A rush of blurred images appears on the video wall. At the count of eight, video feeds began to slow into recognizable shapes. By the time Rich has reached zero two insects already face the building. The third faces down and away as the pilot hunts for control and the proper orientation.

Web is amazed at the detail of the video. He sees texture on the scallop-shaped balconies with their ornamental concrete baluster railings. Some balconies have puddles of standing water. Years worth of dust, dirt and weeds have taken hold. Straight ahead, the insects reveal the building's dark interior through balcony openings into individual apartment spaces.

"Which floors are we looking at?" Web says, the words just coming out of him amid the rush of adrenaline.

"We'll get there," Rich says. As he speaks, images of the building's face come into sharper focus, giving the illusion of higher resolution. At Rich's direction, the SUAV with the longest battery life flies a search pattern, rising and then descending, until spotting the graffiti of the gorilla. Rich directs pilots to the proper floor. From there, each insect flies toward the open face of a different balcony.

"This is incredible," Web says, looking to Patch for agreement.

Patch doesn't move. He is fixed on the visuals playing out in front of them.

Web turns to Rich. "You pull this off and I'm giving you a bonus that will make me weep."

Rich smiles, but stays focused on the task at hand. "There!" he barks. Pilot two has discovered flickering light beyond the open doorway of the residential unit it has entered. Flight continues forward, passing through the dark room into a dimly lit hallway. The SUAV turns toward the light. Two men sit at a table a few meters down the hall.

"That's it. That has to be it," Web says. He feels a rush of emotion and unconsciously places his palms on the top of his head. He stands and takes a step toward the video wall.

"U-two, hover there," Rich says calmly into his headset. He has the tone of a seasoned airline traffic controller. "U-one and U-three, find the hallway."

Seconds later, another view of the guards appears on the video wall, but from the opposite direction. Soon the third view locates the guards, this time from immediately in front and to one side of where they sit.

"Park three," Rich says. It takes the pilot multiple tries, but insect three finally lands on the floor in the proper orientation. The camera is now still. It rests approximately eight meters from two men at a table.

There is a lit candle between the men, who everyone assumes are guards. That candle, and a small amount of ambient light from open doorways, is enough for one of the guards to read by, and for the flying insects to see a closed door behind the two men. An AK-47 leans against the wall just behind them and to one side.

"Patch, you seeing this?" Web asks.

"Park two," Rich says.

Another SUAV finds a place to land. "U-one, we need eyes on the other side of that door. Find a way in."

The pilot of the mosquito expertly heads for the ceiling, then flies against one wall. He advances. Images of the hallway ceiling, inches from the lens, are blurred, but even in the dim light the two guards remain in view.

The mosquito approaches the closed door and flies slowly down one side to the floor. "Can he make it through there?" Web asks. He sees a space on the video, no more than a centimeter or two, between the door and an unfinished dusty concrete floor.

"I don't see why not," Rich says. "It's either that or we wait. We've already lost a lot of time."

The mosquito lands inches from the opening and then seems to leap forward a centimeter or two at a time until it is inside.

"It's pure black in there," Web says.

"Wait for it," Rich says. He adjusts contrast of the video feed, but they are still unable to make out shapes. He taps his headset. "Bring U-one upward a few feet," he says. "I know you're flying blind, but do what you can."

"We need infrared," Web says.

Rich ignores the comment. He is busy adjusting the video and audio levels. Soon they hear a familiar voice in the darkness. Ginger's German accent is unmistakable. She is asking someone if he has ever been to New York.

"Ginger!" Web shouts.

"Yes!" one of the techs yells.

"Shut up, everyone!" Rich yells. "U-one, find a corner, park, and hibernate. We just need audio. U-two and U-three set image intervals at two minutes and save those batteries. Tallis, park the quadcopter somewhere on the roof. It may be a long night."

"Rich!" one of the techs in the op center shouts. He stands and points toward his workstation monitor.

Rich rapidly taps commands into the control panel and shows, on the video wall, what the tech is excited about. The guards outside the utility closet are now standing. "Fire up U-two," Rich says loudly. The stationary insect drone switches to full video. Two other men approach the guards. They carry a large cardboard box.

"U-one, be ready," Rich says.

The guards talk for a while in the hallway. Tshua translates. Casual banter, nothing of value. Moments later, a guard opens the door. Two guards carry the box into the room. A small flashlight held by a guard illuminates all five crew members.

Techs in the op center gasp. Some cheer.

"Quiet!" Rich shouts again. Everyone in the op center stares at the video wall as unit one gains elevation and flies away from the guards. Crew members are huddled against the walls of their small room. They share two mattresses. A five-gallon pail is present, apparently so they can relieve themselves. They are cuffed. They look exhausted, dirty, and fearful. Joe is slumped against Ginger's shoulder. But they are clearly, gloriously alive. Despite Rich's order for silence, the room erupts in exuberant cheering.

When the guards leave, Rich orders pilot two to follow them. U-two rises awkwardly and follows two guards away from the table and down the dark hallway. A minute later the hum of a generator becomes audible. Light shines from behind an open door. A tangle of cables snake from somewhere down the dark hallway into the open room.

When he sees the cables, Patch sighs.

Web shares the feeling, but doesn't say anything in the crowded room.

Pilot two follows the insurgents through the open doorway and hovers there, panning left and right before heading back into the darkness of the hallway. Rich rewinds that section of video and scrubs forward slowly through what appears to be the insurgent's control room. It has two tables that support laptops and other equipment.

"U-two, give me another pass across the doorway. We need to know what's in there."

Men sit in front of equipment stripping cable ends and connecting them to a control panel of some type. Snips of cable and wire are strewn all about them on the table and floor.

Water containers and boxes of dried and canned food sit at the far end of the second table. Two semi-automatic pistols rest on a towel next to a machete. Equipment, bags and boxes are stacked against the wall to the right.

The pilot hovers the SUAV in several places then looks for a place to land in the crumbling ceiling. In the op center the monitor shows a video camera on a tripod facing a large white sheet nailed to the wall.

"You need to park quickly and switch to reserve. Keep audio active if possible," Rich says.

Patch waves for Web to follow and they leave the control room. They go into the conference room and shut the door.

"I know what you're going to say, Patch. Let's hear it anyway," Web says.

"Tripod and video camera mean media coverage. We've seen this before, Web. He has American advisors to the Thai military as hostages and he's parked in one of the most recognizable landmarks in Bangkok. He knows what he has and he's capable of gruesome violence."

"The cabling?"

"No doubt about it. Demolition gear."

CHAPTER 40

Web calls Sam and says, in coded language, that he has run into some friends he's been missing for a while. Sam sounds incredibly relieved, but when she hears they are not home yet, she wants to know more. She wants to help.

"I'd rather you went with Sonny to Bali," Web says, and they argue. Sam refuses to leave Bangkok. Knowing how serious she is about staying, doing anything she can do to help, Web sends Brick to get her. After dropping Sonny at the airport, Sam and Brick join the crew at the op center, where planning for the rescue attempt is already in progress.

CHAPTER 41

The demeanor of everyone employed at Tuck Webber LLC is that of resolve and concentration. Even employees in other areas of the world are on heightened alert, and communicating frequently to determine what, if anything, they can do to help.

By 1600 hours on the day they discovered where their crew members are being held, everyone in Bangkok has an assignment and is working feverishly to prepare for their role in the rescue. Tables are piled high with sodas, Domino's pizza, and assorted cut vegetables and fruit. Both coffee makers run nonstop in the office. Techs analyze the tower and nearby streets for entrance and exit options while Brick prepares tactical kits.

Web is the coordinator for all support activities, while Patch guides preparations for tactical operations. Everyone is focused on maintaining heightened operational security. Travel to or from facilities is restricted. The Hmong linemen have gone to ground with orders to communicate only through trusted clan connections until further notice. Some choose to stay, to assist with guarding insurgent prisoners or, even more dangerous, to man positions near the tower. A contingent of Hmong quietly recruit restaurant and hotel workers to watch for potential insurgent spotters.

Web is physically and mentally spent. His trip to and from Dubai, and everything after his return, has robbed him of vital energy. His legs burn and twitch, but to avoid grogginess he puts off taking much-needed medication. Often his eyes blur and burn. The sensory problems he faces are dismissed in the face of what is at stake for his crew. What he doesn't report to others, or even want to acknowledge in himself, is tachycardia. His heart races even at rest, from lack of sleep, possible dehydration and mounting stress.

"You don't look right," Patch says. Sam, who has insisted on remaining with the team, agrees. Together they convince Web to take five in their conference room.

Resting his chest on their table, arms folded under his turned head, eyes closed, Sam rubs Web's shoulders and back. Her touch, as much as the massaging itself, releases waves of tension. But it also makes him drowsy. Web drifts in and out of consciousness.

Meanwhile, Patch sits at the command table in the op center, discussing options with Rich and various pilots. A runner circulates among other technicians gathering answers to Patch's tactical questions about the tower and surrounding buildings. The techs recalibrate equipment and prepare for whatever will come next.

Patch checks the time often, anxious to hear from Tshua. So much of the operation depends upon his connections that planning without him is an exercise in faith. When he does return, he wears a telling grin.

"Can't fool me that easily," Patch says to Tshua, returning the grin. "I can see in your eyes that you're as tired as I am."

Tshua sits heavily, but laughs. "We are no longer young men," Tshua says. "But we continue. I have men for the mission. Good men."

"Absolutely no disrespect intended, but this next operation calls for top-tier operators. I've cycled through options a dozen times. Called men in Australia. Hunted through all my contacts. I'm not going in with aging warriors."

Tshua scoffs at the suggestion. "What did I just say? Good men.

I knew you would say that, Patch. My elders are fit, but I agree. How many men do you have, and how many do I need to provide?"

"The minimum is ten. Honestly we shouldn't even attempt penetration of a structure like this one with fewer than twenty-five, but we don't have that option. My contacts will all take a long time to get here. What did you come up with?"

"There are military families in our clan. Some of the men are very well trained. I can't get ten but I can get six Thai rangers, with equipment."

"That's a lot to ask," Patch says. "You've lost a man already. To lose a child or grandchild would be devastating. I can't ask you to do that."

Tshua's eyes soften. "This is not just the enemy of your crew. We stand with you and Mr. Webber. What equipment will they need?"

Patch hands Tshua a copy of his list and begins to read. "Night vision equipment, lids and LEDs, close quarters weapons. We'll need a few stun grenades and probably sting balls. We should carry a boomstick, maybe a donut launcher."

Tshua interrupts with an awkward look on his face. "Stop. I don't know some of these terms."

"Sorry. Boomstick is just a shotgun for breaching locks and doors, pump action is fine. The donut launcher is slang for a rifle attachment that fires rubber rings. It's a non-lethal weapon used in riot control. We want to take as many of the bad guys hostage as we can."

"Like a bean bag gun?" Tshua asks.

"Close enough. We won't shoot to kill unless we have to.

"Lids are helmets. The LEDs in this case are little infrared lights that help us identify who is who. They attach to helmets with Velcro. Any Thai Ranger will know what I'm talking about."

"Infrared LEDs? People won't see them unless they have night vision equipment?"

Patch nods and continues. "We need secure headsets, ammo, body armor. I think we have rope and harnesses around here somewhere, but you should get a length of that with rappelling gear. Most important, we need men who can handle themselves with and without the equipment. You understand what I'm saying. Give that list to your guys, tell them which building, and they'll know exactly what we need."

"I understand. How soon? I can have them here within a couple of hours."

"Not here," Patch says. "Have them slip into the warehouse, plain clothes, gear in boxes or something inconspicuous. Brick will fill them in on the plan when they get there. He'll also rehearse them. Make sure they know he is the man in charge."

Tshua steps away to make calls as Patch turns to Rich. "Call up images of the tower again, please. Let's focus on the upper floors."

Rich cycles through photographs and video of the jagged rebar jutting into the sky from walls designed to one day support a dome.

Patch makes a call to his pilot friend for another big favor. He needs his former jump instructor, with his DHC-3, to do a flyover of some property during the night. Without knowing more, Patch gets solid assurance that Proctor will be fueled and ready when Patch arrives.

Patch barks to techs on the main floor. "Somebody get Web out of the office. Tell him to suck it up. We're on."

"I'm already here," Web says. Patch turns to see his partner and Sam standing together, ready to rejoin the mission.

At 1930 hours Patch calls for everyone's attention. He points to the video wall and images of the Sathorn Unique Tower.

"We're getting close, people. I need you to listen up for last minute instructions." Pointing at the video he says, "That's our theater of operation. The bad guys have all the advantages, or at least they think they do. They can see for miles in four directions. In an operation like this there's nothing worse than fighting uphill, especially on an exposed concrete stairway. We're going to take that high ground away from them. I've lined up a pilot. Tallis and I will skydive onto the roof and conduct recon as we clear the tower on our way down. To make recon faster and more efficient, Tallis will fly small UAVs out ahead of us. You're good with those, right, Tallis? Because I'm not."

Tallis raises his eyebrows and stares at the images of Sathorn Unique Tower. "That's a pretty nasty-looking landing zone."

The crew looks at a round section of roof with tall sidewalls. Jagged rebar juts into the air from each weatherworn wall. Even the available landing areas are cluttered with uneven and rusted construction materials.

Patch folds his arms across his chest, a look of disappointment quickly vanishing from his face. "You have an Airborne Badge, don't you? Even a jump chump could do this. Trust me. We'll talk later.

"Anyway, we'll work our way downward from the top floors to the floor just above the hostages. We'll take up positions on floor twenty-one. Somewhere just above the hostage location, we'll drop two secured rope lines over the edge of the balcony. The rope lengths will pass the twentieth floor, reaching two of Tshua's Thai rangers on nineteen. They will use those lines to climb up to where the insurgents have their generator and control room. When they are in, Tallis and I will move those lines to where the crew is currently held and rappel down.

"That accounts for Tallis, me and two of the six Thai rangers. Brick and the remaining four rangers will work their way from the ground upward, beginning in the parking ramp adjacent to the building. I don't have to tell you all how dangerous this mission is, so if Rich or Web ask you to do something, don't question, don't hesitate, just do."

Rich wants to know where Brick will be when Patch and Tallis rappel onto the guard's floor.

Patch answers the question while addressing the whole team. "Brick and his guys have to neutralize lookouts, guards, whatever they encounter, beginning with the parking ramp. It's a big order. As Tall and I work our way down, he has to work his way up.

"Throughout the mission, go commands will come from Web. Whatever he says goes. Getting into the building and neutralizing the bad guys is phase one. Freeing our people is phase two. Getting them out and away is phase three.

"You all saw the condition of Joe, him leaning on Ginger like that is a bad sign. Getting everyone out at the same time is the goal, but you all have to be prepared for contingencies. Joe is a big guy. We may need to carry people or flat-out stash someone in a hide and come back later.

"When we've assessed the condition of our team, we will all move to rally point one, at the north end of the hallway on the 20th floor. From there, we travel downward, as a group, to rally point two. That's the floor where our Hmong family encountered the lookouts. Brick and a couple of rangers will escort our crew members. The rest of the rangers will control insurgents. Tallis and I will take point during the extraction.

"I don't have to tell anyone that we will have to be extremely careful in that building. There are places where a slip or push could send someone to their death. Railings are missing. The floors are covered with debris. The elevator shafts are open and unguarded. A rat or a dog could jump out and startle someone at any time. We don't want this rescue mission to be the cause of three more."

"You'll have night vision goggles, though, right?" Rich says.

"Rescuers yes, the rescued, no. We can use flashlights only if we are completely sure we've cleared the building of insurgents. That might not be possible. Point of fact, we may have to fight our way out of there.

"Tshua, you'll have to arrange for transportation and secure the ramp. Send a scout as soon as possible so we know what we're up against.

"Again, everyone, rally point two is at the top of the escalators. Assuming we all get there in one piece, it's down the escalators, into the alley, into Tshua's vans and home."

"I assume we're using grenades. They make a lot of noise," Web says.

"That's the one thing I'm still working on," Patch says. "Not sure we can do anything about the noise. Best would be to have a loud diversion outside, noise to cover anything that happens inside. I'm open to ideas."

Patch turns to Sam. "I need you to play a role, Sam. Are you willing?"

Web objects. "No way she's playing a role anywhere outside of the op center."

"What do you need?" Sam asks. "I want our people back as much as anyone. And by the way, Web. You can't decide for me.

Not today. I want to help."

"We need you in the ramp to translate," Tshua says.

"That's not going to happen," Web says, getting to his feet. "We'll work on that one in a sec, but I need us to back up a minute. How the hell are you going to skydive onto the roof? You'll be shredded to pieces or impaled on all that rebar. I know you have all the training in the world, but what about Tallis?"

Rich reaches for his keyboard. Patch forcefully cuts him off. "We don't need the images, Rich. We've all seen them a dozen times, especially Tallis. You've got something like a hundred jumps, right?"

"Not really," Tallis says.

"We're jumping, no matter what," Patch says to Tallis. "You have more skill than you realize, but if you're uncomfortable, maybe we can land on a terrace. Rich, show us the front face."

"At night? It's all dangerous," Web says.

Patch gives Web a look. "Let Tallis and me worry about the jump, all right? You're scaring the crap out of him unnecessarily."

One of the techs holds his hand up like a schoolboy. "Yes," Patch says.

"Do you think our people are all right?"

Web moves closer to the rail, ready to take the question, but Patch waves him off. "I want to say yes. When we first heard Ginger there was very little stress in her voice. Of course, we don't know, could be a shit storm up there right now, but my guess is they're still very much alive and mobile. Does that answer your question?"

The tech nods.

"How do the rangers get into the building?" Tshua asks. "I have to tell them the plan."

"Brick will do that. There's a walkway over the alley."

Rich brings up the image of the walkway that spans the alley, connecting the parking ramp and building. Patch says, "They'll cross over on the roof of that walkway. You can tell by the chain link barrier on the other side that others have done it in the past. They'll pass over, cut their way through the fence, and subdue the lookouts. While this is going on, one of your men will have a mil dot on the guy who waved his gun at our family."

Rich pulls up photographs and video of the front of the building. Patch points. "Everyone see this? Can we get over our Nervous Nellies now? The terrace will work just fine for a landing." He points to an area of the building where the balconies are oversized, and largely unobstructed. "Tallis and I will drop in there. We will have to recon the floors above us before continuing down. Hopefully they aren't expecting anyone to enter the building from that high up."

"We don't exactly have overwhelming force," Rich says.

Web laughs. "You don't know Patch."

"You're right, Rich," Patch says, apparently annoyed at Web's flattery. "We don't have overwhelming force. Trap them in a hallway and we're good to go. If we're lucky, their people won't have the training of our team. But no one should underestimate what we are up against. Anything goes wrong, if this thing turns into a free-for-all, we could be in for a lot of hurt. Everyone good? That's it."

The techs go back to work. Patch turns to Rich. "I know you will, but preserve the insect drone batteries as much as possible. We will need visuals in the seconds before we strike."

"When are we going in," Web asks Patch.

"Tall and I go wheels up at 2300 hours. Brick, and the rangers need to be equipped, rehearsed and in position in the ramp by 2400."

CHAPTER 42

Web paces in the op center. For nearly twenty years he's taken pride in doing everything possible to protect his people. He's seen the pain families face when lives are lost and he mentally vows, each time, that it will never happen ever again. Now five of his crew members have been taken.

One of the techs takes him aside. "We're sending seven or eight men into a wired building to save five. The bad guys could flip a switch and blow up the whole building."

Patch overhears the conversation and interrupts. "And?"

Web thanks the tech for his concern and agrees. Wanting to help the technician come to grips with what is about to happen, he adds, "It is no longer a question of math or strategy. Focus on what matters. Everyone going in has been given the opportunity to say no. Your job is to stay alert."

The tech returns to his workstation. Web is well aware of the calculation and tries to push similar concerns from his mind. "Why Sam? I don't like it."

"She's the only English-speaking person we have at the moment who understands enough Thai to be a go-between."

"Tshua can take care of that."

"Tshua has his own people to manage."

"So I go in and she stays here."

Patch gives him a look. "You speak Thai now?"

"What about the techs?"

Patch waits.

Web exhales. "We're short-handed as it is. I get it."

"I need her, Web. She won't be in the building, She'll be in the ramp and none of us will enter the ramp unless it's secured. If it makes you feel better, we can get a couple of Tshua's old guard to sit with her, but I need very clear English-speaking lookouts on the ground. We can't be babbling over comms wondering what the hell someone just said. Come up with a better solution in the next twenty minutes, I'll reconsider, but she's our lookout."

"I don't like how this all came down."

Patch stiffens, chin raised. He takes a deep breath through his nose. "Anything else?"

"Yeah. You make me sit here while the rescue is taking place, I'll go crazy. Rich has been calling shots like a pro all day. He can handle it. I'll sit with Sam in the parking ramp."

"Oh, please!" Patch says. "We stack bodies, he'll freeze. You saw him at the warehouse. I need you right here at the command table calling the shots. It's not fair, it's a damn slap in the face, but that's the price of leadership."

"Whatever," Web says, feeling helpless.

Patch steps away from Web and addresses the room again. "Listen up, everyone. One last thing." It takes a minute to get everyone's attention.

"I know how tired you all are. One way or another, we're going to find the energy to keep going. That's just how it has to be. If you feel like you're going to sleep, want to tap out or something, see

Web or Rich. I'll leave special candy with them." The techs laugh, already giddy from stress and weariness.

Tshua interrupts. He holds up his phone. "We have the equipment. It won't be missed until tomorrow," he says, smiling. "My men have arrived at your warehouse."

Patch walks to Tshua and in an uncharacteristic gesture, bows.

"Where are you getting parachutes?" Web asks absentmindedly.

Patch shakes his head at Web. Nothing has to be said.

"Sorry. You have that covered."

Patch shouts to the room. "You all know what to do. Stay frosty. Good luck." He turns to Tallis. "Let's go into the hangar. We need to talk."

CHAPTER 43

Proctor's skydiving plane leaves Don Mueang airport at 2230 hours and quickly climbs to six thousand feet. Patch and Tallis are the only passengers on board. Patch repeats instructions given to Tallis in the hangar.

Beginners train with flat open landing areas. Young guys especially like to SWOOP their landings, come in hot, flare hard and hit the ground running. It's more fun to do and more exciting to watch. Unfortunately, the practice doesn't teach the operator how slowly they can manipulate the canopy when a difficult landing requires finesse. This is one of those moments. Come in too slow and Tallis will not reach the balcony. He'll crash into the side of the building with unpredictable results, none of the options being acceptable. Come in hot and he will land too far into the balcony and smash against its concrete back wall. The latter is preferable to the former, but could still end his vital role in the mission. The ideal is anywhere in between, a landing area about twenty feet across, high on the side of the tower.

The plane slows over residential skyscrapers and the wandering Chao Praya River just west of the Sathorn Unique Tower. The river winds like a black snake through the otherwise brightly lit city, void of light except for the occasional dots of light emanating from riverboats. Wind whistles into the plane's cabin through an open door.

"How accurate are these?" Tallis asks. He fumbles with the diamond rig tacked to his chest, fingers quivering slightly. "In the service we had whatever that GPS was called."

"Accurate enough," Patch says. "And the acronym you're fishing for is SAASM. If it makes you feel better, I'll have Rich activate the quadcopter at our landing spot and turn on the lights. But either way, I'll guide you in."

The jump light switches from red to yellow.

"But we're diving with like Google GPS, right? We're trying to hit a dinky terrace at night," Tallis says.

Patch bangs Tallis hard on the top of his helmet. "Man up! We're going to be fine. If we had military gear you wouldn't walk away with a story worth telling."

"Good point," Tallis says.

Patch heads for the open door. His dark jump suit rustles loudly in the wind. He rests his hands on the railing above his head and rocks back and forth. Seconds later a green light flashes and he steps into the sky above Bangkok. He drops through the rush of air with his arms at his sides and legs splayed like the tail feathers of a hawk. With a large bag of weapons, ropes, tools and other equipment attached to his belt he quickly accelerates to over 100 mph. Tallis follows a few seconds later with a bag of small UAVs, extra batteries and flight controllers.

As planned, the operatives stagger their chute openings. They use the brightly lit Krung Thonburi Road and bridge to guide their descent.

At 2,000 feet Patch opens his ram-air chute and activates his night vision goggles. He stays in communication with Tallis through every moment of the fall, rattling off instructions and assurances.

Through the night-vision equipment, the tower comes into clear view. Patch focuses on the upper balconies, picking a narrow landing spot guarded only by a railing. From images obtained through the quadcopter earlier in the day, this is the only place he feels Tallis can stick his landing.

Upon approach, Patch controls his canopy by tensing the front risers of the chute. He easily adjusts for a light breeze, flares at the right time, narrowly passes over the balcony's ornate railing and lands without incident. He clears his chute, turns in the direction of Tallis and taps a small penlight, which to Tallis, wearing his night vision equipment, may as well be a mini-flare.

Five hundred meters out and coming in hot, Tallis voices concern. Patch continues his instructions. "Smooth toggles, smooth toggles. There's no wind up here, nothing to worry about. Take it easy." An inexperienced jumper, especially in the life-or-death scenario Tallis faces, tends to overreact with each shift in the breeze, the inability to judge distance, or the realization that speed has become a factor.

Tallis comes in slow and low. He swears in Latvian moments before impact. Despite anything he or Patch can do at the last second, he smashes chest-first into the outer ornate concrete railing of the balcony. His torso, legs, and a bag of equipment dangle below him. He slips quickly, clinging for life to a rounded dusty concrete railing cap.

Patch grabs a fistful of paracord in the instant Tallis falls. The cord races through his hand until he can slow the fall. "I've got you," Patch says into the headset. "Talk to me."

"Fuck!" Tallis says and then immediately calms. "I need a couple more meters."

"Don't move," Patch says. He collects his strength and a few more strands of cord. He inches forward until his hands are pressed painfully against the railing. "That will have to do."

"It's good. It's good, but I have to swing."

"Fucking do it already!"

Seconds later, Tallis finds the railing below with his toes and he is able to press forward and drop to safety. "I'm coming to you," Patch says. "Stay there." He releases the chute and takes a deep breath. He touches a button on his headset connecting him to the op center.

"Piece of cake," he says.

In the op center, Web and Rich have watched Tallis's rough landing through head-cam feeds and cheer Patch on in relief. "Good luck gentlemen," Web says. "We'll have clean undershorts waiting for you at mission's end."

Patch and Tallis carry standard cell phones as backup, but communication between each other, and with the op center, is conducted via secure military headsets. It takes over forty minutes for Patch and Tallis to make their eighteen-floor descent. At each level, Tallis sends a UAV out ahead of them to scan hallways and open areas. They see areas where squatters have settled, but no one is encountered. The assumption—insurgents have chased them off.

Guided by op center pilots, a single-prop fixed-wing UAV holds a surveillance pattern between Sathorn Unique Tower and the State Tower located one mile away. Its cameras are fixed on the exterior of the building, delivering a constant feed. Patch steps onto a balcony to verify their location. He turns an LED to strobe until Web confirms they have one more floor to clear. Web also confirms that Brick and Tshua's men are ready to enter the parking ramp. The Hmong scout, already present there for nearly two hours, had given the all clear.

Tallis switches out batteries on the UAV he's been working with and sends it out of the building and down two floors. He expertly scans floors below the insurgents, beginning with level 19. They encounter cabling on every floor. It runs vertically down a shaft, but they don't encounter any additional insurgents. There are no lit rooms or visible guards. If intrusion detection equipment has been installed, it can't be seen.

Maintaining flight controls in the dark and navigating among the construction that was left incomplete challenges Tallis's skills. But with focus and a bit of luck, floors nineteen down to fourteen are declared clear.

At the twelfth floor that changes. Insurgents have removed partitioning walls near the interior central supports of the tower. Broken and crushed drywall lies in piles near solid concrete supports. A team of three insurgent workers is spotted. They are busy wrapping concrete columns with explosives, thick rubber mats and cyclone fencing. Cables run from each support to the central shaft, where they disappear upward into a large opening in the ceiling.

Web has seen enough. He orders Tallis to withdraw the UAV before it is spotted. Tallis sends it down another floor, to eleven. There they see another guard. He is apparently asleep, propped up against a wall, resting in a chair. A rifle rests across his lap.

Not wanting to speak unless absolutely necessary, Patch sends a text to Web.

Patch – *getting this?*

Web – *yes*

Patch – *scrub equip for brand*

Web – *will do*

In the op center, Rich has already started that investigation. He rewinds video of men wiring the tower, zooms in on the closest column, and captures stills. "Are you familiar with this equipment?" Rich asks.

Web nods in the affirmative. "Those explosives have detonators embedded into them. The lines run up through a duct to a control panel upstairs. Normally that equipment would never be located inside the building. They are either going to blow the building out from under them or possibly use a cell phone. Maybe all we have to do is cut cables. That would do it, I suppose, but I want confirmation."

"And how do you propose we get that?"

Web checks the time. "I can't think straight right now. What time is it back in the States? Twelve hours, right?"

"Where?"

"Anywhere," Web says, irritated.

"It's like mid-afternoon, I guess. Why?"

"Go online. Find me a few demolition companies and get someone on the phone."

Rich laughs. "That's why you get the big bucks."

Three minutes later Rich cues up a company in Texas. He points at Web. "Yes sir," the man on speaker phone says.

"This will be the strangest call you'll ever receive, but we need your help and you can't tell anyone about it."

"Your guy filled me in, Colonel. How can I help?"

Web looks at Rich and mouths the word 'Colonel,' making an interrogative gesture with his shoulders. Rich smiles and salutes.

"Check your inbox." Rich gives him thumbs-up and within a few seconds the demolition expert acknowledges receipt of three photos, two detailed shots of the actual explosives and men working. The third photo presents a view of the insurgents' control panel.

"They've wired the twelfth floor of a fifty-story building under construction. Controls are on the twentieth floor. If we cut the cables, what happens?" Web says.

"Give me a second," the expert says. "I have to dig into my catalogs here. Everything is online these days, but I still go to print."

Web and Rich watch images Tallis sends to them from remote areas of the tenth and eleventh floors.

"Sorry about the delay," the expert says. "Cut all the cables at once and they're dead in the water. Thing is, green lights will turn red with every cut. They're going to know something is going on. Best thing would be to pull the detonators, get them away from the explosives, but that would take you a hell of a long time from what I can see in these pictures."

"Does that control panel support remote detonation?"

"Could happen," the Texan says. "You could jam signals, but then you're probably jamming your own communications at the same time. I wish I could tell you more."

"You've been a great help already, more than you know. Sorry you won't be acknowledged for your service, but know that you may have saved lives today. One last question. If we drop a grenade in their control room, might that set off the explosives?"

"Not likely." The Texan goes on to explain why it might be a viable strategy, then points out that after that explosion, no one should move anything in that room until the detonators have been removed.

Web ends the call and transfers the information to Patch, via text. Patch responds with a text of his own.

Patch – *understood. send in the rangers.*

CHAPTER 44

Sam, Brick, five rangers and two older Hmong warriors are sandwiched into the back of a delivery truck parked a kilometer from Sathorn Unique Tower. The interior is bathed in soft red light to preserve night vision.

The scout in the ramp is armed. He sits immediately across from the floor where the first guard still rests beneath his blanket. He reports being unable to spot a second person.

Web places a call to the van and the driver backs into the darkness of Alley 51 just far enough to block clear views from the street. Brick and two rangers raise the back door and climb down from the van. They pull a ladder from the side of the truck and place it against the parking ramp. Everyone but the driver quickly climbs up and over the concrete railing. They take the ladder up with them.

Minutes later the best of the Thai shooters joins the scout and takes a prone position on a stack of pallets. He points a suppressed Remington 700 into the tower and does a visual scan of the area, using his night vision scope to peer into every crack and crevice. He confirms that the woman who had been there earlier in the day, has gone. The shooter lays crosshairs on the sleeping lookout. His orders are to incapacitate the man if he reaches for a phone. At his discretion, he will shoot to kill.

Sam joins the scout and two Hmong warriors at the shooter's side. She wears a headset. Through it, she reports progress to Web, saying that Brick and one ranger have gone to the roof of the elevated walkway.

Brick and the ranger carefully cross the roof. Using cloth between the blades of his bolt cutter, Brick cuts through the cyclone fence. Once through, he moves deliberately into the tower and across the open floor toward the sleeping lookout.

A dog barks somewhere in the building. The sound echoes off the bare concrete. Brick freezes with his weapon pointed at the man. The lookout stirs, but doesn't stand. Brick waits. The sniper, able to see the man's face clearly through his scope, gives a motion to Sam.

"Keep going," she says into her headset.

Brick approaches the sleeping guard. He wakes, but it is too late for him. Brick attacks viciously, rendering the man unconscious. He cuffs him and tapes his mouth. He and the ranger drag his unconscious body to a back wall and lash him to one of a dozen drainpipes. They cover him with his own blanket, denying him vision and further inhibiting sound. Once secured, Brick and the ranger who crossed with him take up defensive positions to protect their team.

The shooter leaves the Remington in place for Sam to use, and joins the other rangers in the tower. Her assignment, as Patch instructed her, is to use that scope to keep an eye on the disabled lookout and watch for new arrivals. The Hmong warriors with her watch the alley below from various vantage points on the same floor of the parking ramp.

Web and Rich focus their attention on Brick and the rangers. They watch video feeds originating from helmet cameras as the team of operatives cut through the new cyclone fence and move upward into the tower, toward their next objective, the sleeping guard on the eleventh floor. When they arrive on that floor, Brick calls for more recon. Tallis flies a UAV out of the building and onto the eleventh floor. As he sweeps the floor, his video feed is sent to Brick. The guard still rests in a chair that leans against a wall, chin on his chest, arms lax.

Brick studies the floor carefully for obstacles and picks his path. He charges forward with a violence of action that quickly takes the man to the floor. As he attacks, a ranger rips the guard's rifle from his lap. Two rangers bind, gag and secure the shaken guard and Brick sends word to Patch that they are ready to climb stairs to the twelfth floor and take on the demolition workers.

Patch replies – *fast and furious*

Brick – *give me eyes*

Tallis flies his SUAV out of an opening on the eleventh floor and enters the twelfth. Video confirms the insurgents are still busy working and unaware of being watched. Brick and his team of rangers quietly commit to a plan of attack. Though the room is lit by two bare electric bulbs, the workers wear headlamps. The rangers ascend an open staircase and disburse quietly.

Brick – *set*

Patch – *on my signal*

Patch taps Tallis on the shoulder and motions for a discussion. He whispers, "Can you fly into the one nearest the gun? Could give Brick a couple seconds of advantage."

"Definitely."

Patch – *be ready*

Tallis flies the SUAV through shadows, positioning for a run at the worker. Video shows insurgents to be fully engrossed in what they are doing.

When Patch gives the word, Tallis flies the UAV directly into the skull of the nearest worker, startling him. Simultaneously, rangers rush in, each with a target and task. All three insurgents make a move for the same rifle, but they are all too slow. Brick and the rangers quickly intersect their path, muzzles pointed at their chests, and they immediately raise their hands in surrender. They too, are restrained.

"This is too easy," Rich says, watching from the comfort of the op center.

Web doesn't reply. He knows better. The worst is yet to come.

Brick confirms their success and reports to Web. "Workers contained. Ascending to rally one. ETA twelve minutes."

One ranger remains on the twelfth floor to ensure the demolition workers don't get loose. He carries the bolt cutter in his kit and wraps a dozen or more cables with detonation cord in preparation for an emergency cut.

Brick and the remaining rangers climb carefully through darkness and rubble to the nineteenth floor. Two of the most capable rangers make their way to balconies on the north face, between and below the hostages and their control room one floor above. A quick burst of infrared strobe verifies that they are in position. When confirmed, Patch and Tallis lower lines to them and they climb up to the twentieth floor.

When they arrive, they carefully advance from the balcony they have rappelled onto toward an open hallway. Patch and Tallis move to balconies above the room nearest to the guards and their captive crew members. They set anchor lines and ready themselves for a fast rappel.

The rangers that climbed to the twentieth floor carefully make their way to the hallway, check to be sure it is clear, then advance quickly to the generator room. They tap their headsets, signaling to

Sam they are ready to cut power, then wait in the dark, just meters away from the insurgents.

Brick and his team ascend a stairwell at the end of the building and approach the hallway. Brick glances quickly around the corner toward the open door of the control room then sends a message that they are in position.

Patch double-checks his friction hitch and places the free end of his coiled rope on the railing. He and Tallis prepare flash-bang and sting-ball grenades for quick deployment. They wait for Web's signal.

On Web's order, Sam places a call to Brick's Uncle Gunner. Within minutes, the street in front of the tower fills with motorcycles. Bikers approach from two directions, each group acting as if they are meeting an opposing gang on their own turf. They slow their bikes, rev their engines, shout at the top of their lungs, doing donuts and wheelies in the street. Their high-display and revving engines, some backfiring as the rider backs off the throttle, generate an incredible amount of noise.

"Positions," Web says into his headset. The communication goes to the entire tactical team.

Brick leads his rangers up the hallway to the edge of the insurgents' open control room door. They turn off night vision gear and ready for attack. Ahead of them, past the dimly lit open door, the other two rangers emerge from the generator room and give thumbs-up.

Brick taps on the microphone of his headset four times. Patch echoes with four taps, then he and Tallis rappel to the twentieth floor and make their way rapidly through an empty room toward the hallway. They move to within ten meters of the guards, the door and their imprisoned crew members.

In the op center, Web watches the action unfold. His pacing stops. Brick is in place. Patch and Tallis are ready. "On my command," Web says. He takes a deep breath.

"Web!" Sam says. "Web?" The audio comes into the op center through the speaker system.

"Hold it. Stop," Web says into his headset. Adrenaline races through his system. "Everyone just hold up."

He touches a button on his headset and speaks directly to his wife. "Quickly, Sam."

"A van just pulled into the alley," she reports. "Two men for sure, maybe more."

CHAPTER 45

A vehicle has backed into the alley between the parking ramp and the tower. The two Hmong men with Sam spotted the vehicle first, and went to intervene if given an order to do so. Now, Sam seeks instructions from Web. The truck is parked. Two men climb out of the cab. Open the back door, and grab supplies.

"What are they doing?" Web asks.

"They are going through the fence into the tower," Sam says.

"Weapons?"

"Don't know. One has a box, the other a huge jug of water. They're inside now."

"I hear the motorcycles through your headset," Web says. "Where are the Hmong?"

"They went down there."

Web struggles to understand why the Hmong warriors left their post, a fact he quickly realizes is irrelevant to what must happen next. He forces his mind back into action. "Those men will be on the floor opposite you in a minute. I'm going to give the attack order as soon as you have them in your sights. I don't want to put this on you, but they're soon going to see their cuffed lookout. Can't let them make a call."

"What are you asking?"

"Get into a position. Find them in your sights. Do it now."

Sam wraps the Remington's sling around her arm and tightens the rifle butt to her shoulder. She steps to the sidewall of the ramp and rests her elbow on the concrete. "I don't see them yet," she says, her scope focused on that area of the floor across from her where the men will most likely appear.

"Tell the Hmong to take control of the van," Web says.

Sam switches channels and passes along the information in Thai. As soon as she speaks the Hmong run from the shadows of the ramp to the passenger door of the van. Without hesitation, two shots are fired from one of the Hmong warriors' pistol. The sound echoes through the alley and into the parking ramp and lower floors of the tower.

Sam touches buttons on her headset. She stares down at the roof of the insurgent van. She says, "They shot someone." The Hmong open the passenger side door of the van. "They shot someone, Web. One is getting in the van, the other one is standing in the alley."

Sam looks up just in time to see two other insurgents are directly across from her. They've put their supplies on the ground and run toward the alley, weapons in hand. Sam steadies herself, places a mil dot on the fastest runner and pulls the trigger. The rifle kicks into her shoulder and she cycles the bolt, loading another cartridge into the chamber. When she refocuses, heart pounding, arms shaking, the second insurgent is no longer visible.

In a flash of fear, she drops below the concrete barrier. He'd been armed. He would have known where she fired from, if not precisely by the muzzle flash, then instinctively. There are few other places where her shot could have come from.

"Web?" she says, voice shaking.

"Hold," he says to her.

Web switches his headset to the operatives.

"Cut power. Go. Do it now."

High above the alley, Brick signals the rangers to attack. The generator stops and men rush forward.

Below, Sam regroups, crawls quickly to another location, and raises her rifle. She scans the tower for any sign of the second insurgent. Her ears ring. Adrenaline races through her system. The smell of spent powder fills her nostril and she fights to steady her breathing.

Her scope comes to rest on the man she just shot. He has fallen on his back and tries to crawl, using the elbow of one arm. His other arm and hand are pressed against a dark stain on his upper abdomen. He weakly calls for his friend to help. The effect of seeing the wounded and obviously dying man is immediate and visceral. Sam approaches shock. She gasps, chokes back a scream and nausea, and looks away.

Below, one of the Hmong drives away in the insurgents' van. The other enters the tower on the run.

CHAPTER 46

Brick throws stun grenades. Instantly, everyone in the insurgents' control room is temporarily incapacitated. He races forward and rips cable from the demolition controller as the rangers rush in behind him and take control of the insurgents.

Patch and Tallis bounce sting grenades off the walls of the hallway just outside the prisoners' door. They bounce on the floor at the guards' feet and explode. The guards are rendered helpless and struggle for consciousness through the shock and pain.

They race forward through the acrid smell. The guards' table is obliterated. The rifle that was leaning against the wall is now on the floor beneath one of the writhing guards.

Patch yells for Tallis to close his eyes. He disables his NVG, turns on his flashlight, and pounds on the hostage door. He yells. "It's Patch and Tallis. Stand down. We're coming in."

Tallis cuffs and gags the guards.

Inside the close quarters of the utility closet, the crew huddles in one corner. The stench in the room is overpowering. Joe doesn't wake up as Patch enters. Patch carefully clips their cuffs and helps each of them to their feet. He brings them, one by one, into the hallway.

Lee kicks one of the guards in the face. Patch tells him to cool it.

Ginger rattles off her assessment of the crew's situation. "Joe has a concussion. He's been out of it for hours. Jimmy is out of it, too, but mental. We'll have to keep an eye on him. Anish, Lee and I are all able. Jawad is in a high-rise somewhere, possibly nearby."

"How do you know?" Patch says.

"Skype. We all saw him on Skype. There are glass windows and an expensive television in the background. Cabinets are high class, like a ritzy hotel. Tall buildings just outside the window."

Patch calls in the information and they complete the crew member assessment. It takes six minutes.

Tallis drags guards down the hall behind Patch and the crew.

Patch and Anish support Joe as they walk. He is only slightly aware of his surroundings, dazed and struggling for clarity. By the time the crew reaches rally point one at the end of the hallway, the bearded, cuffed and gagged guards are nearly compliant and able to walk under their own power.

The team does another assessment. None of the rescuers report injuries. The captives, except for an older man in the control room, are all able to walk. Insurgents are arranged into two groups, and roped together.

"We're coming out," Patch says into his headset.

"Belay that," Web says. "Destroy the control panel and descend to twelve. Cut cables but don't go lower until I say. Stay above rally point two. Copy?"

"Copy. What's going on?" Patch asks.

"Not now. Stay above the open floors."

Rich streams Sam's voice into the op center communications system. "Talk to me," Web says. Sam gasps for air. She is in trouble.

"I shot him," Sam says. "He's not dead. He's just, he's just on the ground. Web?"

Web gathers his wits. "Where are the Hmong?"

Sam takes a deep breath and returns to her scope. "One of them drove off with the van. The other one is in the tower somewhere. The guy I shot is dying, Web. We should do something. I don't know what to do."

"It's horrible, I'm sure. But stay with me. Can you see the other insurgent? We have to find him. Focus."

"I've been fucking looking! He's going to die!"

"I'm sending our people down. Do not fire on anyone with a light."

"That Hmong guy doesn't have a light either."

Web sighs. "I'd rather he got out of there. You're doing great. I'll be back with you in a minute."

Web switches comms back to Patch. "Here's the situation. We have two insurgents at rally point two. Sam knocked one down, the other is somewhere in the tower, at least for now. One of the Hmong is in there after him. He's not tagged."

"She what?"

"Just know she may hit the wall any minute."

"Fuck's sake," Patch says. "Get our guy out of there. Tell her to yell if she has to. It will help. When we come down those stairs that bang stick has to be on the ground, Web. Hear me? Tell her we'll take it from here and bring up the vans."

Web calls Tshua. The Hmong return to the alley in their step van. Gunner's team continues to provide cover. Assuming their noise will soon draw the attention of police, they gradually move their faked battle blocks away from the tower.

In the tower, Brick and the rangers frantically disassemble demolition wraps and pull detonators to ensure there are no other ignition devices.

On Web's command, Sam yells toward the tower for the Hmong warrior to return. She continues to scan for the second insurgent, but spots no one. She yells repeatedly.

When the explosives are disarmed, Patch leads everyone down

treacherous flights of stairs. He and Tallis take point, hunting for undiscovered combatants. Their crew, led by Brick, follows. Behind the crew, the chain of insurgents is led and followed by rangers. One ranger lags behind by a floor, covering their retreat.

As the teams and captives nears the second rally point near open floors, Web calls for Sam to put down her rifle. As she does, the Hmong warrior exits the tower.

"He's out," Sam says. "Our man just came out."

"You did the right thing, Sam," Web says. "Stay where you are. Patch or Tallis will come for you."

He gives Patch the order to proceed with caution, informing him of the presence of an insurgent still in the building, possibly armed.

Patch and Tallis come down the exposed stairway first. They scan the area with night-vision goggles, then advance. They scan the floor again and Patch takes a knee.

Tallis approaches the downed insurgent, now unresponsive, and removes his weapon. He turns the man onto his stomach and kneels behind him, gun raised. They wait and listen. A full minute later Patch calls to Brick. Brick replies. "Joe is out again."

"Bring him," Patch says.

Brick hoists Joe over one shoulder and heads down the stairs. Ginger and the rest of the crew follow. The rangers orient their captives and prepare to descend.

As Brick reaches the bottom step, shots ring out.

The missing insurgent runs full speed toward the team. He attempts to empty his clip, but Patch and Tallis return fire, instantly killing him. Brick drops Joe on the concrete and clutches his shoulder.

Tallis runs to his aid, replaces him at the head of the crew, and hustles everyone toward the escalator.

Web calls Sam. "Things have changed. Get to the alley now."

Sam picks up the Remington and runs.

In the tower, just before reaching the escalator, Ginger trips. Tallis grabs her arm, helps her up and they continue down the escalator, across the floor, across the rubbish and into the alley where vans wait.

Rangers push the captured insurgents into one of the vans. They climb in with them and the van leaves. Sam makes her way into the alley where she, Patch and the crew climb into the other van.

Brick is wounded and in pain, sprawled on the floor next to Joe, who is only partially responsive, but cogent enough to make a joke. He says, "Someone give Jimmy a roll of toilet paper."

As the van pulls out of the alley giddy crew members speak all at once, so grateful to be rescued. Tallis finds the med kit and cuts away cloth to get to Brick's shoulder.

Then Lee discovers that Ginger has been hit by a round from the insurgent's gun. She clutches at her bleeding abdomen, straining to breathe.

The driver accelerates. Now Brick and Ginger are flat on the bed of the van and Joe is propped against one wall. Tallis and Sam do what they can to stop Ginger's bleeding. It is painfully apparent that color has left her cheeks and arms.

"Fuck," Ginger manages to say, weakly.

"We have you," Tallis says, pressure on her wound. "On the way to the hospital. Man up, okay?"

Brick turns his head toward Ginger and begins to recite the Lord's Prayer. Patch takes Ginger's hand. "You did good," he says.

"You got your people through."

The van continues on but Ginger does not. As the sun rises she closes her eyes and exhales for the last time.

CHAPTER 47

At the rail yard warehouse, rangers and Hmong warriors secure the newly captured insurgents. Those taken from the Sathorn Unique Tower are isolated from the rest of the captives. They lie on their stomachs, blindfolded, legs and arms in nylon cuffs. The rangers are clearly relieved that their mission was successful, and that none of them were injured.

At the far end of the building sits the insurgents' van. The body of the driver has been removed, leaving only bloodstained seats and blood spatter on the windshield and dashboard. The insurgent's body will never be found, nor will the Hmong warrior that took his life ever be found by police.

Everyone waits anxiously for the second van to arrive, but it does not. They are aware of Brick's wound, but no one believes a man of his size will be unable to handle a simple shoulder wound. Going to the hospital is a formality. But when the van does arrive, things change. A woman's body is carried by her friends to a table and she is covered with a white cloth.

Twenty minutes later, Web arrives at the rail yard warehouse to be with his team and console his wife. The Thai rangers have just finished packing their equipment when he drives in. There is no exuberance now. The once excited rangers are somber and subdued.

Web joins Patch and Sam at the table where Ginger's body rests. Sam's eyes are swollen from tears. She takes her husband's arm and collapses into his chest.

Web calls his team together, shakes their hands and personally apologizes for the lapse in operational security that led to their ordeal. To a person, they all reply with how grateful they are having heard the lengths the team went through to rescue them.

Tshua and the rangers approach. They bow toward Ginger, toward nearby crew members and then to Web and Sam. Their sincerity is expressed in wordless gestures Web will never forget. He bows back to them and then shakes hands with each of the men who helped rescue his friends. When they leave, Web turns to Tshua. "We owe the Hmong a great deal," he says. "I don't know how we can ever repay you."

"My men are getting older," Tshua says through a mischievous smile. "Old men run out of stories. If you want to help the people somehow, that is different. I trust you will find a way."

Web bows. Tshua bows. "Consider it done," Web says.

Patch puts Tshua in charge of guarding insurgents until it is determined how to turn them over to General Phang. Tshua also volunteers to provide transportation for crew members as soon as it is determined where they will go.

As Tallis drives Web, Sam and Patch back to the op center, Web debates whether to have Tshua deliver all his people to the airport and get them out of the country. Instead, he has Rich place calls to tourist-heavy seaside resorts. They book their crew members into these resorts in pairs and Rich relays orders. Their new protocol is to blend in with tourists and check information on a particular website every day for updates.

Meanwhile, Tallis takes side roads to the op center. Additional guards have already been posted. It is there he will meet General Phang, possibly the last professional meeting of his career, certainly one of the most difficult discussions in his life.

But preparation for the general will have to wait. Web thinks first about the people who helped them. He places calls to Gunner and the skydiving club to thank them personally, and settle accounts.

In the case of the bikers, he volunteers to purchase a new Harley Davidson they can auction off during their next charity run. A donation to the skydiving club settles that debt. During the call, the pilot asks a couple of times what the mission was about. Patch interrupts the call to say it was a friendly prank. His long-time friend and pilot knows better, but stops questioning.

Web also leaves a message on Volkov's phone. He says, "It's done. The second payment will go through within hours." In the back of his mind, he also plots how to get his money back. Just business.

Patch helps the last two remaining pilots secure gear in the hangar, as Web sits at the command table inside typing notes. As soon as the equipment is locked down, Patch sends everyone away, retaining only Rich to keep systems running and data flowing.

Meanwhile, Web is more exhausted than he's been in twenty years. He can barely keep himself from falling over, so Patch sends him and Sam to the conference room to rest.

When they are alone, Sam says to Web, "We should just leave. You don't have to explain anything to anyone. Patch will handle all of that."

"You did an incredible job today," Web says absentmindedly, slumping into a chair. As soon as the words come out of his mouth, he knows he has said the wrong thing.

Web has never seen Sam react the way she does. "No! Web! What has become of you? I shot a man. I took his life! I have to live with that now. And Ginger is dead. She's fucking dead! You! You have to live with that! This isn't what we set out to do."

Web stands and tries to comfort her, to hold her, but she pushes him away. She pushes him and says, "I'm going home. When you come back to the States, if we can even leave, if we're not in jail, you better be ready to retire. I mean it!" As she speaks she breaks down crying, pushes her fists into his chest and then surrenders to his arms.

"I'm so sorry," Web says.

They hold each other for a long time, then sit. Web falls asleep, head on the table. It seems to him like hours, but fifteen minutes after dozing off, Patch is at his side, telling him it's time. "Choochai called," Patch says. "Not good. The general has MPs with him and they will be here in maybe four or five minutes."

Web splashes cold water in his face then joins Patch in the open hangar. As expected, the session begins with confrontation. The general and an entourage of colonels and military police drive into the open door facing the tarmac and screech to a halt in front of Patch and Web. It's clear the general intends to unleash holy hell on the two men, and then arrest them, but neither Web nor Patch budge. They stand firm until the general has finished delivering what he came to say. It's a litany of abuses that wanders between English and Thai—loud, angry, unyielding.

The verbal attack turns into a heated discussion. Perhaps because Web and Patch remain calm the general's posture settles. Civility returns and he demands an explanation.

Web describes their mission in detail, including how they captured many insurgents. He doesn't mention rangers, but says instead his crew pulled off all missions. Patch adds that they saved the city from an explosion that could have killed hundreds, and certainly would have brought fear to millions.

Patch hands a packet of information to the general. It contains a bullet list of the arguments they just presented, along with times and locations. He says, "It's all in there. We didn't capture Jawad, but the information we gathered will inevitably help you do that. Some of my men are hunting him now. You should assign a team to move quickly."

General Phang flips three pages of information before landing on dozen photos. The pictures show the insurgent's destroyed control room, their crew members in confinement, and captured insurgents next to mounds of plastic explosives and wrapped concrete columns in the tower. Another photo shows the floor of a van. He sees Brick and Joe in the hospital then stops at a photo of Ginger's body on a table.

The general closes the folder and hands it to one of his aides. His demeanor, at first angry and combative, has calmed considerably, but he is still a formidable leader who cannot afford to be disobeyed, nor appear to be weak in front of his men. He says, "This does not explain why you acted without contacting me first. It's unforgivable!"

"May we have a word in confidence?" Web says. He glances at

the general's men.

Web, Patch and General Phang step away. Patch hands over a second folder, this one containing forensic evidence of the traitor in the general's inner circle. It shows how the man stole information using a thumb drive and gives linguistic evidence proving it was delivered to the insurgency. "We're sorry we didn't get in touch with you," Web says. "Under the circumstances we couldn't be sure who could be trusted."

"You can trust me!" the general barks, but then he turns his head. The disappointment and betrayal that the general must feel is obvious to Web. "Why would he do such a thing?" the general asks.

There is no answer. Nothing more Web can do. He and his crew are now at the mercy of the Thai military, but there's one more thing to say. "General, it would be better if you claimed to have conceived and run this operation to save the city from Jawad's attack. We want to continue our work for you, but we can't do it if exposed in the media."

General Phang's expression shifts slightly as he considers the implications of Web's request. He signals for his men to wait in their vehicles and says, "Let's go inside. I want to see what you accomplished before we dismantle everything."

Web's heart sinks. He's lost a great friend and employee, has two more in the hospital, and now has lost the project entirely.

But the general continues to speak as they walk. "After the tour of this facility, I need ideas on how we better protect your staff in a new location."

CHAPTER 48

Web sets out to contact Ginger's family, only to discover that her single surviving relative is her grandmother, seventy-eight years old and living with terminal cancer. Instead of describing to her what has happened to Ginger, he arranges for a substantial payment to the facility with the goal of making the elderly woman as comfortable as possible. The payment is accompanied by a note saying how much Ginger loves Thailand, how much she loves and misses her grandmother. He ends saying how Ginger hopes to see her grandmother soon.

Patch tells Web not to worry, that he'll take care of the cremation.

"I don't want her dropped off somewhere, Patch. If we were going to do that we could have left her at the hospital. She deserves better. How would you like to go out? Not in a damn incinerator."

"I understand," Patch says. "I'll take care of things."

The next day at sunset, on property owned by General Phang, Web and the crew salute the arrival of a Unimog troop carrier. Thai rangers, in full dress uniforms, lift Ginger's stretcher to the ground. Her body is wrapped in white linen. They carry her ceremoniously to a funeral pyre composed of timbers crisscrossed atop a large rectangular flat stone edifice used for such purposes.

Buddhist priests perform the ceremony, ringing bells, chanting and bowing. Those gathered, including General Phang and dignitaries, along with Choochai, Tshua and many Hmong, offer food and candles to the monks. They place thick bundles of incense on the pyre. Sam weeps as the flames rise.

The lights of Bangkok glow in the distance. A pair of UAVs circle far above, like eagles.

Rich leans heavily on the railing of the observation deck. The weight of the guilt he carries over his security failure brings him to tears and he cries unabashedly.

CHAPTER 49

Jawad sits in an expensive suite, Chatrium Hotel Riverside. He is registered under his birth name, Sarab Najjar. He wears soccer attire and an outlandish pair of green sunglasses. The suite features a view of Chao Phraya River and the Krung Thonburi Road Bridge. He gazes at the Sathorn Unique Tower.

The night before he placed a call to arrange the final step in his plan. Earlier this day he trimmed his beard to stubble at the side of the road in the Ban Lot District. Now he sits in a chair, reviewing video clips of captured Americans. He looks out through the large plate-glass window of the hotel and pulls drinks from the mini-bar, a luxury he can't afford in his life as Jawad.

After a few drinks Sarab opens a phone and enters a number. He sets a small video camera on a table facing the window and presses record. He paces, thumb on the send button of the phone in his hand. In his mind he sees video circulating among the news venues of the city, indeed the world. American interventionists captured, humiliated, locked in a building that explodes into millions of pieces on top of them.

Resting his forehead on the glass, eyes on the Tower, he raises his arm and presses the button. Nothing happens. He keys the number again and presses send.

Fear and anger race through him. He dials a different number and waits for Akara to explain his failure and make things right. The call is answered, but no one speaks. He waits, listens then asks, "Are you faithful?"

The man on the other end of the call answers the challenge incorrectly. Jawad ends the call immediately and heads for the bathroom. He pulls the battery from the burner phone.

Jawad quickly shaves his face to the skin, pulls on a baseball cap, and leaves the building. He is unaware of being followed by two Hmong elders. Outside he hails a taxi. The taxi pulls forward and Jawad gets in.

"Where are you going?" the driver asks.

Jawad wants a ride to the airport. He says he is about to miss his flight so they have to hurry.

The taxi pulls away. "What's your name?" the driver asks, and adjusts his interior rear-view mirror to look his passenger in the eyes.

Jawad doesn't answer.

The driver slowly pulls a pistol from a bag on the front seat and points it through the seat toward the passenger. He says, "We're taking a shortcut."

Jawad rides nervously for ten minutes then realizes he is not heading in the right direction. "Turn around," he demands. "I want your name!"

The driver apologizes and says he is sure they are heading in the right direction. "But if you want my name, I'll give it to you. People call me Tshua."

EPILOGUE

A caravan of two trucks and a Range Rover travel twelve hours along Route 105 to northern Thailand, near Mae Hong Son. Brick rides in the back seat of the Range Rover, arm in a sling, looking out the window. Tallis sits next to him, thumbs engaged with a hand-held simulator.

The trucks leave the highway at 0100. They rest until dawn and then continue west through wild country toward Pai River. Their destination is as far back in time as it is off the trail, a remote Hmong village carved among rising hills. Any farther west or north and they would be in Myanmar.

Children swarm the trucks as they enter the village. Brick and Tallis hand out boxes of fruit as the Hmong unload the trucks. Colorfully clothed elders emerge from thatched and metal-roofed homes. The village comes alive—cooking, milling about the trucks, laughing. These are former combatants from the Secret War. They fled certain death years earlier to raise their children and grandchildren in Thailand, in peace. In the eyes of Web and Patch, no people have ever been nobler.

The caravan carries water purification equipment, small gold bullion, satellite phones and building supplies, as well as a crate of M1 carbines. Tallis asks for a particular woman. Translators help him find her.

She slowly emerges from her hut, hair in a tight bun on her head, smiling through darkly etched skin.

Tallis punches numbers into a satellite phone. He smiles and holds the phone to the old woman's ear. As she listens, tears and smiles alternate across her face. It is her son Tshua's voice.

Two days later, Web watches his wife sleep. Tallis watches television in the adjoining room of their hotel suite, assigned to their protection. Web quietly opens a glass sliding door and steps into the night air, the streets of Bangkok below and an uncertain future ahead. He places a call to his brother.

"How are you holding up?" Sonny asks. "I hear Sam is really shaken."

"Can you blame her? Speaking of that, I'm going to take some time just to be with her. Patch and Rich can cover things here. I need you to take care of the office while I'm out of pocket. Good with that?"

"Of course," his brother says. "Take as much time as you need."

They talk for a while longer, handing over authority for various projects, and then Web ends the call. He places the phone in his pocket, closes his eyes, and takes in the smells and sound of Bangkok. The breeze quickens against his face.

He leaves the balcony, closes the door against pending rain, and returns quietly into bed. Sam's sleep is restless. He touches her hair then lays a hand on her shoulder. The touch calms her, but as she drifts back into deep sleep, tremors continue. No one knows better than he how close his team came to losing more lives, and how vulnerable they will continue to be during the remainder of the contract.